Aubade Rising

Hayley Pierce

Published by Hayley Pierce Writes

First published, 2025

British Library Cataloguing in Publication Data available

978-1-0681684-0-6 – Paperback
978-1-0681684-1-3 – eBook

Printed by Amazon.
Edited by Author's Pen.
Typesetting and proofreading by Helen Jones.
Cover design by Aby Thompson.
Interior map by: @shepengal

To the new mums, in the thick fog of post-partum,
hang in there.

You're not alone.

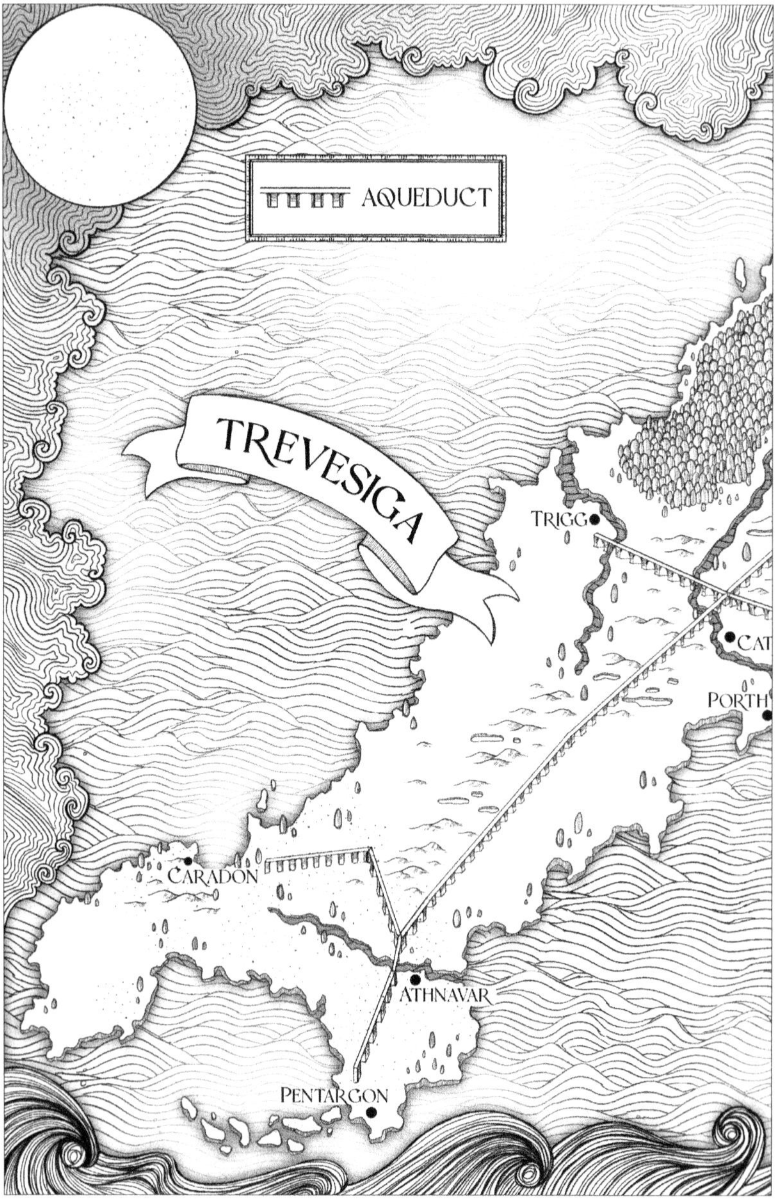
AQUEDUCT
TREVESIGA
TRIGG
CAT
PORTH
CARADON
ATHNAVAR
PENTARGON

AICHE
THE HAAG
TANWEN
RESTORMEL
THAIR

Prologue

Years of my life. Total isolation. Set-back after set-back. So much potential smothered. So many voices silenced. But a tidal storm is coming. Strong winds of change are gathering and new sunlight will burn away the stagnant waters.

Chapter 1

Irrevocably changing the world is a fool's dream. For most people anyway. But not for me. I'm teetering on the edge of something incredible. The sun flickers out from behind heavy clouds, coating my face with a weak winter warmth. My meagre magic stirs. It knows what's coming. Waiting any longer is impossible. I promised Dervla I wouldn't do this without her. But as the sun vanishes, leaving me cold, I falter. If this experiment doesn't work, if my theory doesn't hold, then I don't want a witness to my failure. I straighten my spine. It will work; it has to.

A small lump of quartz, veined with copper, weighs heavily in my palm. I place it on my workbench and retreat across the laboratory. My theory is simple: I've been searching for a material that can absorb magic, to hold it in stasis until it's called upon to be used. For Aubades like me, with such little magic, succeeding means we will be able to stand on equal footing with the Mordros, our rulers, and demand they lift the many restrictions which keep us bound to poverty. But I'm getting ahead of myself. Magic is forbidden in Trevesiga and it's critical I keep this research secret. I steady myself with a deep breath and lock the laboratory door. I turn back towards the workbench, failing to quiet the bubbling excitement from my magic as it fizzes in my chest. It's been years since I've dared to let it out.

My hands rise, twisting in shapes learnt in secret from my mother before she died and I call my magic forward. It comes gladly, filling my palms with white light. I shove it towards the worktop, aiming for the stone sat on it. The magic sizzles through the air and into the quartz. The bright light vanishes and I hear my heartbeat loudly in my ears. Smoke starts seeping through the copper veins towards me and I dart behind a large storage cabinet. The room shudders and I'm thrown against the wall.

The fall-out from the blast leaves me covered in a fine metallic dust. Eyes watering, head throbbing, ears ringing, I flex each of my fingers in turn and flinch at the numb hollowing in my chest where my magic is housed. It's completely empty. I've failed.

The workbench, at the epicentre of the destruction, suffered the most. Its top has disintegrated along with one of the legs. The three remaining legs smoulder, covered in dark ash, an awkward triangle of kindling. The storage cupboard behind leans unsteadily to the left, threatening to fall over. Its doors have been ripped away and measuring instruments warped by the heat spill onto the floor. Vast swathes of scorch marks radiate across the stone walls. Every window has been blown out, shards of glass sprinkled on the floor. I feel grateful to be alive.

My hand presses against my sternum, grounding me, my lungs push against it while adrenaline washes through me. Deep breaths. I inhale the metallic dust and struggle to suppress a coughing fit. It's important to focus, to be certain nothing else will catch fire. I stumble towards the workbench legs, grabbing my cloak from the cabinet to smother the embers. My throat burns as ash billows at the movement.

I need a cover story for the destruction. Some disturbance is expected in a research laboratory but I can't get away with such a substantial explosion; the broken glass windows alone will draw attention. Thankfully, it's late enough in the day that the neighbouring labs are empty; no one bangs on the door to check on me but the smell of smoke will raise questions in the morning.

I peer blearily out of the empty window frame. The last few rays of sunlight are disappearing over the domed roof and towering spires of the Academy. My hands move in repetitive, practised motions, summoning the last few seconds of sunlight to me to replenish my magic for the night ahead. A warmth spreads through my chest and my magic hums contentedly, happy to have been utilised for the experiment instead of being suppressed as usual. My magic doesn't care about failure, it only cares about escaping the tight leash of control I'm forced to maintain.

My legs shake as I attempt to sweep the shattered

glass into a corner; cleaning up feels overwhelming. I wrap myself in my spare cloak, leaving the one covering the workbench legs well alone, and turn the collar up to protect against the winter gales.

The laboratory is a chaotic mess: very little is salvageable. Tomorrow I'll make a note of what needs to be replaced and how much it will cost. It won't be cheap and I'll need approval from my sponsor, Dervla. Once the door is closed on the destruction, I check it's firmly locked before leaving.

To say today was unsuccessful is an understatement. It's been a long time since I've had an experiment fail and, even then, they don't blow up half the room.

Defeated, I head down the worn, stone steps out of the Academic's wing and almost make it across the central courtyard before a man's voice rings out.

"Sage, a moment," the please is conspicuously absent. Honestly, it's not even really a request; it never is with Principal Alemond.

I stop walking but refuse to concede any distance and walk back towards him. His nose twitches as he recognises my counter power play. Intentionally irritating him has been one of my few joys. My latest scientific paper gained quite a bit of notoriety in the Academy and it rankles me that he takes credit for the initial idea. So I relish no longer pandering to his rank and stand my ground where I can.

"The explosion just then. Should I be concerned?" A simpering smile accompanies his shout, louder than needed. He remains fixed in place, his words reverberating intentionally. We both refuse to take a step towards each other.

"A small miscalculation." My refusal to apologise irritates him more.

"I hope you can afford to repair the damage. Athnavar Academy is a historic building and we must treat it with care."

I deflect with an internal eye roll. The Academy is barely older than the founding of Trevesiga, maybe one hundred and fifty years at most; granite stones and wooden rafters, nothing precious. Just a home for second-rate, under-achieving academics.

"If it's too much of a disturbance, I could always follow up with the Academy in Pentargon? They did seem keen to accommodate my new research." It's a cheap shot, name-dropping the illustrious Pentargon Academy, but he started it and it feels good to take my bad day out on someone.

The conflict is visible across his face, and, if I had been in a better mood, I would have enjoyed watching him struggle whether to take the bait and continue this argument in public or to acknowledge I have bargaining power now and leave me alone. There's no one around right now but the Academy is never truly empty. He takes it.

"I do hope this isn't a sign that you're a bit of a one-hit wonder. With all this additional attention, there are a lot more people to disappoint." Smugness radiates from him in greasy, thick waves.

"One-hit wonder? I hardly think Sage needs to prove anything anymore." A voice from behind me, soft on the breeze but dripping in derision. It belongs to Dervla

Cairbre, my sponsor and the only person who holds Principal Alemond in a lower regard than I do. "She is working at the frontier of scientific development. Not many Academies have researchers that can claim the same." Casually examining her meticulous fingernails, I notice a touch of irritation in her tone.

"Good evening, Ms Cairbre," he greets Dervla with a false smile, almost a grimace.

"Goodnight to you too, Principal," she says, effectively ending the conversation. She turns and links arms with me, steering me back towards my demolished laboratory.

All thoughts of running from my disastrous day and having an early night are abandoned when Dervla surveys the destruction and picks her way through the room, somehow managing to avoid spoiling her clothes.

"Clearly you decided to go ahead without me. I take it this was the result of our pet project then?" She lifts one dark eyebrow and gestures to the chaos. "How much is this disaster going to cost me to fix?"

I sink against the dented storage cabinet and fold my arms, "I haven't added it all up yet but it won't be cheap." All of the laboratory equipment will need to be replaced, not to mention finding someone to fix the windows without asking too many questions.

Dervla has extensive business interests across Trevesiga and so, while she is my sponsor and closest friend, I don't have a monopoly on her time and attention.

"It will be worth it when it works. I'll move a few

things around; you should get the funding by the end of the week." I smile gratefully, relieved that she's taken the explosion and damage in her stride. She shrugs delicately and surveys the detritus littering the floor. "Although, I maintain this is not the best place to conduct these sorts of experiments. You got lucky today, but it just takes one person to discover what you're doing…"

She's not wrong. My laboratory space isn't exactly desirable. Athnavar Academy begrudgingly upgraded me after my last publication but before the explosion my predecessors' ancient books and equipment cluttered the room. Now, tattered pages lie strewn across the floor and the old equipment is unsalvageable. With all of this cleared away, the space is still small and cramped. It's not suitable for clandestine explosions either.

She gets to the point, checking her watch. "Is there anything I can do to make you consider that position in Pentargon?"

We'd put this to bed several times before, but she will not let it go. I should know by now that nothing stands in her way when she wants something. "No, nothing. Despite what I say to wind up the Principal."

"I don't mention it because of the funding. There are other benefits to taking up a position in the capital. Easier to conceal your work, more secure accommodation, better facilities and you'd be making it clear where your allegiance lies." I observe her closely. This level of persistence is unusual, normally she trusts my judgement when it comes to the research part of our arrangement.

"And the drawbacks? More security means being watched, making it harder to achieve our project, unlimited funding comes with input and others' ideas and perhaps I don't have political aspirations." Relocating to Pentargon sounds like punishment, constantly being observed and monitored, no autonomy or independence. And, with my family's history with the city, it's better avoided.

"I know it's not what you want right now but I want you to seriously consider it. If you're discovered here, I can't protect you. Pentargon would give you more freedom than you know." The thinnest hint of frustration starts to show through her tone now. "I'm concerned for your safety."

"Safety?" I say sharply, taking greater note of Dervla's expression. "Why are you concerned about my safety?"

"There's been more activity from the rebel groups since the assassination." My stomach drops. Trevesiga was rocked when a small group of rebels penetrated the palace security and murdered the King. They were caught and severely punished but it seems that wasn't enough of a deterrent for the others.

"They seek a way to make magic more accessible, to turn it into weapons against us. If they knew what we were working on…" She pauses, uncertain, tightening the leather straps of the falconry gauntlet she wears on her arm. "They're rallying now. It's only a matter of time before a mistake like tonight draws their attention. Or worse, attracts the Mordros."

"What if I don't care what the Mordros think?" I've never reacted well to being cornered. I force myself to remember that Dervla cares about me and snapping at her is not productive. I centre myself with a deep breath and rub my aching chest with my knuckles again.

She patiently watches me gather myself and smother my growing anger. I know what happens to people who threaten the Mordros and, despite my resistance to moving, a slow prickle travels down my arms, the hairs standing to attention.

"My answer is still no."

She hides her disappointment well, covering the small deflation in her body with a nonchalant shrug as she makes for the door. I grimace, recognising she doesn't consider this conversation finished, just adjourned.

"Get me an inventory of the damaged equipment by the morning and I'll ensure it is replaced. And don't leave the laboratory in this state again – anyone could have discovered it."

Suitably chastised and shivering from the icy wind blowing through the empty panes, I survey the damage and resign myself to a late night tidying and cataloguing. There's not much I can do to hide the smashed windows but the rest I can tackle.

Chapter 2

Completing an inventory of the damage took a lot longer than I wanted and my shoulders and neck are aching by the time most of the debris is piled into a corner. Dervla was right to insist that the mess was cleaned up; my exhaustion made me sloppy and the mess could have easily been found and questions raised.

I retie my long ponytail ready for the windy walk home, thankfully clear of glass shards this time, when the earth begins to shake violently and all sound cuts out.

A pulse travels through my body and knocks me to the ground, vision blurring and ears ringing. My hands and knees are grazed and dripping blood from broken glass I've overlooked. Noise trickles in, but all I can decipher are screams and shouts of distress. The vast flagstones on the floor have cracked in half, deep grooves running under my hands and towards the door. Someone shakes my shoulder urgently, pulling me round to face them. Dervla has returned and her dark skin is ashen as she pulls me to my feet. Her mouth is grim and her hands are steady. She's remarkably calm considering we've been attacked. Thick smoke creeps round the doorframe's corner, curling towards us.

"We need to stay hidden." She repeats it twice more and I realise, through the ringing in my ears, she's waiting for my response. I manage a small nod before my vision fractures again and I lean on her shorter frame for support. She keeps a tight hold on my waist and pulls us out into the courtyard, away from the main entrance. As soon as I'm able to walk unsupported, she picks up the pace, leading me deeper into the older wing of the Academy, where the faculty work, along winding corridors I scarcely knew existed.

A few shell-shocked people brave the corridors too, stumbling around, all injured. Through the acrid stench of burning smoke, a cloying sweeter smell of burnt meat permeates and my stomach roils. Dust and mortar fall from the ceiling and my vision flickers with black spots. Through the shattered windows, I can see fire spreading from the buildings around us.

We don't stop for anyone, avoiding eye contact and Dervla is walking faster and faster, almost running. We reach the bottom of a narrow flight of stairs and Dervla checks we are alone and looks at me with a sort of nervousness I haven't seen on her face before dragging me into an unmarked office.

It's empty and a thick layer of sticky dust grips my shoes to the floor. She strides across the room to the dark wooden panelling. I don't see how she does it but a door opens and she gestures to me to go through. Confused and still dripping blood from my hands and knees, I venture through the doorway, into the total darkness and Dervla seals us in.

"You've channelled today?" she whispers fervently. "We'll need your light."

I don't think to question her, even though using my magic in public is a capital offence, and summon a flash of light from my palm. Our faces are illuminated and before her pupils shrink and adjust, I catch a fleeting glimpse of fear in her brown eyes.

She looks at the flickering ball of light I'm holding. "We need to hurry." It's not clear whether the rush is because she doesn't believe my magic will last or if she thinks there's someone chasing us. I'm too afraid to ask.

She pushes me ahead to lead the way through the damp stone tunnel as it slopes gently downwards. We move in silence for no more than a few minutes before the tunnel opens into a small, underground quay. This must be an offshoot of the river that surrounds the city, as the water smells clean and fresh.

Dervla passes me, sinking her hands up to her elbows into the flowing stream. I assume she's channelling until I hear her muttering under her breath and moving her hands in a complicated series of movements. I realise she's wielding magic.

She halts abruptly and turns to face me, the glow from my magic highlighting the concern on her face. "We need to get out of here. I'm going to take you to Pentargon but it will be risky."

"To the capital?" I'm confused and frustration rises despite my fear, "but my home is here, my work."

"Sage, there's been a massive attack on the city. Until we know more, we need to get somewhere secure. I need to keep you safe and this is our best option." Eerily calm, she keeps her hands in the water, channelling now, and drawing immense amounts of power if the sweat on her face is anything to go by. The light in my hands stutters and extinguishes completely.

Dervla grabs for my arm in the darkness, startling me, "Listen to me carefully. I've sent a message to Pentargon and I'm going to ferry us there via the aqueducts. I travel this way all the time but I've never done it with someone else before and it will be draining. If my magic fails, keep floating. People will look for us, eventually." Her grip is vice-like and feels like a manacle round my wrist.

"If you fail?" A wave of dread rises from the bottom of my stomach.

"If my magic runs out."

"But Pentargon is days away!" I can't fathom the amount of magic required to wield for that long.

"Not using the aqueducts." She guides me forcefully to the water, taking my lack of resistance for compliance and I stumble. In the deep blackness, I feel my way into a small wooden boat. A precarious little ferry, built for one. I feel Dervla climbing in behind me; we're back-to-back, presumably so she can use her hands like rudders to steer us through the water with her Mordros magic. The boat rocks dangerously, water lapping at the edges and spilling into the bottom.

"Don't move. If you rock the boat, I may not manage to hold us." With that last discomforting instruction,

I lock my muscles in place and barely breathe, desperately trying not to make this any harder for Dervla than it already is.

The tunnel keeps us in perpetual darkness. I can tell we are moving by the brush of air against my face and the rocking of our fragile ferry on the current. Ahead I hear harsh screams and shouting. My eyes adjust and squinting hard I see a warm, orange light which glows brighter as we approach. Still floating, we emerge from the tunnel onto the main river, slipping into the faster current. I look up at the burning banks of the river to the chains of people frantically passing up buckets of river water to quench the fires. It's an impossible task. There aren't enough buckets, or people to help.

The ancient city is made of stone for the most part, but the residential areas are all wood and have been hit the hardest. We wind through the city and I see more and more devastation. The anguished screams are at odds with the rhythmic sloshing of the water as we rock and shudder through the eddies. I close my eyes, clenching my teeth to smother the guilt of abandoning the people in need and resist the anxiety that rises to the surface when I think of the currents beneath us. We're not out of danger yet either.

Out of the city we leave the main river and divert into the aqueduct system. These towering stone structures are the pride of Trevesiga, the visible reminder of the Mordros superior magical and engineering abilities. The imposing aqueducts ensure every citizen has access to clean water and apparently, I've now been permitted to learn, allow the Mordros to travel and communicate over large distances.

I can breathe a little easier once we've navigated into the aqueducts with their high, impenetrable walls. Despite the unforgiving speed of the currents, the water is at least calmer and flatter. A strong breeze glues salty tears to my cheeks which stings as we pick up speed. Overhead, I hear the harsh hunting call of a bird of prey.

The waning moon breaks through the drifting clouds at points throughout the night. We travel in silence, muscles cramped and barely moving. The bird continues to call out, following us, hidden in the darkness. I hope it's Kaens, Dervla's kestrel. They're never far apart and I hate the thought of her pinned under the rubble, wings savagely broken.

Sleeping is impossible in this floating prison. The constant wind and slapping of water do not provide much comfort as the night wears on. I try not to think of the attack, of the sheer power of the blasts and the people of Athnavar we've left behind. Shame at running away, at not staying to help, starts to eat at me. I consider turning around, asking Dervla to take us back but what would be the use? I have no resources to help, no place to shelter anyone. My home was in the middle of those burning districts, surely burnt to the ground now. Time passes slowly, the winter night stretching ahead of us.

The few stars that have peeked through the clouds to keep us company begin to fade. Dawn comes but every moment is drawn out when there are no distractions. I seek apricity in the rare winter sun on my face when finally, it rises over the raised walls, replenishing my magic after the long, dark night. Distracted by its encouraging warmth, I startle when we reach a standstill. A small floating quay, attached to a stone doorway in the aqueduct wall, is out of reach.

"You did it." I turn to smile at Dervla but she looks broken: her body curled inwards, hunched protectively over her hands, protecting them from the brutal wind. She raises haggard eyes to meet mine and I think she attempts to smile before collapsing backwards into the water.

I launch clumsily after her, every limb seized and aching. The icy cold rips the breath from my lungs and my feet struggle to find purchase in the frigid shoulder-deep water. The current is vicious. I cling to Dervla, holding her lolling head above the water but the current drags at us both, sweeping us away from the quay.

Guards appear on the quayside and the first leaps into the water and takes Dervla from me. He holds her hands in the flowing water and supports her head gently on his shoulder, her smaller body dwarfed by his muscular frame. Water flattens his dark hair over deep, caramel eyes.

"We need to get her to the waterfall." The remaining men lift Dervla out of the water, carrying her through the doorway at the edge of the quay.

"Come with me," he snaps, pulling me viciously behind him as he exits the water. He grips my forearm tightly, ignoring my shivers and steers me down steps wet with water dripping from Dervla's clothes.

I glance through a small window in the aqueduct wall to Pentargon below. Resentment bubbles to the surface at being forced to return so unexpectedly to the city I've been avoiding for years.

Chapter 3

The same four walls stare back at me through the unsettling darkness. The incessant sound of racing water highlights the monotony of being imprisoned. I think I've been held here for days, left to stew over Dervla's fate.

I recognised the insignias on the uniforms of our rescuers – they were from the palace. We were separated before Dervla regained consciousness and I was taken underground and escorted to this cell. My nerves were shredded after the first few hours.

Darkness has never been a friend to me and I'm left alone in a stone cell, shivering. The temptation to reach inside and draw out the tiniest bit of light, of warmth, nags constantly at the edge of my attention. My magic writhes inside, resisting being imprisoned and wanting to be released. I don't dare let it out, not even the smallest fraction. That's one way to guarantee I'll never leave this cell alive.

Other than the echoing footsteps of guards changing shifts, I have no way of knowing how much time has passed. Initially I tried calling out to them, asking if

Dervla survived, begging for food and water. But I haven't received a single word of acknowledgement. A balloon of fear continues to swell in my stomach, compressing my lungs and making my chest ache.

Two guards arrive when I'm barely strong enough to stand. They fasten heavy, iron restraints to my wrists and secure them to the table that's brought in behind them. My magic shrinks inside my chest, cowering at being trapped in this cell. Neither of them acknowledges me, nor speaks a single word, their actions well practised and efficient. My legs are left unbound but I don't even consider trying to escape. I have barely a fraction of magic compared to everyone else. It's not even close to a fair fight. Satisfied that I'm properly incarcerated, they leave.

The heavy door heaves open slowly sometime later, startling me. An older man, with a thick white streak in his hair, enters with the sort of confidence I've found, only occurs in people who are used to being obeyed instantly. He places a flickering oil lantern onto the table and my eyes take a while to adjust. He's well dressed and small in stature, but the warmth from the light contrasts with the cruelty around his lips. He grabs the chains holding my restraints and yanks them towards him, the skin on my wrists ripped away by the motion as I slump forward in forced compliance.

My stomach growls again and reminds me how long it's been since I've eaten. I risk a glance up at the man but find no pity in his eyes. I summon my strength to ask if Dervla is okay.

"That's none of your concern. I would worry less over

her fate and more over your own." His voice is harsh and unyielding, with the clipped aristocratic accent I'd grown up hating. Contempt fills the lines in his face as it turns into a sneer, ageing him substantially.

"Tell me who helped you organise the attacks on Athnavar," he commands.

"What?" I pull against the manacles in shock, a rabbit caught in a snare, my whole body resisting the accusation.

"I don't ask twice." Each word punctuated with barely concealed hatred, the old man leans forward, hard lines drawn around his narrowed eyes. I back into the wooden chair, bruising my spine to increase the distance between us.

"I don't know what you're talking about." I smother my rising panic. When he doesn't relent, the panic takes over. "My name is Sage Dewnam. I'm a researcher at Athnavar Academy. I work for Dervla."

When he doesn't react, his mouth still sneering at me, I can't help looking around desperately to see if there is anyone else to hear my pleas.

"You are an Aubade," he says, as if that is a crime by itself. To him I am a waste, a pointless burden on society with my useless magic.

"And that automatically makes me guilty of the attacks on Athnavar? I haven't done anything." I shout, hoping the guards at the door will come to my aid.

"What do you know of pain, Sage?" he whispers, leaning towards me, his hot breath on my face turning my body to ice. I'm trapped down here, utterly at his mercy.

The cell door opens, a silhouette of a tall figure slips into the room. They remain shrouded in darkness and stand, unmoving, in the corner. Any hope I have of them coming to my rescue is cruelly slashed when the old man looks over his shoulder and says, "Begin."

For a moment nothing happens and I pause in expectation, body tense and my focus split between the known danger in front of me and the shadow lurking in my periphery. Then I'm hit with a fire from within. Every fibre of my body is forced into an agonising vice. It goes on and on. Never-ending. My head pounds, and blood trickles from my mangled wrists where the metal of the restraint bites through my skin. Then, the awful pressure recedes. I'm left panting, forehead leaning on the table.

"Good. Good." A guttural rasp, almost a laugh, comes from the old man watching me squirm in fear. "Again."

The shadow obeys and my body is wracked with agony.

"Confess you were behind the attack!" his eyes are alight, gleaming with relish.

I press my lips together, locking my jaw so I don't bite my tongue. I remain silent.

My muscles cramp and burn as the vice tightens, the larger ones in my thighs spasm whilst the smaller ones in my hands and feet sting like I've plunged them into an ants' nest. I hear my throat shatter with the cry that is ripped from it.

"Go gently now, ease off a little. That's it." He coaxes with pleasure, at ease with my agony. The silent shadow obeys.

"Why did you bomb Athnavar?" His glee is evident now I'm being punished in a way he clearly believes I deserve. I summon enough energy to open my eyes and see a grim smile pulling back to reveal pearly white, perfect teeth.

I couldn't reply even if I wanted to. My brain can't focus on anything other than pain.

They repeat the process: pain then relief, questions then more pain. Waiting for the next wave, anticipating the wracking spasms throughout my body, is worse. The pauses in between feel like I'm dreaming, the ghosts of torment linger in my fried skin, so over-sensitive that the sensation from the cold metal manacles feels agonising.

The person in the shadows never wavers, nor reacts to my screams, only applies the pressure again and again.

I know when I've reached my limit: the blackness of the cell turns to welcome me and my vision dims and goes black.

Vaguely, I hear the scrape of his chair against the stone floor, "Very well. We will resume tomorrow." and then I drift into blissful nothingness.

The same procedure follows the next day, the shadow in the corner burning my muscles and organs without leaving a mark and the old man questioning me about the attacks until my brain is ready to give out. I resent my old self for hating the cold, quiet loneliness of the cell and I wish I could return to the isolation and be left alone in the darkness. I never speak; my voice is only used for screaming until eventually that too gives up.

A distant banging and shouts infiltrate my fading consciousness. I don't dare move, desperate not to bring attention to myself in case it triggers another wave of pain. I'm not ready for more torture.

My eyes are loosely closed, the side of my head rests on the cool, iron table.

A violent slam of the door reverberates through me, the unexpected noise piercing the haze of pain, ricocheting around my brain.

"Get out! You have no authority here!" The old man lambasts against the intrusion, infuriated by someone interrupting his enjoyment.

A welcome voice, full of fury, penetrates my cloudy mind. "Does the King know you've hidden her in the darkness and tortured her? When I demanded that she be protected."

She came. She's alive. I can feel Dervla press her cool hand gently against my forehead, tilting my gaze up to her. I feel a small wave of relief at seeing her. That's about all my poor broken body can manage before I slump back on the table. I keep my gaze locked on her though; I don't dare to blink in case she disappears.

The old man falters, confidence draining from him in the face of her rage.

When he remains silent, I see her eyes fill briefly with tears she doesn't let fall. Two narrow jets of water shoot from her hands into the manacle locks, shattering them violently and the walls echo with the noise. She pulls me to standing, an action which exhausts me – my legs are too weak. I lean heavily on her small frame and desperately try not to think about my shaking hands or how broken my body has become.

As we make our way to the door, the old man is frozen in place. Dervla tugs me along, before he can object. The shadow is nowhere to be seen.

Our pace is excruciatingly slow. We climb floor after floor, resting frequently, each pause shorter than I would like before Dervla hauls me to my feet, encouraging me to continue. Her anger is icy cold and tension radiates through every one of her steps. Each time she sees me stumble or my muscles spasm in an aftershock, her lips purse threateningly.

She leads me upwards through a beautiful palace I recognise from childhood stories, Chi An Mor, the heart of Pentargon city. It's built into a bleached yellow sandstone cliff with the rest of the city separating it from the ocean. I've heard it has over one hundred floors but climbing these stairs feels like a thousand.

We pass through cream sandstone corridors, each with a shallow stream, about a hand-width wide, running along channels carved into the floor. The water is sparkling and clear and it takes everything I have not to fall down and drink from it.

Finally, Dervla pulls me into a suite of rooms and locks the door. A soft futon in front of me tempts me, begging to be slept on.

"Do you need to channel?" Dervla whispers.

I assess the dregs of magic in my chest and nod.

"Quickly then."

I stumble to the window to replenish the void in my chest. The sun is hidden behind thick clouds, casting a sombre shadow over the city below. No matter – I don't need much. My aching hands rise and call the daylight to me, replenishing my magic and wiping away some of the exhaustion from the cell.

"Come. We must go," Dervla snaps the moment my hands stop moving, her posture tense. She unlocks the door and drags my weary body back out into the palace.

The climb is gruelling, each flight of stairs deepens my exhaustion and a glance at Dervla tells me she isn't faring much better.

"Keep going Sage," Dervla pants. "Not much further. We have to get to the King first." Her pace falters as she struggles to bear my weight. I must rest but the resolve in her face tells me it's not an option.

"What happened to you?" I gasp as we reach the top of another flight of stairs.

"I burnt out." She pauses and looks around to check we are alone. "My magic got us here but I had nothing left. The waterfall underneath the palace restored me but it took days."

Days of channelling magic to recover? That's a staggering amount. I've come close to burnout before but it takes me moments to replenish. The amount of magic she must be able to store defies all of my preconceptions. I regard Dervla warily, realising for the first time she might be one of the most powerful Mordros in the Kingdom.

"I came for you as soon as I could. I didn't realise my

message had been misunderstood. They thought I had brought you in for questioning. That I apprehended you when I escaped." She turns to me, her dark brown eyes wet. "It's my fault you were tortured."

"You were the reason we escaped Athnavar and the attacks. You can't blame yourself for what happened next." I reach for her hand, clasping it tightly in mine. I don't blame her.

We stagger upwards, holding hands, ignoring our cramping, weakened legs.

Chapter 4

Dervla continues walking once we've reached the top of the stairs and leads me along a long sandstone corridor. With every step, I watch her compose herself and don a mask of blank neutrality. She halts abruptly in front of a large, wooden door and releases my hand. The action causes me to stumble. My hands plunge into the narrow channel of icy water that runs the length of the corridor. I swear aggressively as the dampness spreads up my clothes, spreading the grime from the dungeons further.

"Sage. This is important." She pauses in front of the door. "Whatever you do, do not lie to the King. He can tell. Do you understand?"

I nod, not able to bring myself to care that I'm about to meet the most powerful man in Trevesiga in ruined clothing, smelling of the dungeons.

The door partially opens to reveal the guard from the rescue, the first one in the water. He towers over both of us, his broad shoulders blocking the doorway. I might be exhausted but I note that he looks as good now as he did in wet uniform. One of his eyebrows rises at my disgusting appearance but he doesn't comment, and opens the door widely.

The room is a vast space: large panes of glass cover three sides and I take a minute to absorb the views. I expected to see the city and ocean beneath me but on the north side is the great expanse of the River Targon, lazily disappearing under and around the floor of the chamber. I could walk straight out and onto the surface of the water.

To the left and right of the river are the tops of two show-stopping waterfalls which hug the external glass walls before thundering into the city below. I'm confused. Growing up in Pentargon I remember the river appearing at the base of Chi An Mor, the palace breathing it into existence. These beautiful waterfalls are completely hidden, disappearing into wide tunnels that are buried between the palace and the cliff-front – another Mordros secret. This room and the upper floors of the palace are recessed into the cliff and instead of a city view to the west, I can see the curved arm of the archipelago stretching into the distance.

Once I've adjusted to the unexpected view, the other people in the room draw my attention. Dervla smiles weakly, her dark skin pallid and ashen from exhaustion and her hands pulled tight behind her back. One of the two men sitting opposite me is the old man from the dungeon. My lungs constrict, feet frozen in place. Adrenaline rushes through my body, screaming at me to run. My body listens and I back away, only to find the guard from the rescue blocking my exit.

Trembling, I turn to face my torturer. His face is

flushed; he must have set quite a pace to arrive before us but still he manages to look derisively at us. I keep him in my peripheral vision and take in the final occupant sat behind a large reflection pool.

He must be King Cado; a thin metal circlet adorns his head, the pale gold contrasting with his dark hair. My unease remains as I take him in. He's tall and long-limbed, classically handsome and looks completely at ease leaning back in his chair, a half-smile playing across his lips. Actually, I think he's smirking at my sodden state. I doubt he'd still be smiling if he got close enough to smell me though.

"Welcome to Pentargon and Chi An Mor," he says archly, surveying me from head to toe, noting my bedraggled appearance. "I hope you're feeling well since your ordeal."

My fear dissipates at his poor choice of words and I work to stifle a sarcastic response. Which ordeal is he referring to? Being bombed in Athnavar, being imprisoned in *his* dungeons and tortured? It's been quite the week.

Evidently, he can read my feelings from my face; he laughs softly.

"I need you to confirm a few things for me." His soft, melodic tones are at odds with the firm line of his full lips. The atmosphere in the room turns frigid. Someone is on thin ice. I nod cautiously, trying to work out who.

"A simple yes or no will suffice. Since your arrival in Pentargon have you been mistreated?"

"Yes." The water in the pool moves, the current swirling in lazy circles.

"By this man?" He gestures to the old man.

"Yes" I hate how soft my voice sounds, barely echoing in the chamber.

"You were tortured?"

I pause, my throat thick and hot with anger. I look directly at the old man sitting beside him, glaring daggers at me.

"Yes."

"Did you have any knowledge of the attacks on Athnavar, Porth or Cathair?"

Three separate attacks. The two largest cities in Trevesiga, and Athnavar. I'm floored by the extent of violence that I forget that the King is looking to me to answer.

"No."

"Are you a traitor to this kingdom, to Trevesiga?" The old man leans forward expectantly, hands clasped tightly.

"No."

Silence. Both Dervla and the old man look at the King. He is studying me carefully, evaluating my every breath. I square my shoulders to meet his gaze. Despite the reflection pool between us, I make out the amber flecks in his green eyes. Rare eyes indeed, a royal trait I suspect.

Without releasing me from his stare, the King announces, "Lord Bal, you are hereby relinquished of your position as the King's Almanac."

Relief pours through me briefly – he believes me. It is quickly superseded by thick dread. I was tortured by the second most powerful man in Trevesiga. All positions on the Concord are meant to be equal but it's the Almanac that speaks for the King. The water in the reflection pool goes cloudy and churns between us.

"You cannot do that! Appointment to the Concord is a lifetime position." Lord Bal is incensed, spittle flying from his thin lips.

"You served my father well, too well. But I have no need for you. I'm allowing you the dignity of resigning. Don't make me change my mind." The King's voice starts off carefully neutral, his handsome face devoid of all feeling at the mention of his late father, but the lethal threat is apparent when he finishes talking. I feel the shock radiate through Dervla and barely breathe as Lord Bal walks carefully around the table and stops in front of the guard.

"You'll regret this," Lord Bal promises, shouldering his way out of the room. The guard sidesteps as Lord Bal barrels towards him, avoiding his trampling path.

"See he leaves Pentargon by morning," the King instructs the guard. "I don't expect him to go quietly," he adds.

The reflection pool is bubbling, steam rising, water sloshing over the edges. No one else pays it any attention but I ease backwards towards Dervla to avoid the hot spray.

I look round the room, unsettled by the old Almanac lurking in Pentargon.

"When can I go home?" My enquiry is tentative. I do not want to be involved in lethal palace politics.

"That might prove difficult," a deep voice sounds from behind me. The guard's arms are loosely crossed and he leans casually against the doorway. "The Academy suffered badly in the attack. Barely half the buildings are standing," he adds dispassionately. "It may never reopen."

"Captain Eskar Devath, the King's Verax," the King explains, giving the Captain a cautionary look. The Verax is a truth-sayer and the Kingdom's moral compass.

The Captain continues, ignoring the King's warning "Your apartment in Athnavar was also a target in the attack. The whole street was destroyed. There's nothing there for you to return to."

I sway on my feet, fighting to remain focused and present, my hand automatically pressing into my chest.

"You will need to remain here. Under supervision," the Captain continues, oblivious to my growing distress.

The King interrupts, "It seems I'm in need of another Concord member." Dervla twists towards him in surprise but his eyes are fixed on me.

"Would you consider becoming my Alchemist?"

Concern remains etched onto Dervla's forehead. She looks at me, desperately trying to communicate something with her eyes, a warning? The King's face is carefully neutral, the expression of a polished politician but I catch his eyes flicking to the wounds on my wrists from the manacles which are slowly dripping blood onto the floor.

Reeling from the Captain's words, I take a moment to think. My life was at the Academy, everything I owned was in that apartment. I need somewhere to live, somewhere to work and clearly some protection if the rebels are targeting me. I don't know if I can bear to live in this palace, above the dungeons that is, but my options are extremely limited.

Tucking my bleeding wrists behind me, I ask, "I can resign at any point? You won't force me to stay in the city."

His smile is unexpectedly warm, as if he knows what's running through my mind and I'm struck by how much younger and lighter he looks. He's the same age as Dervla and I, but a year of ruling has already written fine lines around his eyes. "Yes, you can resign at any time, although I'll do my best to make sure you don't want to."

His eyes twinkle at that last comment. Evidently, he is used to getting his way. As he holds my gaze, the reasons I resisted coming back to Pentargon feel distant.

"I accept."

Dervla's shoulders sink, resigned.

"Welcome to my Concord then, Alchemist," the King announces smugly.

Chapter 5

"You can both leave us now." The King's tone switches, the clear command ringing out across the empty Concord chamber to Dervla and the Captain and I startle when I realise, he intends for me to remain.

Dervla's eyebrow rises at his tone, displeased with his blunt dismissal. Their gazes lock together in a battle of wills before she concedes defeat and sweeps out of the room, silently followed by the Captain.

"I want to know why you think the rebels are targeting you, Sage? Why have you caught their interest?"

"I have no idea." The lie feels heavy on my tongue but he doesn't call me out on it.

"What does Dervla need you for that caused her to save you from a burning city, even when her magic was so depleted?"

I stay mute and our gazes battle it out. Amber sparks in his eyes flash and I feel the air grow hot with magic. My body shudders under his command. His kindness has limits: he will not stop until he has an answer. I glance at the reflection pool, buying time while it churns impatiently.

"You'd have to ask Dervla."

"I plan to. Now, I have one more thing to ask of you." The King's voice is softer now, coaxing.

Instinctively my arms cross and I take a step towards the door.

"I would very much like to see your magic, if you'd be willing to show me?"

Whatever I thought I was going to be asked, it wasn't this. Breaking the Difan law, in front of the King, is tantamount to a death sentence. My magic is forbidden for a reason.

"You won't be punished for it," the King whispers, and patches of red appear high on his cheekbones. We both know his family is the reason my magic is unsanctioned. The Mordros claimed Trevesiga as their own years ago, wiping away any resistance with their vast oceans of water magic. The Aubades that remain are disparate, scattered across Trevesiga and not permitted to practise our magic. The Mordros claim our paltry magic is dangerous, uncontrollable and chaotic, the antithesis of their superior abilities, whereas, wind-channelling Zephyrs were banned because they posed a threat. The majority of us live with our magic hidden, constantly battling the temptation to let it break free.

My mind recoils against the King's request, even as my magic rises to the surface, begging and pleading for a chance to be released. Demonstrating my magic feels personal, intrusive, after a lifetime of cloaking it. Until our escape, I'd never used it in front of anyone.

I take a steadying breath – the turmoil of the last few days has me on edge, my control brittle. Magic may escape whether I choose it to or not.

Misinterpreting my struggle, the King approaches me as if I were a wounded animal, hands raised in placation. He thinks I'm worried about the ramifications of letting my magic free. The irony of punishment after the torture I've endured extracts a half-crazed laugh from my throat. I'm not worried; I'm angry. I don't want to share something so personal with someone I should hate – the cause of mine and my people's suffering, long before I was subjected to a torture chamber. I lost my family to the Mordros' negligence long ago but the prospect of sharing my magic with him is what breaks me.

My hands clench and burn hot, magic ripping through me, my anger turning to ecstasy when I let go. Magic sings and hums through my body and bright, white sunlight erupts, unrestrained from my fingertips. This isn't the meagre ball of light I produced in the tunnels under Athnavar, or the beam of magic I used in my research that caused the explosion. This is a release unlike any I've felt before. I've never loosened control and relished in it. But it ends. All too soon. The light sputters out.

My hands tingle, fried from the release of energy and I clasp them to my chest and feel myself slumping towards the floor.

The King darts forward, catching me, cradling the back of my head to his chest.

I pull away; his chivalry is unnerving. His stare is fixed on the horizon through the large glass windows, green eyes murky. The silence between us thickens and

I slip out of his grasp and stumble to my feet, leaving him lost in thought as I escape the Concord chamber.

Chapter 6

"What the hell were you thinking taking a position on the Concord?" Dervla's voice is icy cold from outside the Concord chamber where she lies in wait. I ignore her, stumbling ahead.

I have to get out of the palace, to find somewhere quiet. Everything is gone and I just showed my magic to my biggest enemy. My breath is ragged, it echoes along the corridors. I run, blindly searching for somewhere private to breakdown.

"Sage! Stop!" Dervla wrenches my arm, pulling me round to face her. I avoid her dark eyes and stare out of the window, focusing on counting the islets of the archipelago in the distance, nails biting into my palms.

"Are you alright? What did King Cado want?" Her voice is soft, gentle even, despite the vice-like grip on my arm and I let it envelop me.

Words tumble over each other in my mouth but none make it out.

"Come, let's get you into the daylight." Instinctively knowing what I need, she leads me through the palace via quiet back corridors, away from prying eyes.

The day is fading, shrouded by low clouds, the sunset struggling to scatter its last light. We huddle against the winter chill, at the edge of the formal gardens while I turn my face and hands to the remaining sunlight. My hands move of their own accord. The meagre warmth on my face counteracts the adrenaline running through my body and settles my restored magic. It's fretting, looking for another release, a way to burn off the fear and uncertainty. I wrestle control; I can't risk a light show here of all places, even a small one. Dervla reads the struggle on my face and waits patiently until the sun slips below the horizon. My magic calms, irritated but resigned.

"Better?" She breaks the silence, eyes furrowed and concerned.

"Yes. No. Maybe. A little." Swirling emotions lurk at the edges of my mind, threatening to overrule me. I wipe the thin film of sweat from my forehead. Her first question lingers, the smallest crack in our relationship.

"I had no choice. I have no home, no way of making a living. The Almanac…" I stumble on his title as shadows grow around us, my mind threatening to take me back to the dungeons. "He made it clear how little an Aubade matters in his city."

She reaches for my shaking hand, holding it tightly. "It's not his city. And we're working to change that, remember? I wouldn't have let anything happen to you." Dervla's consolation rings hollow, the crack widening to a chasm. To be a Mordros and an Aubade mean very different things. it's not only our different magics causing the schism. She has influence in this city but she's not invincible. The image of her collapsed in the water when we arrived in Pentargon is still fresh. As a member of the Concord, I'll be untouchable.

"I know what I'm doing."

"I really hope you do." Her eyes stare into the distance, attention caught by something I can't see. "Your research is critical and we don't have much time."

Her comment makes me bristle. For the first time, I wonder whether my friendship with Dervla is a little one-sided.

"I'll arrange for a new laboratory to be set-up. Somewhere private where you can work uninterrupted. Be careful who you trust in the palace. People are rarely what they seem, especially King Cado or Captain Devath."

Noted – not that I was planning on making friends here anyway I scoff privately to myself.

Dervla pulls on my arm, commanding my attention. "I'm serious, Sage. I grew up with them both and yet I still feel like I hardly know them anymore." I pull away. I've had enough of being told what to do today.

"And Cado? What did he want?" she asks.

"To see my magic. The novelty of it, I suppose." I start to tell her I disappointed him with whatever he was hoping to see, but a loud bird call sounds out a warning and Dervla tenses. My heart soars as she extends her arm and Kaens lands heavily on the leather gauntlet encircling it, russet feathers ruffled and amber eyes gleaming. She made it out of Athnavar safely.

Dervla nods at the majestic bird, communicating

back and forth in their silent exchange of gestures before she turns back to me, whispering curtly, "We're not alone out here. I have to go now; I have urgent business. Promise you'll do everything you can to solve your research. I'll be away for several days, but we'll speak more when I'm back."

They disappear into the blackness, heading for the city and I savour relief that Kaens made it through the attacks unharmed.

Chapter 7

The suite of rooms I've been given in the palace are beautifully spacious: the lounge alone is bigger than my whole apartment in Athnavar. Such compensation for being accused of treason and tortured. After Dervla's abrupt departure I was left disorientated and still disgusting from the dungeons. A servant found me wandering the hallways and after realising that I had nothing to my name – no clean clothes or belongings and no idea of where to go for food – they took good care of me. I now have a new wardrobe of clothes, paper and pens to write with and a selection of books from the palace library to occupy my time while my wounded wrists heal. Over the last week, when it's not been cloudy, I've watched the sun set over the city and archipelago, but this morning as I sit in the shaded windowsill, I prefer the sunrise.

In keeping with the Mordros disdain for frivolity, there is no artwork or decoration on the walls and the rough stone should feel unfinished but, with the scale of the rooms, it doesn't. The floor is heated underfoot and I uncurl my toes to savour the new sensation.

I summon the strength to venture outside my rooms, to leave my heated floor behind. I have no choice but to attend my first Concord meeting today. My feet trip over the long ceremonial robes as I trudge up the endless stairs to reach the Concord chamber. The cream stone walls blur as I fall, bruising my knees badly. These bruises will match the shadows under my eyes. Sleeping has been hard; every shadow or movement in the corner of my eye makes me flinch and sends my heart racing. But the shadows stay as they are in the stairwell, the pain never comes and I press my knuckles into my sternum to bring my breathing back under control and climb again. I am safe. The darkness can't hurt me.

The door to the Concord chamber is unwelcoming. I shrug off the vice of nerves compressing my straining lungs. I refuse to show weakness in front of the Mordros and steel my spine as I push through the doorway.

The members sit in a loose circle surrounding the large reflection pool, with several vacant spots. I expected to be made unwelcome and for their disdain to be palpable. But as I venture further into the spacious chamber, I am completely ignored. My presence is inconsequential compared to the ongoing argument.

"That is unacceptable." The lethality of the tone cuts through the discourse and silences the room. The King's jaw tenses but he does not comment at the Concord member who takes control of the room, rises to his feet and lifts an outraged finger towards him, careful not to point it exactly in his direction.

"I will not stand for the constant request to repeal the

Difan, nor any other law pertaining to magical access in Trevesiga." The man speaking is polished iron, every feature hard and smooth, a toughened veneer of privilege.

"Your opinion is noted," the King responds dryly, ignoring the vitriol and gesturing for small stone discs to be distributed to every person in the room. "As I was saying, shall we take a vote." My body flushes hot. I'm unexpectedly late and underprepared to cast my vote.

Historically, Concord positions were purely ceremonial, a way for the King to recognise loyalty, not expertise. With King Cado's ascension last year, he disavowed dictatorial decision-making and decreed the fate of Trevesiga will be decided upon via democracy. This landmark decision initially kindled hope outside of the Mordros, but was quickly extinguished when the status quo remained. Why he's elected to include me on his Concord still remains to be seen.

"We can vote on this issue at every meeting from now until you force my resignation like you did for Lord Bal. My position and the others will not change." The temperature of the room drops and goosebumps prickle across my skin as gazes turn to the King. He doesn't rise to the challenge, face frozen like marble. The water in the reflection pool swirls ominously. King Cado doesn't react except to turn to me.

"Sage, take a seat." I tense as one by one members of the Concord deign to recognise my presence. Some let their disgust roll across their features, others maintain a poised neutrality. Fixing my expression with a sneer that mirrors the worst of their derision, I survey each one in turn, my nerves well hidden. My gaze catches on Captain Devath and a flinch breaks through my steely resolve. His face remains blank, no trace of recognition, so I pass the empty seat to his left and take my time settling myself as far from him as possible. Dervla would be proud of my nerve, but I tuck my hands deep into my robes so no one catches them trembling. The Concord member to my right, a woman with a sleek, twist of grey hair leans over and mutters under her breath, "The King is pushing for the Difan to be repealed. We are all requested to vote." I nod at her kindness in clarifying for me and fold my hands neatly in my lap, mirroring hers whilst the voting tokens are distributed

The vote is called and one by one, the other Concord members' stone discs are tossed into the reflection pool in the centre of the room. White for disagreement, black for alignment. White to maintain the status quo and suppression of all magic other than the Mordros, black for equality.

I drop my token in the pool. It sits lonely, a shadow surrounded by light counterparts until Captain Devath's casual flick has his black disk spinning through the air and splashing into the pool with a flourish, ripples spreading wide. I catch a subtle glimpse between him and the King and the smallest of nods exchanged before the final member casts their vote. The King abstains. Regardless, one additional vote would not have changed the outcome, the Captain and I are sorely out-numbered and I release the breath I'd trapped inside. The Difan could have been repealed right now, the lives of thousands changed irrevocably.

"Now we can begin." There's no trace of disappointment in the King's face at the outcome, casual nonchalance emanating out across the assembled Mordros. They expected the result and all I've done is reveal my intentions.

The discussions are tense. The topics vary: from mining and farming to taxes and trade agreements, or lack thereof. My silence is assumed and the barrage of arguments flies back and forth between Concord members. Several more votes are called, but nothing is achieved or agreed upon. One member will make a proposal, others will indicate their support only to be chastised by someone else, reminded of an alternative bargain and forced to withdraw. A complex web of allegiances becomes apparent with each faction fighting only for themselves. This does not bode well for King Cado's reign as discontent simmers beneath the surface, the reflection pool coming close to boiling. A kingdom without consensus terrifies me more than a brutal dictatorship.

Recess arrives after several hours and the Captain is the first out of his chair, heading straight for freedom beyond the Concord chamber door. I follow suit, the breeze from the winding corridors chilling my flushed cheeks as I run from the squabbling and self-interest. I cannot hide in my rooms, I'll be summoned back to the meeting, so I venture down the stairs, deeper into the soul of the palace.

The library is hard to find. A small antechamber, buried into the rough cliff edge is manned by a stern-faced librarian. The room is barren, save a small desk and heavy tome serving as a visitor's log. The librarian gives a cursory glance at my Concord robes and I'm waved through to the shelves behind.

It's a subterranean cavern and the only place in Chi An Mor where water doesn't flow. The towering stacks of books disappear into the deep shadows that cloak the long aisles and obscure the depths. I shudder as the edges of the shadows reach for me. Libraries are never truly quiet: the tomes creak with age and the shelves sigh with weight. My fingers skim the brass plate descriptions. If I'm going to hide down here, I may as well make good use of my time.

Another lone figure flits through the stacks. I skirt them in the gloom until their Concord robes are illuminated by the oil lamps. As they draw closer, their hood falls back, revealing a woman my age. Intrigued, I venture into her line of sight. The woman startles when she notices me; our eyes catch and I see recognition spark in hers.

"The new Alchemist?" Her whisper carries over the breeze, the edges of her dark braid flutter. I nod and a smile breaks over her face as she turns so our paths intersect.

"I'm the King's Archivist, Haelyn." She greets me warmly and with a conspiratorial grin adds, "Already looking to skip out on your first Concord meeting?"

I laugh for the first time since returning to Pentargon. "Guilty, but then it looks like you are too."

"Well, we already have something in common then." Her tone is light but I shiver as the breeze picks up around us.

"Can I help you with anything in particular?" she queries. "Because there are better places to hide in Chi An Mor."

"No, thank you. I'm just getting familiar with my surroundings."

Haelyn nods and walks past me towards the exit, her long, intricate braid swinging behind her.

"Would you like to join me? I don't plan to wait down here for them to find me."

She's read my mind. "I'd love that."

"Come, let's visit the Koes Dowr. I think you will appreciate it." She waits for me to reach her, raising her arm to link with mine.

Chapter 8

The formal gardens are bland, all barren twigs and brown mud, waiting for spring. Haelyn leads us away from the palace and towards the southern boundary wall. A small, stone bridge with a delicately wrought ironwork entrance is cloaked from the rest of the gardens by a twist in the path.

She pauses halfway across the bridge and explains, "Koes Dowr means River Garden in old Mordrish." This is the ancient language of the Mordros – typical for them to be so literal in their naming. They aren't exactly renowned for their artistic creativity. "This is the King's personal refuge, but it's ours for the day."

I peer eagerly ahead as we cross the bridge and enter the garden properly. It is extraordinary. Sheltered by the external palace wall on one side and a tributary of the River Targon on the other, it is completely separate from the rest of the palace. Tall trees obscure the lower levels of the palace from view and the air smells of forest moss. Small brooks bubble through the garden, with stepping stones of smooth pebbles creating winding pathways. Birds nest in the trees, braving the cold air to swoop down and pick at the remaining berries peeking through the undergrowth. It's heavenly and I feel so at peace.

I turn to smile at Haelyn, "It's truly perfect."

"If I ever need to hide, then I come here. It's my favourite place in the whole city."

She looks at me, expecting to be judged, and continues. "With the ocean so close, not many plants thrive with the salty air and I miss the forests where I grew up. Coming here grounds me when life in the palace feels overwhelming." A breeze blows over my skin as she talks, with enough pressure that the weak warmth of the day is lost on my bare skin and it hits me. Haelyn isn't one of the Mordros, she's a Zephyr, an outsider like me.

I turn to her in shock and she shrugs.

"What do you have to gain by turning me in? I imagine you need an outlet for your magic too sometimes." I wait for the paranoia, to rise to the surface but nothing comes. The corner of my mouth lifts in a faint smile instead, my magic bubbling eagerly to the surface, excited to play. Small seeds of light, like dandelion seeds, materialise from my fingers and get caught in Haelyn's breeze. We stand for a while, surrounded by calls from the nearby birds.

"Where are you from?" My comment breaks our reverie, a single cloud passes in front of the sun and I rub away the goosebumps on my arms.

She smiles wistfully and watches the seeds of light as they flow through the garden. "Tanwen. The last town of civilization before the Haag." That's in the East. The

Haag is a vast, misty moorland that occupies about a third of the kingdom and separates it from the rest of the continent. On the edge of the moors, the forests are so dense and dark that rumour has it you can't tell day from night. Not a place I'm keen to visit.

"You're far from home then?" I wonder how often she travels back and why she left in the first place. In my experience, ambition makes you dream of faraway places but ties to home are strong and not easily broken.

"Working at the palace is a privilege." Her smile falters and she doesn't elaborate. I don't question it. "It's the second most coveted job for a librarian," she continues promptly, skimming over the pause in conversation.

We share a conspiratorial grin. It's widely known in any academic circles that Pentargon Library is the most acclaimed. However, the librarians there don't take kindly to outsiders and positions there are lifetime appointments. Haelyn is in agreement with me: libraries are there to be used and should be accessible to all.

"I'm going to request access to Pentargon Library soon. You wouldn't happen to be interested in coming along for a visit, would you?" It's the best way I can think to thank her for showing me Koes Dowr.

"Oh, I would love to." A devilish grin appears on her face as she springs into action and begins to lead the way deeper into the garden. "It would infuriate their librarians no end."

I laugh and follow her footsteps. Several hours pass quickly, as Haelyn tells me about life at Chi An Mor.

She's full of stories of people at the palace, who's who and who to avoid.

The tepid sun reaches its zenith as we walk up the central steps to the palace entrance, having exhausted every corner of the garden. From the stories Haelyn has told me, most people consider her invisible given the situations she's witnessed over the years.

She has me bent over in hysterics in the doorway, regaling me with a tale of how she accidentally interrupted a couple engaged in scandalous activity on her library desk last night, one of whom was the King's Verax, Captain Devath. Apparently, libraries are a popular location for trysts. She said she won't be able to look him in the eye for weeks. I'm losing it over how blasé she is about the indecency but how aghast she is over the fact they didn't even move the books and now the spines are damaged.

Right at the point when I beg her to stop the story because it's too much and tears are streaming down my face, we hear a deliberate cough behind us. The Captain is lurking in the shadows and our peals of laughter dissipate. He's clearly been in the barracks training given the amount of sweat on him, working off the frustrations from the Concord meeting. He's quite a sight and my cheeks flame red; Haelyn's are worse. There's no way he didn't hear us gossiping about his exploits. I force myself to calm down. If you don't want to be gossiped about, then you really shouldn't be cavorting all over the palace.

"I thought it was best to announce my arrival," he says, and I swear I catch the hint of a smirk playing around his lips as he notices our warm cheeks. His eyes regard me closely before shuttering.

"A word, Sage," he orders, dismissing Haelyn rudely. To my surprise, she cowers a little and backs off, wishing me good night.

"That was rude," I respond, watching Haelyn hurry down the corridor. He raises one eyebrow conveying his complete lack of regard for anything I say.

"Too busy gossiping to attend the remainder of the Concord meeting?" Disapproval drips from his lips.

He rolls his eyes when I don't respond. My focus is entirely on the bead of sweat running down his neck on to his muscled shoulders. "Dervla is returning to the city tonight. She sent a message ahead asking me to escort you to the islet where your new laboratory will be ready. We will go tomorrow." I can feel the irritation rolling off him at playing messenger but it's immaterial as, at the excitement of having a new laboratory, my shoulders straighten. Dervla requisitioned use of an old outhouse on an islet and promised to have it outfitted to my exact specifications. Working outside the city and the palace will give me the privacy I crave and allow me to cause as many explosions as I need to solve this damn problem.

Chapter 9

The climb up from the islet's small quay to the laboratory is breath-stealing. Wind whips my cheeks as I venture higher, easing the nausea from the crossing. The unforgiving path is treacherous, lined with loose slate. A single misstep will see me tumbling over the cliff edge. Dervla leads the way, sure-footed and confident, all trace of weakness from our aqueduct escape gone. Captain Devath glowers at my back, resentful at being my escort. His family own this islet, which is why I assume he's continued to follow us up the cliff. He probably wants to make sure I don't stick my nose somewhere it's not wanted.

"How was the Concord session yesterday?" Dervla probes. I'd rather have this conversation in private considering the last time we spoke. I wait a few steps whilst I consider what she wants me to say.

"I… left." I feel as if I'm about to be told off. The fierce breeze from the ocean slaps me in the face, I don't need more rebuke. Captain Devath snickers at my admission.

"Oh. That's surprising," her voice fades, inviting me

to elaborate.

"I'm taking time to adjust." It's the story I'm telling myself, and the other Concord members who have accosted me this morning. None have been friendly but they aren't above scouting out how my vote could be bought.

Behind us the Captain's snicker has turned into a full-on scoff and I turn to him in anger.

"Would you like to join the conversation, since you clearly have an opinion? I thought you'd already made your disapproval evident."

Despite being several steps ahead of him on the hike up the cliff front, Captain Devath is at my eyeline and those eyes – the colour of delicious caramel – are taunting.

"I'm here for the view," he retorts, his mouth quirking into a half-smirk.

My eyes widen and I force my face to glare back at him. I have no intention of becoming his next library conquest, splayed out all over the reading table. Dervla's stony expression greets me as I turn around.

"I'll make sure I attend in full in future." She nods, disapproving and we continue the climb.

It's the first time I feel as if I've disappointed Dervla. In the years she's been my sponsor, she's never criticised or complained when our research hasn't gone to plan, yet skipping out on my new responsibilities has riled her. I can't ask her while the Captain is lurking at my back but perhaps, she is worried about the new Concord's lack of action too. It's been nearly a year since the old king was assassinated and the hope of change, we all had for King Cado's reign is fading.

Even though agreeing with the Captain vexes me, the view as we continue to climb in silence is stunning. On this side of the islet, hidden from the city, all I can see is the edge of the archipelago and the ocean, all shades of cloudy grey above and deep navy dusted with white frosting in the waves below. The sea spray continues to chase us up the path and I concentrate on placing my feet so I don't slip and slash my hands on its slate shards.

My nausea from the bumpy crossing has finally faded as we reach the top of the cliff and brace ourselves against the large reinforced steel barn doors of the islet's largest outhouse. The Captain unlocks them and proves himself useful by heaving them open.

A loud bird call sounds before we enter and we raise our heads to find Kaens circling. Dervla grins and extends her arm and my breath catches as the beautiful bird of prey plummets towards her leather gauntlet. At the last second, she flares her wings and lands, forcing Dervla to absorb the shock and slither down the path a little. A half-crazed laugh erupts from her lips at the bird's antics and pieces of slate tumble into the ocean.

Kaens pecks at Dervla's short braids in apology and extends her leg so Dervla can untie a small glass canister with a message inside, before turning to the Captain and calling sharply, "Eskar, you're needed at Chi An Mor."

His face becomes stormy and darkens. Kaens clucks sympathetically and takes to the skies, scouting overhead as the Captain takes his leave. Dervla wistfully watches her fly over the archipelago and into the distance.

Chapter 10

My shoulders, hunched from the hike up here, drop as I breathe the smell of freshly sawn wood. The laboratory is everything I could have asked for. I run my fingers over the new workbenches that don't wobble and turn to Dervla, whose grin matches mine.

"What do you think?" she asks. "A small step up from sweeping lab floors for extra credit?" She will never let me forget how I lambasted her for walking over my freshly cleaned floors the first time we met. I've never been a natural networker and foolishly agreed to clean floors for one of the more senior academics in the hope he would take me on as an assistant after I graduated. He didn't. In fact, he made it his personal mission once he was promoted to Principal to get rid of me. Dervla frequently stepped in to prevent that happening.

I like to think she took a shine to me because no one else in her life would ever talk to her like that. She says she has a weak spot for adopting irritating strays. Agree to disagree.

The airy, open outhouse with its high, vaulted ceilings has been transformed with all the testing equipment and tools I could ever need. The shining worktops are unmarked and everything is clean and organised. My every specification has been met and it only took her a matter of days to achieve. I knew she was influential but this is some feat.

Dervla sees the gratitude in my eyes and shakes her head. "This wasn't just me you know. You, or rather your position, commands a certain level of authority too. The Academy was only too happy to lend equipment to the new King's Alchemist. Donations have been flooding in too. You have your choice of research topics to return to once our work is completed. You'll never be out of work again." My joy at the laboratory dims and I chew my lip. This isn't a gift – the laboratory is a golden shackle.

"Are you ready to begin? I was hoping you had some new ideas to try out whilst I've been away."

My chest feels heavy. It's only been two weeks since the failed explosion in Athnavar and barely a week since she rescued me from the dungeons. I've been hiding in my rooms, summoning manuscripts from the library and meticulously trawling through them, looking for anything that might explain why my theory is failing but I've got nothing to show for it.

"There's a flaw in my theory. I just don't know where it is yet. Everything I've read so far tells me it should work. Or at the very least it shouldn't explode."

"Was the explosion in Athnavar the first attempt?" she asks.

"Yes…"

"Well then, let's try again whilst I'm here. What's

the worst that could happen?" Her rueful smile is too relaxed for my liking. I survey the pristine space, calculating how I could minimise the damage.

Dervla perches on a workbench while I get to work setting up the experiment. Either the experiment will explode again or I'll be able to spot something different which could give me a new lead. Worst-case scenario, cleaning and sweeping all afternoon beats another day spent hiding in my room.

Once I'm ready, we stand clear of the experiment and share an anticipatory glance. There's always something exciting about the moments before you start a new experiment: you could be on the edge of a breakthrough, to achieve something that no one else has before you. My magic bubbles under my skin, ready to play. I take two deep, calming breathes before summoning everything to my palms and thrusting it towards the lump of quartz in the middle of the room.

The light blinds us and our hands grasp for each other. Dervla shudders next to me as a shockwave passes through us and then there is an echoing boom.

My new laboratory is covered in shards of quartz and fine dust rains down from the ceiling. Disappointment highlights the empty hollow where my magic lives. I don't know why I let myself expect something better this time.

Dervla sits dazed on the floor. Shaking my head impatiently to clear my vision and stop the ringing in my ears, I try to explain that I expected this to happen. She doesn't look particularly relieved at my assertion, picking debris from her hair and clothes. The lab hasn't fared too badly, the benefit of preparing properly. At least this time I had the foresight to move all essential equipment out of range, but I'll need to do something to stop the smoke from causing permanent damage.

"So that's where we are so far. In theory everything should work but..." I'm distracted by a final falling thread of debris; red hot, it scorches the workbench where it lands.

"Sage, you are one of the smartest people I've ever met. No one else could have developed this theory. I don't even understand most of it, though you've explained it enough times over the last two years. But sourcing the right material? That isn't your area of expertise. Perhaps it's time to reach out to an expert." Dervla struggles to form the words, leaning heavily to one side as she stands.

I glare at her, anger rising up my body.

"An expert on materials, not a fellow researcher," she corrects hastily. "I know a geologist who might be able to help with the material that we're trying to imbue with magic. He might be able to recommend another material, other than quartz, or help source purified samples."

I grimace; she has a point about sourcing samples to experiment on but I am hesitant to try and explain the theory to an outsider, as it poses a risk that they will work out what we're researching.

"It's worth a try. With the rebel activity and you being a target, we need to solve this as soon as possible. I'm not suggesting we tell him any of the details, but I really think we need his help." For the first time, I see worry lines on her dark skin. I suspect I have the same now as well. I nod carefully; at this point I'm out of other ideas.

"I'll write to him today." She continues, "Can I ask a question? Why do you transfer your magic so violently?"

I stop sweeping up the debris and turn to face her. "I don't understand?"

"Watch." She closes her eyes and a wave of serenity encompasses her features. A ball of water materialises between her outstretched hands. It's large and as I peer closer, instead of being solid like the acorn of power I house, hers resembles a ball of watery yarn. Each strand of magic is carefully constructed and woven together, the ball of magic spinning lazily.

My mouth drops open at the sight. It's beautiful, seeing pure Mordros magic calmly rotating in front of me.

Dervla barely moves, keeping her eyes closed, her posture relaxed. "Everyone in the Mordros is trained in it from birth. It's called the Gallos, which means control. Without it, we would have no way of managing all of our power."

"Then why have I never heard of it?" My eyes are glued to the ball of magic in front of me.

"It's not common knowledge. We learn it as children and it becomes as instinctive as breathing. The threads are a basic building block of magic. We can layer them when we need to wield more but they remain as strands inside us, ready to be employed when needed. I think that's what you should be doing, gradually building up the magic, instead of blasting it."

"Another Mordros secret." I sound bitter, ignoring the glimmer of excitement her suggestion creates.

"Yes, I suppose." She's not apologetic, just matter of fact. The ball of magic makes a final rotation then fades into her hands.

"Most of the Mordros prefer to home school their children; knowledge like this is passed down so I don't think it would occur to anyone to share it."

I can't halt the sneer which flits across my face, forbidden knowledge striking a nerve.

Dervla rolls her eyes, exasperated. "Yes of course it's because the Mordros are superior. Nothing to do with preventing children with access to that much magic being allowed to run around unsupervised." Icy sarcasm drips from every word.

"I'm sorry," I reply. I guess incorrect assumptions are irritating to everyone. I return to cleaning but Dervla surprises me: she picks up a broom and starts to sweep.

Chapter 11

The handwriting on the letter sitting on my desk is vaguely familiar. I'd ignored it initially, assuming it was a petition to support one of the aspiring Mordros families in whatever endeavour currently held their interest. The volume of requests increases each day, a clear response to being unable to corner me in the dining hall or elsewhere in the palace. Between my laboratory, the palace library, compulsory Concord meetings and sheltering in my rooms once the sky turns dark, I've avoided all interactions.

I open the letter and my heart drops at the signature and name neatly printed at the bottom: Cedar Dewnam. My older brother. We've been estranged since our parents were swept out to sea in a flash flood a decade ago. We argued before I left to study in Athnavar and haven't spoken since.

Our parents came from small families and met when they were young. By the time they had children, they were the only family each other had. Our father cleaned Pentargon's streets and our mother dreamed of working as an assistant in a school.

Being Aubade in a kingdom ruled by the Mordros made life difficult. With our magic suppressed and our numbers dwindling, earning a living was hard. Most Aubades make the most of the little sunlight Trevesiga receives, so tend to stick to farming or outside work, very little of which can be found in a city. Steady, reliable employment and opportunities to improve oneself are rare.

Escape, for me, came in the form of studying. Our mother believed in the possibilities from a good education, even for an Aubade. I had to commit to studying to keep up with other children whose parents hired the best tutors money could buy. All that studying meant Cedar and I weren't close. My only focus was to excel so my magical ability, or lack of, would be disregarded. But only Athnavar Academy was willing to accept an Aubade and I bitterly compromised at this second-rate Academy. My test scores were exemplary but the admissions' scholars were blinded by prejudice. I vowed to be exceptional and when the offer to move back to Pentargon came earlier this year, I knew I'd made it.

My parents were overjoyed and I made plans to leave that summer after I turned eighteen.

When our parents died in the flash flood as my mother walked my father home from work, my brother wanted me to give up my place in Athnavar and stay in Pentargon. Family should remain together, he said. But I couldn't see a future where I stayed and became a street cleaner like him and my father.

Our arguments escalated, cruel words thrown by

both sides and eventually I accused him of being selfish and left. Part of me was angry that he couldn't support me after I'd worked so hard; the other part was relieved to have an excuse to leave the city and its memories. I felt guilty that he didn't have the same.

I clutch the letter tightly in my pocket, protecting it from the mizzle as I walk through the grounds of Chi An Mor, towards the palace quay.

Chi An Mor is separated from the city by a bend of the River Targon. Growing up, I've seen ferries transport people back and forth, but I've never stood on this side of the movable, floating quay before. The gentle rocking conflicts with the ominous creaking from the wooden planks as I tread across them.

It occurs to me if the city was under attack, the palace quay could be disassembled quickly and no one would be able to seek sanctuary there. Chi An Mor is a fortress, but an isolated one.

The small crossing to the city feels hazardous. The ferryman guides the ferry with skill against the strong gusts that try to tip us into the water. The skiffs provide little shelter and the incessant wind drives salt spray over the gunwale where it blisters against my exposed skin.

I gratefully accept the outstretched hand of the ferryman and place my feet on firm ground. My legs are steady but my hands tremble. No one notices my arrival; the harbour docks are busy with fishermen unloading their catch and with travellers queuing to embark on large ferries that will take them around the coast to Porth and other cities in Trevesiga. The salt crusts on my cheeks, mixing with tears that I blink away. I force myself to move, to hurry through the busy crowds, away from the slipways where my parents perished.

Leaving the harbour gates behind, the city and the constant smell of the ocean beckons me home. So much remains the same and the tension in my shoulders loosens. Bleached bunting connects each side of the cobbled streets; food carts clatter along the causeway, empty after a successful day. Recognition shadows my footsteps as I encounter familiar marketplaces, familiar streets.

The city is a calamitous mix of experimental building styles, which strive to withstand the winter gales and sharp sea air. Algae grows on the wooden structures, sea salt splits stone in two. Nothing is untouched by the sea in Pentargon. In late winter, it's every structure for itself, gripping the ground to withstand the violent season. If the buildings survive past the spring floods, the focus will be on repairing before winter comes again. It's a vicious and constant battle with the unforgiving sea.

I knock on the door and it's opened promptly by a face so similar to mine that I take a moment to adjust.

"You came." Cedar exhales loudly and welcomes me home. He looks like our father, autumn red hair, a sprinkling of white in his stubble and light grey eyes that match mine.

"I did. Your note was convincing." I thumb the creased envelope in my coat pocket. I didn't expect him to reach out, to extend an olive branch after all these years and my nerves calm at the sight of his warm smile. He leads me into our old family home. Embers from the fireplace cast a cosy glow and my fingers sting as the blood pumps back through them. Very little has changed, and a lump in my throat forms when I see he's laid the table and assigned me the same spot that I had as a child.

"I meant every word. I've missed you."

I avoid his eyes, taking in the meticulous collection of clean pots and pans hanging above the stove, the leaves of paper and charcoal technical drawings neatly piled on the desk, looking anywhere but at him.

"You never wrote before." I face my older brother, voice cracking. There was a time, when I first moved away that even thinking his name made my heart ache as badly as the memory of my parents. Alone in Athnavar, scorned by the other academics, I wished he had written.

"Neither did you." His mouth twitches wryly as he leans against the countertop, crossing his arms and I remember that he's only a couple of years my senior. Not much more than a child when our parents died either.

I guess we are both too proud for our own good. "What changed?"

"I heard you were back in the city. And the attacks… Well, life is fragile. I don't want to let grieving words from a decade ago keep us apart." He turns away, busying himself with tidying the spotless countertop.

My hand drifts across the cutlery laid at my spot on the table. "I'm glad."

He turns back, grey eyes damp and envelops me in a warm hug. We cling tightly to one another and a piece of my heart unfreezes for the first time in ten years. I need my older brother.

"Let's drink." Cedar pulls a bottle from a cupboard and we raise a glass to each other.

Chapter 12

The night air is calm as I leave Cedar's home. The wine sits heavy in my stomach, causing the streets to sway. Wine is a rarity, I've never had money for anything frivolous. But the headache tomorrow will be worth tonight's celebration.

"I got my brother back!" I announce to the litter dancing along the street with me. A thread of connection stitches itself between me and this city I've thought of with dread for years. It's not too bad after all, I muse, scuffing my shoes on the dirt clasped between cracks in the cobbles. Grime coats them and I stagger around trying to scrape it off.

Recklessly, I take the most direct route to the palace quay, liquid courage sustaining me as I brave the shadows. Pentargon wasn't a dangerous city when governed by the ruthless old king but I feel a sense of unease now and quicken my footsteps.

The moonlight vanishes briefly behind a large bird's wing and I freeze, ears straining. It's too early for the taverns to empty but long past the closing time of the merchants around me. I haven't seen a soul so far and other than my thrumming heartbeat the city is too quiet.

Only a few hundred steps to the harbour gates and the city quay a short distance beyond. I resist the calming lull of alcohol and quicken my pace, eyes fixed ahead, spine rigid and alert.

A single silhouette waits at the quay. The moon flickers from behind a cloud and I recognise Captain Devath's sharp features above the high collar of his woollen overcoat.

I'm not inebriated enough to withstand a lecture on why I shouldn't be out in the city alone and turn from the quay, preferring to risk the dangers of the city. My foot catches on a cobble and I go down hard, ego bruised.

His warm hand pulls me back up and I pray my wobbly legs don't give away my drinking.

"Thank you." I grit out, cheeks flooding with warmth. My cloak tangles between my legs and I fumble to right myself.

"You're drunk," he accuses darkly, stepping closer and my neck extends to meet his gaze.

Caught off guard at his perceptiveness, I retort, "Am not."

"And childishly irresponsible." His caramel eyes are stormy and unimpressed and he crosses his arms as I struggle.

"And definitely none of your business." I try to shove him out of the way, giving myself room to breathe and I stumble. He's close enough to catch me, his strong arms wrapping around my waist and placing me gently back on my feet. His hands linger for long enough that I can feel their warmth through my coat before he breaks away, shaking his head.

"It is my business when you're roaming around drunk and unchaperoned." He thrusts his hands deep into his pockets.

"Again, it's none of your damn business. I can take care of myself!"

"I am the King's Verax – I'm making it my business." He stares down at me, eyes gleaming with menace. The last dregs of alcohol drain from my body.

"I was visiting my brother. Not that you deserve an explanation," I hiss, finally sorting out my cloak and pulling myself together.

"I wasn't asking for one. Nothing you say would justify you being out here alone." His voice comes from the back of his throat as he closes the gap between us, ensuring we can't be overheard.

"You don't trust me?" I seethe, my magic spoiling for a fight at the injustice. I take a deep breath, calming the roiling mess inside. This is why I shouldn't drink: my magic becomes unpredictable.

"I don't trust anyone, not even other Mordros. It's my job to find and eradicate the rebels. I would question anyone alone at night." His voice steadies, "It's not personal. From now on, you'll have an escort into the city."

"I will not!"

His eyebrow rises, "Good luck getting the ferryman to take you without one. You could always swim." He gestures to the dark river separating us from the palace. The current is violent and the water frigid – I wouldn't stand a chance.

"The King vouched for me; does that mean nothing?" My throat closes, I can't bear to be trapped in the palace. The dread I felt at returning to the city and the harbour pales compared to being trapped mere floors above the dungeons where I was tortured.

"The King may trust you but I have a rebellion to deal with and no guarantee that you're not about to join it!" He sweeps a hand through his hair, pushing it out of his eyes and I notice the bruises under them. He's not sleeping either.

"I am not a rebel," I spit out. "I will not sacrifice everything I've worked for, what little security I have in this cruel kingdom for some idealistic mission backed by a few explosives." I've seen first-hand now how reluctant the Mordros are to change. Aubades will never repeal the Difan and get other archaic restrictions repealed without gaining power of their own. My research is the answer, not a rebellion.

"Then you shouldn't have a problem with being escorted." His crossed arms tell me he considers the matter closed.

"I have a problem with being treated like an irresponsible child!" I'm not going to let this go easily.

"Have you forgotten that your home was a target in the attack? It's for your safety too!" he shouts, then checks over his shoulder to make sure we're still alone. His polished facade cracks and I get a glimpse of the weight he's carrying, keeping the Kingdom safe.

"A coincidence. Hitting the residential district was

bound to cause the most chaos. My apartment was collateral damage." My words sound weaker than I'd like. But I refuse to believe any different.

"You're too clever to be that naive. Why take the risk? You have everything you could possibly want in the palace."

"You don't know anything about what I want or what risks I'm taking."

"And yet you charmed the King into offering you one of the most coveted positions in the Kingdom after one meeting?" Something flashes in his eyes as he scans me from head to toe.

"It's not coveted by me. I don't even want to be here." I throw my hands up in exasperation.

"Then. Why. Stay?" he grits out.

I avoid his gaze, unwilling to admit what we both know – that I have nowhere else to go.

The painful silence extends for the ferry ride back to the palace, neither of us willing to break the stand-off.

Chapter 13

Captain Devath is infuriating. None of the ferrymen look me in the eye when I next implore them to take me across the river. Not even kindly old Diogel, my personal ferryman. He is happy to take me to the laboratory, but gives me a sympathetic smile when I plead to go to the city.

"It's not worth my job and I happen to agree with the Captain. The city isn't as safe as it used to be." His eyes crinkle with concern as he regards the city across the river with dismay.

I resort to badgering one of the palace guards to escort me. I'm assigned a guard who looks half my age, fresh out of training. I feel so very safe…

We make an odd pair, traversing the city towards the address Dervla gave me for her geologist contact. Taking his duty of my safety seriously, the young guard scans every road junction and crossing, frequently holding me back so he can check for danger. It's ridiculous and now I'm running late. What on earth is he actually even looking for in the middle of the day as we walk through the market? I highly doubt rebels are lurking in each alleyway, waiting to grab me.

I'm relieved when we reach the address and make our way up the steep stone steps to the wide doorway. But the guard reaches to knock before I can. "What do you think you're doing?" I hiss. "Your role ends here. Wait outside until I'm finished."

"But Captain Devath instructed me to be your escort."

For ocean's sake! It's bad enough that Dervla has commanded me to ask for help from a Mordros. I'm not going to let another one witness this moment. "That doesn't entitle you to my personal business. Feel free to pass that back to the Captain." I summon ice into my voice and glare at the guard until he sensibly retreats to the bottom of the steps.

I knock on the door and wait.

A willowy young man throws open the door, dressed from head to toe in an impeccably tailored, rich burgundy tunic, his light brown hair perfectly coiffed. He looks like he would be right at home in the shopping district of Pentargon.

"Howl Karek. It's a great pleasure to meet you." He shakes my hand keenly, welcoming me in.

We stride down a long corridor to his office, feet tapping on the polished stone floor. An immaculately tidy desk commands the space. Howl leans casually against it with a beaming smile and gestures for me to sit opposite. I lower myself cautiously onto the futon, careful to avoid crumpling the soft cushions, all too aware that everything in this house is fastidiously tidy and ordered.

"Now tell me exactly how I can be of service?" His smile is a little too big, the warm reception unwarranted. I wonder what exactly Dervla told him about me.

"Dervla mentioned you are something of a geologist and that you owe her a favour." I glance around, expecting to see some evidence on the shelves to validate this assumption. Perhaps a collection of rare rocks or gemstones but the room is bare – tasteful but minimalist.

I turn back to see him covering his surprise at my question.

"Well, I wouldn't call myself that exactly…"

Embarrassed, cheeks flushing at Dervla's mistake, I go to stand.

"Hold on, I didn't say I couldn't help. If Dervla is calling in her favour then I'm bound to assist." He performs a slight bow, before turning to walk around the desk and takes a seat.

"I'm a purveyor of rare and exclusive goods, most of which happen to be rare gemstones or minerals. I take on very few assignments and have very specific payment terms."

Confusion must be evident on my face as he continues. "I am the complement to Dervla, her business counterpart. There's not much we can't source between us although she's never sent me one of her people before. Where has she been hiding you?"

"I'm an academic and she sponsors my research. I'm not involved in her business interests."

He startles briefly, casting his eyes up and down, evaluating me. But before I question him, he strides across the room, footsteps silenced by the expensive carpet. “Dervla runs the largest and most successful acquisitions business in Trevesiga. She supplies ships, grain, iron, weapons. Whatever you need, Dervla delivers,” he explains. “I am more nuanced. I cater to unique requests. Where you need something a little more special, a little more discreet.” He turns, capturing me with a direct stare. “I assume that’s what you’ve come here for?”

“I’m looking for a mineral, with a very specific set of properties,” I venture.

He pauses, waiting for more information and I debate how much to reveal. Something about the crafty glint in his eye tells me he wouldn’t be opposed to one or two shadier deals if the payment was right. I think that’s what Dervla alluded to when she said he would be able to find what we need. She must be getting desperate.

“I can give you a list of requirements that the mineral will need to have...”

He scoffs, “Well at least that’s something. I wouldn’t want to be hunting completely blind now, would I?”

I shrug, a little out of my depth.

“I suppose Dervla has quite an urgent need for this mysterious item?” I nod and he chuckles.

“Alright, consider me intrigued. I do love a challenge.” His grin widens. “Tell Dervla to consider her favour fulfilled. You can leave me with the list of properties on your way out. I’ll contact you when I have news.” I watch his eyes flicker to the bookshelves lining the hallway as he ushers me out of his house and back into the charge of my disgruntled escort.

Chapter 14

I despise failure. My research: learning the Gallos. I've been surrounded by its constant presence for the last fortnight and it's making me cranky. I've combed the palace library for references, even roping Haelyn in to help. She found a few texts but they all say the same thing: visualise your magic and draw it out of your body. That's it. So simple. Haelyn has begun to master it after only a few sessions. She's as keen as I am to narrow the gap between us and the Mordros. Seeing her sitting calmly in the library with a small tornado swirling in front of her is infuriating.

Today, I've taken a different approach, sequestering myself in my laboratory, determined to make some progress. I sit cross-legged on the cold floor and close my eyes. That little acorn of light sitting in my chest, perks up at being noticed, itching to be used. It's a clear day for once. There's no need to keep my magic locked away when I can replenish it easily. I need to focus – until I have this under control, my experiments are going nowhere and I've had enough of clearing up debris.

The problem I have is not being able to visualise my magic. I never have. The day draws to a close, but nothing is working. Head and back aching, I pick myself off the floor.

As arranged, Diogel waits at the foot of the cliffs, ready to escort me back to the palace. His presence is a comforting constant as I travel back and forth to the islet, braving the rough seas. He guides the ferry skilfully through the currents, avoiding the worst of the eddies. Today, the creases in his forehead are deeper, thick brows furrowed.

"She's a bad one," he nods towards the dark clouds gathering on the horizon. "No doubt about it." There's nothing particularly special about the looming clouds approaching but I haven't grown up on these waters like Diogel, so I'm not about to claim differently. Instead, I hunker further into the ferry's hull, bracing against the rocking swells and pushing salt spray out of my face.

"Mind if we detour to the city quay? I'd feel better if we help move out the stragglers before she hits." I try to nod but the motion sends a spasm of nausea through my stomach.

As my ferry approaches the quay, Diogel's glance warns me not to disembark. I half-smile; I'm not tempted to sneak into the city alone tonight. And if I was, I'd find a way to do it without implicating him.

While I wait for the other passengers to embark, I notice the river level has dropped despite the churning waves. It's a sign the inland glacial lakes are frozen, a precursor to the devastating spring floods. When the lakes melt, the river swells. A ritual deluge collides with the ocean tides, causing lethal currents to flood the lower city.

Everyone living and working close to the harbour evacuates if they can, staying in taverns or with family closer to the palace, praying they will have a home to return to. Of course, the Mordros are not impacted, closeted safely in their family townhouses, high above the tidal line. I look up to that district in disgust. None of them open their doors or provide sanctuary each year, despite having room to spare. This year I will be one of them, safely ensconced behind the palace walls. That thought sobers me.

The final passengers board and a shadow looms over me. Captain Devath appears at my shoulder, gesturing to take the empty seat next to mine.

He folds awkwardly into the compact space, legs taking up half of the central aisle. I concentrate on ignoring the pressure of his thigh pressed into mine and the lingering scent of tobacco smoke that surrounds him.

His stare travels from my shoes to my windswept hair, likely finding me lacking in some way. For once, he makes no comment. I flinch when my stomach makes an unnaturally loud gurgle, wrapping my arms tightly round my waist, leaving no doubt the noise came from me.

Laughter explodes from the Captain, which turns into a coughing fit, tears pooling at the corners of his eyes at my mortification.

"Well, that's the rudest way to greet someone," he

croaks, voice hoarse from laughing, eyes glittering. The temptation to join him surfaces but I smother my smile, cheeks burning.

"So charming," I retort, refusing to laugh.

"Oh, come on." He's interrupted by my stomach rumbling again and this time I can't help seeing the funny side. A giggle slips out of my mouth, just one, but that's all it takes and then I'm in stitches too.

We're still laughing when the ferry docks and Diogel waits patiently for us to compose ourselves before we disembark. It takes a while: every time we get somewhat under control, my stomach sets us off again. Eventually, we manage to climb out of the ferry.

I'm not sure what comes over me but as we walk up to Chi An Mor together, I ask Eskar if he'd like to visit the laboratory.

"And put my life at risk with one of your explosions? I've heard you're dangerous." Sarcasm drips from his lips like honey, but this time it makes me smile.

"I'll do my best not to blow your head off," I retort, a warmth spreading through my chest smothering the faint hint of unease that my pyrotechnics are known at court.

"I'm sure I can handle some of your fireworks, Sage." He chuckles darkly and I'm intrigued at his change in manner today. He's standing close enough that I can count the salt spray on his cheeks but his expression is shadowed by the long, dark hair that falls over his eyes.

A guard paces back and forth outside the palace doors. He sees us approach and stops, standing to attention. I try not to take offence as Captain Devath's posture stiffens and he pulls away from me. He has a short, whispered conversation with the guard and, before I can overhear a word, he stalks off, squaring his shoulders, all plans to visit the laboratory with me forgotten.

The next afternoon at the lab is a waste of time. I'm clumsy and distracted, looking at the door which stubbornly remains closed. The quiet solitude is unwelcome today and I leave early, frustrated at Eskar's mercurial behaviour. It's a relief to arrive back in time for the hustle and bustle of dinner and I convince Haelyn to join me. We're discussing her latest library acquisition when Eskar calls the room to attention.

A wave of anxiety passes through the servants and members of the court alike and the silence which follows is heavy.

"The people responsible for the attacks on Athnavar, Cathair and Porth have come forward," he announces, hands twitching at his sides. "The rebel group Kevren Gwir have claimed responsibility. This act of treasonous aggression will not go unpunished – the King will have justice." He pauses, surveying the room without fixing his gaze on anyone. "The rebels are to be considered incredibly dangerous. Any citizen found associating or communicating with this group will face strict consequences: the penalty for treason is death. Notices will be posted in every major town and city in the morning." Turning promptly, hands clasped tightly behind his back, he leaves, avoiding eye contact.

"Kevren Gwir? I've never heard of them." I turn to Haelyn as the hall explodes in chaos. Half the room leaves, the other half stay to dissect the proclamation.

Haelyn has gone remarkably pale; her wide eyes, two dark pools of fear. "There's been rumours of Kevren Gwir building strength for a few years. They aren't the largest group of resistance against the crown, but they are definitely the most organised." She pauses, fingers pulling at a loose thread in her napkin "And the most equipped, given the scale of their attacks."

I shudder, and now appreciate the risk I took visiting Cedar alone. The threat feels closer now they have a name. "What does Kevren Gwir mean?"

Haelyn will know more. Nobody knows more about Trevesiga than the King's Archivist. "Why are you asking me? I don't know anything about them." She throws her napkin on her plate and bangs her chair as she rushes to leave.

Bewildered, I stare at her empty place before leaping up to follow. It's too late – she evades me in the chaos and my knocks on her door are ignored.

Chapter 15

Chi An Mor is holding its breath. Since the Kevren Gwir claimed responsibility for the attacks on Athnavar and the other cities, a sombre mood has enveloped the palace whilst we wait for more news. Small groups of courtiers huddle in stairways, whispering increasingly outlandish theories. The snippets I overhear are fuelled by speculation and anxiety over more attacks. I flit between bouts of paranoia, jumping at shadows, and unease. Selfishly, I feel safe in my new home but worry for Cedar and the Aubades on the other side of the river.

It is not a time to make new acquaintances at court and I find myself the subject of increased scrutiny as I pass by the cliques. Before I was an inconvenience to be erased as soon as possible but now, I am despised. I could be a threat. Everything about my clothes, my attitude and my family history are up for judgement and debate. My refusal to allow my vote to be bought at the Concord meetings is not helping my reputation and the pressure to succeed in the laboratory is stifling. To make matters worse, since the winter solstice, Pentargon has been besieged with vicious storms which have rendered the whole archipelago inaccessible. Dervla's been trapped away on business, unable to return. Diogel has been apologetic but no cajoling has changed his stance that ferrying me to the laboratory would be a gamble with death. Each morning, I venture to the quay, only to be turned away.

I must have made a particularly pathetic sight yesterday when I made my latest plea because he offered to share his lunch and invited me into the boathouse for a cup of seaweed tea. It was the first conversation I'd had in over a week.

The isolation feels more acute with Haelyn actively evading me. To start with, I didn't think it was personal – the news about Kevren Gwir rattled us all – but yesterday she turned round in the doorway when she saw me and braved the elements outside.

I miss her chattiness; she's a balm to the unwelcome faces at court. I miss her endless stories and light-hearted gossip about the Mordros at court. It reminds me that they are human after all. Above all, I miss her absolute conviction that everything can be solved if you find the right book. I need her confidence right now.

I resolve to corner her today and get her to talk. There's a Concord meeting scheduled and when the weather is this bad, she cannot hide in the Koes Dowr. She will be in the library. I head to the kitchen on the way. If all else fails, she won't be able to resist telling me off for eating in the library. Dropping crumbs is my last resort.

The library is lit with an eerie yellow glow from the oil lamps that struggle to remain aflame on each stack of shelves – an impractical quirk and a reminder from another time. One where our kingdom was splintered into fiefdoms and when Chi An Mor was a central stronghold where relics were preserved and guarded fiercely. Zephyrs were essential custodians of knowledge, capable of smothering an open flame in an instant. With Haelyn in charge, the tradition continues.

I wander through the stacks, tracing my fingers over the name plaques for each subject. I've never ventured all the way into the caves, worried I would lose track of time and struggle to find my way out of the darkness. But today, I know Haelyn will be working as far in as she can to discourage people from finding her. Steeling myself against the thought of getting lost, I recite the categories as I pass, hoping they will linger in my brain so I can find my way out again.

The peace I find is surprising. Books are quiet company and I brush past the last of those written in modern language and on to titles which mean nothing to me. Aubades aren't allowed to have written records of our history. We have fragments of stories, folklore, passed down through generations but the Mordros are different. They are prolific journalists, archivists and curators, meticulously maintaining records of their rule over Trevesiga.

Wrapped in a heavy outdoor cloak, hunched over a study desk in the gloom is Haelyn. Her magnifying glass pores over a handwritten text and she is totally engrossed. My deliberate cough reverberates through the stacks, announcing my presence and she startles. Once she recognises me, her mouth twists defensively and she closes the book, stepping around the side of the desk farthest from me. I've got her cornered though, trapped by the bare rock behind the desk, glistening with condensation in the lamplight.

"Sage, this isn't a great time. I have to go." Haelyn looks towards the books strewn over the desk and then back to me. She must see the stubborn look on my face because she resigns herself to this conversation, sitting back with a heavy sigh.

"Why have you been avoiding me?" I try my best to mask my hurt.

Her face softens at my question and she chews on her bottom lip before making a decision. She holds her hand up to quiet me and I feel a strong breeze blow past me, whistling through the stacks behind. Haelyn cocks her head, listening intently. As the wind returns – blowing my hair in my eyes – she nods, satisfied. "We're alone, we can speak freely."

A faint scent of parchment and pine lingers in the air as my brain stutters. "That was an impressive piece of magic."

"Thanks. My attitude is what secured me the role here. Unfortunately, using it is necessary for this conversation; I can't risk us being overheard. You have to promise not to share this with anyone?"

"Your attitude?" It's the first time I've encountered the term.

"I'll explain later. I guess I owe you that much after avoiding you. Do you promise?" I notice the dark circles under her eyes and nod quickly. I wait patiently for her to continue and she gestures for me to sit. She's at home hidden amongst the books.

"Kevren Gwir means *old truth* in old Mordrish. It used to be the name of a fanatic group that believed in a different way to channel and wield magic. They believed magic should be for everyone. I'm talking about a long time ago though, over a hundred years. I found out about them because I stumbled across a reference to them in a text in Tanwen Library, before I came here. The original uprising started there." She takes a breath, her shoulders lower as she unburdens herself. "They were murdered. Disbanded during the last attempt at an uprising. But now they're back. Or the rebels have taken that name to carry on their mission. Either way, I panicked when I heard that name. I was worried I'd come under suspicion. Bear in mind it's my hometown. I am terrified of being accused of being a rebel. Things might be different with King Cado on the throne but people are still tortured for information."

I privately grimace to myself, wincing at the memory of my muscles spasming and twitching under the Almanac's instruction.

"Thank you for sharing. I won't say a word." I try to smile reassuringly but feel my face freeze halfway, unsettled by the memory of my interrogation. Haelyn returns my attempt at a smile, but our mouths fail to fully rise as we consider the implications of Haelyn's position on the Concord and her association with the rebels, however tenuous.

"So, what is an attitude? Tell me more?" I try to

change the topic but my effort at distraction is weak and Haelyn remains tense.

"It's not a secret per se..." She looks around and I feel the artificial wind ruffle my ponytail and chill the back of my neck.

Evidently satisfied, she reaches into the bag resting at the foot of her desk and pulls out a large, aged tome.

"This book is the authority on the subject. Magical attitudes were well documented before the Difan was introduced." King Feoh, was responsible for invading Trevesiga and putting Aubades in their rightful place. A paranoid dictator, determined to solidify power in Trevesiga, he created the first decree segregating our classes. Splitting people by magical ability and forcing subservience is easy when you have fathomless quantities of power at your fingertips.

"Every Mordros has an attitude although the ruling families are discreet about theirs. Few records exist of Zephyrs with them, even fewer of Aubades." She coughs delicately, avoiding my stare. "I think there has to be a certain amount of magic stored for an attitude to manifest."

"People's power can manifest differently," she continues. "They inherit a particular skill or trait, like the ability to use wind to sense other's presence, to shut off breath and suffocate or to carry their voice in the breeze over large distances. These are Zephyr attitudes, but this book states the Mordros have them too." Another way Aubades are outmatched then. "I'm starting to learn about them myself, I can lend you the book once I've finished."

I half-heartedly accept in order to spare her feelings, not really wanting to learn more about what I will never achieve but recognising she's offering me an olive branch to repair our friendship.

Chapter 16

I acknowledge I might be more than a little annoyed at the lack of progress when I come close to burnout for the third time this week. Pentargon Library declined my request to visit again. There's no news from Howl on anything that could progress my research. Haelyn and I have tentatively made up but she's starting to get suspicious when I won't give details on what I'm researching. I don't want to lose her again. Above all else, achieving the Gallos feels insurmountable. I refuse to let my paltry amount of magic be an obstacle for my research. I don't even think it's my magic that's giving me problems. I can't visualise it taking any other shape at all. It's like imagining your arm is a leg, or something like that. My mind is completely blank and unless I'm directly looking at something in front of me, then I cannot begin to picture it in my mind. I spend hours upon hours, late into the night, trying to coax magic out of my body in individual strands so I can mould it in front of me: nothing works.

At least the weather agrees with me; the winter storms have given way to incessant, gloomy rain so after days holed up in my laboratory achieving nothing, I crave a change of scenery. As the leaden dawn breaks, I take my bad mood out of the palace and away from work to Koes Dowr. The iron gates welcome me over the bridge to the hidden garden, where a slice of serenity beckons. Each step over the bridge tempts me to leave my worries behind.

With the changing seasons, what was a gently flowing stream with stone pebbles to walk over, is now a gushing river with large parts of the garden made inaccessible. The storms are the warning for the annual floods. Soon the entirety of the city will be swollen with river water. The reminder of how my parents perished is brutal. I'm careful to stay on high ground and take a new route through the garden.

The dark grey sky provides little daylight; the sun hasn't fully surfaced over the high cliffs behind the palace and deep silhouettes drift in the winds. I focus on breathing slowly, to keep my fear at bay, reminding myself they are trees and branches, nothing more. Pushing on, I walk further into the garden, ignoring the cold rain on my cheeks. Though immersed in the little wood, I notice I'm not alone.

The King sits in the riverbed, unbothered by the rushing water or rain, legs crossed and hands submerged. His eyes are lightly closed and peaceful, but faint lines bracket his mouth and his jaw is tense. Damp clothes cling to his broad shoulders. He doesn't only spend his days politicking in the palace, then. I'm relieved he's not able to see my blush as I notice the cut of his arms and shoulders under the wet cotton.

Raindrops runs down his face, changing direction over his sharp cheekbones. Perhaps he was looking for solitude too. I lean against a pine and watch him meditate.

I don't know what draws his notice but his eyes open and his body tenses. He turns and peers through the trees, now on edge. I move out of his peripheral vision, letting him see me, hands up so he knows I'm not a threat.

His bland half-smile is one I imagine he's perfected when talking to his subjects. I suspect he expects me to apologise and back off.

But I have nowhere else to go and, besides, the garden's big enough for us both. I step forwards to continue on my walk but the flooding means I have to venture closer to him first.

I can tell the moment he recognises me because the bland smile disappears and he arches his head. "We have something in common after all, Alchemist. We keep meeting when one or the other of us is in wet clothes." His dry humour masks his emotions and I can't tell whether he's angry or amused.

"At least mine was an accident; intentionally choosing to sit in a river is a strange pastime indeed," I call as I continue past.

"Don't knock it until you've tried it." He adds, "It was peaceful until you came stomping through."

"Well, I'm sorry to have disturbed you, Your Highness." I make sure my tone implies it but I am certainly not apologising.

As I walk off, he calls out, "Join me. You look like

you need the company. I could push you in if you want it to look like an accident?"

He's funny – like normal person funny – and I don't know why I'm so surprised. I turn back towards him intrigued.

He gestures to the water in front of him, challenging me. I truly have nothing else to do other than wander in the rain avoiding my responsibilities so when I see a smooth stone under the water that will make a good seat, I reconsider. My clothes are already soaked through so I guess it won't matter if I wade in. I'm certainly not getting undressed in front of the King.

Stepping into the water, it's as cold as I feared. I won't be in here long. I ease my way over to the stone, slipping several times before I take a seat, feet seized from the cold and unreliable. The further I venture into the running water, the higher the King's eyebrows rise and I see a glimpse of a smile and, before he can wipe his face clean of emotion, I settle facing him.

A violent shiver wracks my whole frame; the parts of me submerged in the river are quickly leaching my body heat and I worry for a moment about catching hypothermia. I narrow my eyes at the King when I see he looks rosy and warm. Gradually, a prickling sensation tickles my toes. The water touching my body warms until steam rises from my clothes.

"Don't move," he says. "I'm only keeping a thin layer of water around you warm." It's too late. I squeal as icy cold water pours down my back; more hits me as I squirm.

"I warned you." He throws his head back and laughs

and then he's hit by the cold water too. I get the giggles at the sight of the King of Trevesiga desperately trying not to swear at the cold water, which scrapes like knives along his skin as he fidgets.

Eventually I find I can talk, provided I hold my body completely still under the water and lower myself until I'm submerged to my neck, the current ebbing away to nothing. The warmth is delicious, easing my aching muscles and wiping away the stress of burnout.

"So, what's brought on the need to come here and escape," I ask, feeling bold.

He sighs and looks to the skies. "Endless meetings and trying to understand how to dismantle my father's legacy, coupled with the threat of the rebels." He tilts his head back wearily and blinks the raindrops away as they fall onto his eyes. "Nothing insurmountable but you've seen how resistant the Concord is to change. I should have pushed to be involved before, but how could I sit there being overlooked at every opportunity. Humiliating. But change is proving exceptionally difficult. Particularly without an Almanac."

I don't miss the arch look he gives me, as if I hold the blame. My body tenses and my breathing quickens. It takes me a moment to refocus on the clear water in front of me, the grey sky above. Anything to keep myself present and tell my body I'm not stuck underground with that monster, Lord Bal – I'm safe.

The water now feels like a dead weight, constricting my chest. My lungs suck air painfully as I blink away burning tears, my magic fights for release.

"Have you heard anything from him…"

"No, and I don't expect to. He's exiled, probably hiding far away. Hopefully causing trouble in another kingdom." Panic gives way to irritation at his emotionless tone, his expression haughty and arrogant.

"Well, I'm so sorry to cause you such an inconvenience," I bite back, staring him down to be sure he feels the burn from my caustic words.

He rolls his eyes, returning to his thoughts and I observe little fish swimming between us.

"Is it awful that I'm a little jealous of his exile? I've never left Chi An Mor. My father kept me prisoner. For my own safety. No one can come to harm within the palace walls, except in the dungeons underground, of course." His gaze is level; this is as close to an apology as I suspect he can manage. It leaves a lot to be desired. "Now I'm charged with running a kingdom I know nothing about."

I'm shocked at his confession and pity his narrow existence. It puts having to have an escort in the city into perspective.

"I committed to being nothing like my father. I vowed not to be a dictator and to give people choices but…"

His sentence doesn't need to be finished. I think he lives in such fear of becoming his father that he's risking the stability of the whole of Trevesiga. I'm surprised when he interrupts the silence.

"What's worse? Perpetual problems ruling by committee, or a dictatorship?" Perhaps he does understand what he's risking after all.

The water levels sluggishly rise as the rain continues.

I watch them, taking my time to answer. The stench of damp moss is overriding the scent of petrichor. Neither appeals. "The world is not always so black and white – you could rule for decades more. Make executive decisions that will win you favour with the people, with your Concord. Then I suspect people will follow your lead when it comes to the committees..." Satisfied with my response, I lean back into the warm water, eyes closed, letting it soothe me.

The pause in conversation lengthens. I sneak a glance at the King and flinch when I see those verdant eyes pinning me in place. His face is predatory and I resist the urge to back away, to run back to my warm, dry rooms.

"Who taught you about power?" His icy whisper travels down my spine.

I shrug off the impact of his stare and break eye contact, examining my shrivelled fingers. "It's the intelligent response."

Sensing the conversation is over, I pick my way to the riverbank and haul myself out. Concern for my family surfaces as I see the water lapping at the underside of the stone bridge. "The spring floods. You know they're coming soon." I point to the water rushing over the cobbles. "That's where I'd start. Protect all of Pentargon and then maybe people will trust you to protect them from the Kevren Gwir."

Chapter 17

I'm not exactly in the best of moods as I make my way through the soaked lawns back up to the palace. My whole body is wracked with shivers and I wrap my arms tightly across my chest, attempting to preserve what little warmth I have remaining.

I'm nearly at the entrance to the palace, craving the warmth of my rooms, desperate to dry my toes on the heated floor, when I'm interrupted by Captain Devath, lurking in the entryway.

"About time." He surveys my dishevelled form and smirks as I drip water on the stone steps.

"Why are you waiting here?" I'm not in the mood to deal with his mercurial behaviour right now.

"You requested an escort today, did you not? You have essential business in the city, I'm told." He leans casually against the palace doorway, his huge frame blocking my way in.

Security has been much stricter since the rebels claimed responsibility for the attacks and I am surprised my request was even granted.

"Yes, but not until later. I wasn't expecting it to be

you though." This day is not going my way; I've had my fill of irritating men.

"I'm a palace guard."

"You're the Captain of the Guards, the King's Verax." I don't buy his excuse for a second. "Well, I have to change. You can wait for me here." I try to shake some of the dirt off my clothes as I walk past him but I don't even make a difference. The salt spray coming off the distant ocean acts like glue and the rain pelting at my back isn't helping either.

"You don't look any different from normal to me," he retorts, looking pleased with his comeback.

I roll my eyes at his obvious attempt to rile me. I'm not going to rise to it today.

Not the reaction he was hoping for evidently and he continues to block my path. "Does the offer to see your laboratory stand?"

I cross my arms and wait for an apology from him for running off last time and ignoring me for so long afterwards. It's been three weeks now. I see him pacing round the palace, glowering. He still makes time over dinner to socialise with different women and is all smiles then, but this is the first time he's acknowledged my offer. Haelyn hasn't mentioned any library trysts, not that I've asked of course, but something or someone has been occupying his time. Although an apology is unlikely, some explanation would be nice.

He is nonplussed and evidently is going to need it spelled out for him.

"You ran off last time without so much as an apology or goodbye. Then you've been avoiding me ever since."

"You want an apology?" His tone is surprisingly cold and my heart beats faster when faced with his unexpected anger. Clearly, I shouldn't have assumed he'd got his bad mood out of his system.

"Preferably; an explanation would be nice too." I'm not giving in on this one. Common courtesy or even communicating like an adult is surely not too much to ask. We must look ridiculous though, arguing by the entrance to the palace, neither willing to concede in the pouring rain.

"You're being absurd." He throws his hands up in disgust and walks back into the palace grounds.

I leave him to his fuming. If he wants to skulk around in the rain, then good for him. Hopefully, at some point, he'll calm enough to see my point of view.

Chapter 18

It only takes one weak link to get what I want. Eventually, I found one ferryman willing to accept a bribe to take me into the city and away from the insufferable men in the palace after the captain didn't show up to escort me. I stomp down the main street of Pentargon, viciously kicking detritus from the late winter storms out of my path. My hands and cheeks ache from the frozen salt hurled through the air by the churning ocean.

I manage to resubmit my request to visit Pentargon Library before it closes, the only positive in my day. I had to amend it to include Howl and the long lists of texts that Haelyn and he wish to view. My own list is somewhat shorter. Howl insists that he needs access if he is to find me the material that I need. Hopefully, this time I've overcome the librarians' relentless bureaucracy and will be permitted inside. My hand is still cramping from filling in their endless paperwork. I shake off the lingering irritation from the King's lack of awareness this morning and the rude and mercurial captain. Both are insufferable. I need chocolate.

My feet carry me further into the city, searching for the confectioner's I used to visit when I was little. On the eve of one of the three annual festivals that Aubades celebrate, my mother would entice me to shut my books with the promise of a sweet treat. She would wrap Cedar and me up tightly, tucking our small hands into her coat pockets to brave the frigid air together before the journey to the little chocolate shop a few streets away. The shop was always warmly lit, glittering with foil wrappers: green for peppermint, blue for sea salt caramels and red for creamy fudge, sweetened with berries. We would huddle in the warmth, carefully selecting one or two treats each, depending on the money my parents could spare, waiting for my father. I always made my decision quickly, loyal to those little crimson-wrapped sweets, but Cedar would take a while. He could never commit to one variety and my mother used to tease him that he'd eat the whole shop empty if he could.

The shop is cold and closed. Flickering streetlights scatter off the marbled glass windows as I press my face close to look inside. It must have been open until recently: the displays are empty but no dust has gathered. Frowning, I wipe away the condensation on the glass, straining to get a better look.

"They closed. Not long after the attacks." I turn, stumbling. Cedar's voice calls out to me from across the street. He's wearing overalls and leans against his street cleaning cart. In the dark evening light, he looks like our father. My throat tightens. I turn back towards the closed shop before the perched tears are tempted to fall.

"A lot of places did." His voice softens and I feel him by my shoulder. We look into the empty shop. "It's Mis Genver tonight."

"I know." After tonight, spring will come. Mis Genver is held one month after the shortest day. Aubades can feel a noticeable difference as the sunlight strengthens in preparation for the warmer months. Traditionally, gatherings would be held to share out the remains of winter food stores, to bolster the village through the remaining hard days. At least, that's what our mother always told us. It's why I feel so unsettled: I'm full of winter blues and my magic and I are cranky.

"Fancy a drink?" Cedar offers as he packs up his cart, having reached the end of his shift. I nod sadly, glancing back towards the shuttered confectioners and follow him deeper into the city.

We sit in companionable silence over a pint of what is supposedly fruit cider, although the fruit used is of debatable origin, given the smell that erupted from the dusty cask. Nevertheless, it tastes better than it looks and it's potent enough to evaporate the winter chill from my bones as my fingers regain sensation. I am surprised that the tavern is open – most of the city is in lockdown, still reeling from the rebels coming forward nearly a month ago but, as Cedar crudely points out, you can't police alcohol and having a good time.

Shifting in his seat, I notice his pint is empty. He's looking awkwardly over his shoulder as the tavern becomes more crowded.

"Got somewhere to be?" I tease, swirling the dregs at the bottom of my glass.

"Yes, actually."

I purse my lips. Mis Genver night is meant to be spent with family. I appreciate we're not close but I'm sure there are not many Aubades in the city who will be marking the occasion.

"I've promised to stop by a friend's establishment. A group of us are planning to celebrate together. One of us is performing."

"Aubades?" I question.

He sighs, disappointed. "Does it matter?"

I shrug. I guess not. He can associate with whomever he chooses, I suppose. I'd rather be alone here in the tavern than in the palace. "You can leave me here. I don't need a babysitter." Immediately I regret the bitterness in my tone. It's not his fault I don't have any friends in the city. I made that choice when I picked studying over socialising and then left for a decade without keeping in touch. Now I have no one to turn to when loneliness creeps in.

He pauses, studying me carefully over the rim of his empty glass. His eyes, so like mine, the palest grey, fix me with a stare that has me shifting in my seat.

"You can come, as long as you promise not to report back to the palace." Cedar's mouth is firm, tone authoritative. I don't think I've ever seen him act like a bossy older brother before.

Intrigued, I smile sweetly and agree.

The establishment he takes me to next couldn't be further from the tavern where we started our night. This one is salubrious and polished. The tables, well-oiled and shiny, not pock-marked from wet glassware rims, are arranged around a central stage. Golden light spills from painted glass lampshades, cloaking the room and leaving the bar at the back in shadows.

Despite the crush of bodies squeezed round the tables, there's no foul-smelling body odour, but a heady mix of perfumes. Cedar finds us two seats at the edge of one of the tables and abandons me with a drink as he greets his companions. They greet me with looks of surprise before dismissing me entirely in favour of a hushed conversation with Cedar. He's relaxed though, even if they are not. Soon, they settle next to us, ignoring me completely.

I decide to leave, uncomfortable with the unwanted stares and lack of conversation but the lights dim and a hush descends. The room becomes so dark, I have to strain to see the outline of our companions before a spotlight illuminates the stage and the curtains open.

Howl sits on a stool, eyes closed. I gasp loudly, causing a disapproving murmuring to ripple through the crowd. Suitably admonished, I remain silent but confused and then he starts to sing.

His voice is heady, intoxicating and everyone in the room is mesmerised. He coaxes the melody out. When I hear it, the rest of the room disappears. He sings of love, of loss, of the dangers of ambition and the temptation of power. I find myself clenching my hands into fists as he reaches a crescendo of one song, only to be soothed by the lullaby that follows. Each song is different. He sings the first thing that comes to mind but the crowd doesn't care; all we want is for him to never stop singing.

Howl closes his set to a standing ovation, and I wipe my eyes as the lights flicker back on and the next performer takes over. I don't notice him slide off the stool and make his way to our table until I hear him exclaim, "Sage? What are you doing here?"

"You know my sister?" Cedar interrupts, swaying away from him.

"Oh! What a coincidence." Howl stumbles, coughing, and recovers himself, turning back to my brother. He couldn't be further from the confident polished Mordros I visited a few weeks ago. "We're vaguely acquainted." He smiles weakly, as if he needs me to intervene but I don't really know what else to add.

Cedar blanches, downing the rest of his drink, slamming the glass hard on the table. "Of course, you are. Absolutely bloody typical. Excuse me, I need some air." He turns from the table, face flushed red.

"Cedar, wait!" Howl rushes after my brother's shadow as he strides towards the exit.

I remain behind, a blush warms my cheeks at the scene I've inadvertently caused. Mumblings and stares continue to be directed at me from the other tables after the pair leave to sort out their quarrel. I glance round the room until my gaze locks on the hard, caramel eyes of Captain Devath. He leans against the bar, his face stony. Even across the room, I can sense the rigid fix of his muscles when our eyes meet. This is not good news.

Chapter 19

Some part of me knows it's futile but I can't help struggling against his firm grip as he pulls me from the bar, into the street, his companion at the bar abandoned. Heavy rain soaks the ground and splatters on my face as he tilts it towards him.

"Why on earth can't you do as you're told!" His voice slices through the raindrops, vicious and sharp.

"Leave me alone. I don't need protection, especially not from you."

"Why do you have such a problem with me keeping you safe?" He continues to hold my face, fixing me in place as the rain rolls down his sharp cheekbones.

"Safe? You don't want to keep me safe! You think if I leave your sight for one minute then I'll join the rebellion. You don't trust me."

"I told you, it's not just about trust," he snaps back.

"I don't need some rude, aristocratic arsehole monitoring my every move. I'm fine on my own." I spit venomously, my loneliness biting back. Howl and Cedar stop their argument a few feet away and Cedar looks at me with concern. I shake my head, not wanting him to intervene and he turns back to Howl who starts gesticulating wildly at him again.

"You're coming with me now." His hand is firm as he pulls me along, gripping my forearm.

Unless I want a nasty bruise, I'm going to have to go with him. Something tells me if I broke free, he'd track me down anyway. "No need to be so nasty." The anger continues to bubble in my chest, and I suppress the tears that form.

"I'm not being nasty or rude. Come to think of it, I'm trying to look out for you. And Howl for that matter. Neither of you has any business being in that place. It's teeming with rebel sympathisers."

I freeze, the realisation that I nearly handed myself to the rebels hits me like a violent winter wind.

"I didn't know," a chill prickles up my neck.

"I know." His grip loosens as he surveys me, obviously deciding I'm not going to make a run for it. "I'm sorry for shouting at you." He runs a hand through his soaking hair, pushing it out of his eyes. "There's so much pressure to keep everyone safe and something about you... I can't help but let you get under my skin." He whispers so softly, leaning closer, I question if I heard him right and my eyes widen.

His shoulders hunch protectively against the blinding rain as it freezes, turning to stabbing icy droplets. "I struggle sometimes with my role," he begins as we start back, putting some distance between us, his hood pulled up against the hail. "It's not one I ever wanted, but I was appointed with my particular skillset, so when it comes to the… ," he grimaces.

I wonder whether his pause is a struggle with how to choose the next word, or how much to reveal.

"... the more unsavoury aspects. I can be difficult to be around afterwards. I didn't mean to let you down about the laboratory."

It's not an apology but it's a tentative explanation. I feel as if I should apologise now. We hardly know each other and I demanded such personal insight into his life. I guess my social skills are rusty after hiding away in Athnavar. "And, I take it, the rebel group coming forward meant there were more *unsavoury* aspects than normal?" I try to be casual, to keep him opening up, captivated every time he speaks. My pace slows and he, ever the gentlemen, remains at my side.

"Yes, and it looks like there will be more to come. The attacks mean they believe support for their cause is growing."

"And what if you don't want to do the role anymore?"

He rakes a hand through his hair and huffs a sigh of frustration.

"I honestly don't know, it's been so long. I don't know who I'd be without it."

Perhaps it's the darkness, or the gloomy weather but I want to reach out and comfort him.

"Have you always wanted to be an academic then?" he asks.

I respect his attempt at changing the subject. I tell him about my childhood and how I always knew I could make it in academia, despite being an Aubade.

Speaking of magic, why on earth is he letting himself get soaked?

When I ask him, I get that mischievous grin again and a bubble of water extends from his hands to cover us both, protecting us from the elements.

"Why on earth didn't you do that sooner? I'm soaked through!"

"Perhaps I like it when you're wet through. Makes you seem more real." He winks, definitely flirting now.

My cheeks flush. "Come to the laboratory tomorrow then."

"I will." One last smile before we reach the quay where there's a ferry waiting to take us back.

Eskar whistles quietly while I work, long legs lazily crossed as he perches on my new workbench. The company this morning has been nice; I've had someone to chat to whilst I set up some decoy experiments. As my cover, I chose a couple of the pet projects that some of the Mordros families wanted to sponsor. None of them are anything more than parlour tricks, but they will make passable distractions in the meantime.

It's been a productive day and Diogel surprises me by knocking on the laboratory door as the sun begins to set.

"Excuse me, Alchemist. I'd better escort you back now if you want to return before dark." I pause in measurements and survey the lab; none of these preliminary tests are so important that they can't wait until tomorrow, so I give him a smile and promise we'll meet him at the ferry shortly.

Eskar leads the way down the steep slate path back

towards the ferry, pausing to extend a hand, assisting me as we climb across sections where the rain has washed the stone away, leaving slippery, exposed clay. The whistling has stopped and I catch him frowning a little as we walk.

"Is everything okay?" I wonder if he regrets spending the day at the laboratory. It's not exactly riveting to an outsider.

"My family own this islet," he begins. "Only the most prominent Mordros families have them. Dervla has her own too. They're considered hugely private. So I can't help but wonder why you needed to set up your laboratory here? Why Dervla called in her favour. The experiments you showed me today seemed safe – nothing exploded. What am I missing?" He turns to me, not quite accusing but not in the mood to be palmed off with a half-hearted excuse.

I struggle to form the words to explain. I cannot risk him coming close to the truth about my research. A film of sweat forms down my back and my cheeks heat.

"Nothing. You're not missing anything. I wanted privacy, that's all." Half lies, half-truth. I urge my heart to slow down, its loud beats assaulting my ears as the wind picks up around us. He examines my face carefully and I stare back, careful not to blink or look away first.

"Then what are you doing in the laboratory that means you come to dinner covered in soot and smelling like sulphur."

"You've been paying attention?" I highly doubt I can distract the King's Verax from his line of questioning;

it's his role to be observant but I'm desperate.

To my surprise, a faint blush appears and he breaks my gaze to examine his boots. "Forget I asked. I just thought it was strange that's all."

The fragile trust between us fractures and a wave of loneliness rises up through me. I don't want to return to isolation, to push him away. I can offer him some truth at least, "I hate failure. I am working on something but it's not going well. It's going terribly actually. But if I get it to work, I promise I'll show you." It's a tentative offer, probably more than I should commit to but I don't want to return to scathing comments and ignoring each other.

Satisfied with my response, Eskar smiles. "I'd like that."

Chapter 20

We make an unusual collective, the three of us waiting outside the hallowed library entrance on the top floor of Pentargon Academy. Howl and Haelyn are about to combust with anticipation, fidgeting and fizzing incessantly. Neither have met before but I'm amused at their similar excitement at securing access to one of the most secretive parts of Mordros society.

The entrance chamber reminds me of a greenhouse: claustrophobic glass walls enclose us on three sides within a wrought iron frame. The glass amplifies the sunshine and it feels like summer on my skin, but without a breeze it's already stifling. It's early in the morning but the intensity of the reflection makes it feel like midday. This room would be insufferable in the warmer seasons.

Eskar escorted us to the library this morning but wasn't able to stay. As soon as he left, Haelyn tried to question me about his friendly behaviour. I had been aware of her silently watching the two of us laugh as he offered me a sweet from his pocket once we reached the city quay, trying to prevent a recurrence of my loud stomach gurgling. I didn't mind his teasing at all but I'm not ready to admit that to her yet.

Thankfully, Howl appears before I have to explain what happened in the laboratory last week. How we spent the entire day together and didn't argue once. Or how he asked about my research and I promised to tell him when I succeed. That's more than I have committed to with her and I worry that her patience is wearing thin with my refusal to talk about what I'm really working on.

We stand, clustered in the atrium, waiting for our appointment. As the clock passes the hour, a rhythmic tapping comes from behind the doors leading to the library, demanding our attention. An imposing silhouette of a tall, slender person wielding a cane appears through the frosted glass and the tapping stops. Silently, the handle turns and the door opens, without a single scrape or creak against the polished floor.

Whatever we were expecting from the Head Librarian of Pentargon, it was most certainly not a gorgeously handsome man in his early thirties with wild, long, curly hair. Haelyn and I are struck mute. Her eyes widen and she bites her bottom lip. Howl is the first of us to react, reaching forward to shake the librarian's hand.

"Sage Dewnam and party, I presume?" His voice is soft like honey and with a faint accent I can't place. "I'm Penn Pyst, Head Librarian of Pentargon Library."

I shake his hand and introduce our group. When I mention Haelyn, a predatory smile creeps into his face and he takes his time surveying her, shrewdly assessing a rival.

Not one to be easily intimidated, Haelyn doesn't baulk. Howl coughs loudly and his awkward interruption breaks their impasse. I have a suspicion that otherwise the two of them would still be glaring at each other.

Regaining his composure and flashing me an apologetic smile, Penn gestures for us to enter the library in front of him.

A library is heavy with knowledge, the air inside thick and oppressive and this one is no exception. In our group, I am the odd one out. Everyone else is completely at ease and they delve confidently into the book stacks ahead. I linger, loath to leave the warm air of the atrium.

Penn taps his cane in front of Haelyn and Howl if they venture from his planned route, corralling them like sheep. Mutely, I follow, noting how the light shines through to the polished floor without a fleck of dust in the air. This library is not one where books are regularly used; it's small and contains the rarest of texts and is more of a museum than a place of learning.

Three ancient tomes are laid out in a glass display case towards the back of the library, their pages crumbling. Penn pulls out several sets of cotton gloves, examining them for lint before passing them round. He watches intently as we pull them on. I don't doubt that he will refuse us access if we don't.

"Given the opaque nature of your request, I had to use some initiative about where to start. But I think you will find these… insightful." I can't make out his tone – whether he cares or not that I've been vague about the real purpose behind my research. I need Dervla to return from her business trip soon. There are too many people skirting too close to the truth and I worry we're going to be exposed. I trust her to handle it, I'm in over my head.

Howl looks to me for approval, rocking back on his heels before darting forward to take the first look. I watch carefully – noting his reactions as he skims the three texts, leaning closer to each one – joining him at the case. Several times my pulse soars when I hear him take a deep rush of air but then, as quickly as my excitement rises, it falls again when he shakes his head and continues reading.

Haelyn is interrogating Penn in the background. "Was it necessary to decline my previous requests in quite such an abrasive manner?" Her voice is tart and not one I'm accustomed to hearing.

"Previous requests?" Penn's response is bland, unphased by her indignation.

"Yes, all eight of them."

"Apologies, it's nothing personal. We receive hundreds of requests from across Trevesiga."

"From a member of the King's Concord?" The shelves closest to us creak and I notice a cold breeze on the back of my neck. Now she's really vexed.

"From people looking for knowledge, a position at court means little here."

"But a family name means something, clearly," she hisses quietly, bitterness leaching into her tone. I turn to see her point to Howl's back and he flinches, as if the tip of her finger pierced the nape of his neck. His hands tense and his cheeks go pink.

"Perhaps he was simply better at following instructions. The required paperwork is quite demanding. Many struggle with it." Penn's tone, previously unruffled and remote turns acerbic.

"Haelyn, I submitted the paperwork. Howl had nothing to do with it," I caution her, irritated at the insinuation and not wanting to anger the one person who could halt my research by denying us access again.

She fixes me with a pointed glare, brown eyes storming. I don't back down until the breeze ruffling my hair ceases. Rolling her eyes, she resumes her silence, glaring at the stacks around her and refusing to acknowledge anyone else's presence.

"Thank you," Howl whispers under his breath as he resumes scanning the texts and I press an encouraging hand on his shoulder.

I move closer to take in the final text but promptly give up: it's in ancient Mordrish. Seeing my frustration and disinterest, Penn steps forward.

"Perhaps I could be of further assistance if I had more details on what you are searching for?"

"I cannot give you any more details."

"I see." A heavy pause follows, as if all the tomes in the library are holding their breath.

"We are looking into geology," Howl chimes in, unable to take his eyes off the material and oblivious to the intense stare from Penn, which fixes me in place. "These texts are incredible. I need more time but the suggestions, the possibilities, they are all there."

"Would another visit be possible?" I pose my question to the head librarian, unwilling to discuss the implications of our research out loud.

He shuffles uncomfortably, putting more weight through his cane whilst he looks from Howl to me and back again, softening somewhat at Howl's eager expression. Thankfully, Haelyn stays quiet.

"You will need to be supervised at all times."

This is unprecedented. The hallowed halls of the library are so conscientiously restricted and I can't help my huge grin as I feel like a breakthrough might actually be closer than we think.

Howl nods eagerly, with reverence, and returns to the texts, awareness of the rest of us forgotten.

Conscious Haelyn and I have limited time to get back to the palace before the next Concord session, I thank Penn and leave Howl and him deep in conversation while we make our way back to the entrance. After I spoke with the King about helping the city during the floods, I'm keen to see if he follows through on my advice. I told Haelyn about my encounter and once she'd masked her shock, she agreed to come with me.

Eskar is waiting in the atrium for us, head tilted back, eyes closed, enjoying the sun through the glass ceiling. I poke him on the shoulder and as his eyes snap open, I can't help noticing whilst his face isn't classically handsome like the King's, or obviously attractive like Penn's, there's something about how expressive he is that makes it hard for me to look away.

Chapter 21

On the journey back to the palace I nurture a small kernel of hope from the progress we made in the library but it is abruptly extinguished when I walk into the Concord chamber. A sombre silence, appropriate for a funeral, snakes through the room. Conversation ceases and the nine seated members of the Concord fix their unwelcoming stares on us.

Their eyes track my movements as I search for an available seat. Haelyn and Eskar flank me protectively. Everyone seated around the table is a seasoned political predator and Dervla warned me not to try and make alliances. I have more to lose than to gain until my research is complete, so for now I attend, keep my thoughts to myself and observe.

I nod to each member, noting those unable to hide their outright hostility at my presence and those that look curious. Not that hostility has prevented their aides from trying to buy my support in whatever agenda they are trying to push. Over the last two months, the only one who hasn't tried to solicit my vote is Principal Fyrdyr, the head of Pentargon Academy.

I don't know whether it's because I declined to work for her before the attacks, or because she doesn't see any value in securing my alliance. She keeps to herself, choosing to live at the Academy instead of Chi An Mor and is always the last to cast her disc into the reflection pool. I've taken to cataloguing the decisions every Concord member makes and am now very accurate with my predictions, except when it comes to her. She often surprises me.

The fading light casts a long shadow over the far end of the table, where the empty seats remain. With a shiver, I follow Eskar past his usual space. He pulls out my chair, looming over my shoulder for a moment before seating himself.

Haelyn shifts uncomfortably. Despite keeping her face carefully neutral I can see how quickly she's breathing. Maybe I misinterpreted their reaction as solely being directed at me; she's been dealing with their rejection for longer. Conversation resumes around us; we're outcasts together.

The King arrives, accompanied by Dervla. A second hush sweeps the room, mildly warmer than the reception we received. His face is relaxed, as if the reaction was expected, and his posture is confident as he addresses the room.

"Concord, thank you for your attendance. Before I open today's proceedings, I have an announcement." Interesting. A faint furrow forms between his eyebrows.

This will be contentious.

He remains standing but leans on the back of his chair, gripping the wooden support firmly. "I want to start today's meeting with the appointment of a new Almanac. Dervla Cairbre has accepted the position and will begin immediately." He pulls back the chair to his left and Dervla takes her place by his side.

Under his breath, Eskar lets out a low whistle and Haelyn gasps. Both noises are drowned beneath the antagonistic shouts from the rest of the Concord.

"What has Dervla done to merit such a negative reception?" I hiss to Eskar.

"It's not about Dervla. Several Concord members have put themselves forward since the old Almanac left. They've been swirling round each other for months, believing they're building alliances, all saying they have the King's ear and are certain they will be selected. They will be humiliated. The King will pay a price for surprising them this way."

Understanding dawns on me: "This is going to be a catastrophe."

Haelyn chimes in, leaning closer to make sure she isn't overheard. "That depends. If Dervla can wrangle them all back in line, she'll be a force to be reckoned with."

Principal Fyrdyr leans over and mutters, "Keep your speculation to yourselves."

"Apologies Principal," Eskar replies as I realise our words travelled further than we'd wanted.

The King waits for the mutterings to die down. He remains standing, surveying each of us in turn. I can't make out his expression clearly but I see him startle when he sees me.

"One final announcement: I've taken the liberty of

offering secure lodging and hospitality at the Guild Hall for those at risk from the annual spring floods in the city. A communication is being shared around the city this evening, detailing where to go and how to ask for help during the floods. I anticipate this will become an annual effort to protect those most at risk." The King sits, as if this news is nothing out of the ordinary but the impact in the city will be momentous: so many lives will be saved.

My shoulders sink with relief; the guilt I felt at being safely sequestered in the palace this year lessens. He listened to me. After one conversation in the river garden, people will be safe from the floods. The solace I feel in knowing the city will be safer is tinged with regret; the situation should never have got to this point. It shouldn't have taken our heated argument for the people to be protected. Nevertheless, I'm taking it as a win.

"So much for democracy." An aggrieved mutter from an older man sat halfway down the table. Panic jumps into my throat as I remember the King's promise never to be a dictator like his father. Would this Concord member actually prevent people from being kept safe in the capital city to showcase his own political clout?

"There's democracy and expediency. Surely you're not planning an objection to housing the most vulnerable in our city during such a dangerous time? The King is merely relaying an update on the situation, not removing any decision from you. I believe volunteers will be required to assist in the rebuilding efforts after the floods – I can recommend you lead that committee if you desire." Dervla's comments are clipped and the disgruntled member twists his mouth in displeasure.

The King smothers a smile before continuing with his address. "Now we are at full complement, I hope this signals our willingness to work together in addressing the instability caused by the rebel attacks and to concentrate on protecting our kingdom."

"The Kevren Gwir. Do we have any idea of their next moves?" A man closest to Dervla is the first to speak.

The King gestures to our end of the table and Haelyn tenses as all eyes turn.

"The prisoners are… resistant," Eskar hesitates and I turn to him in shock. "I have been unable to extract any useful information. All have been able to withstand the… usual treatment." His stare is fixed ahead. Even as the conversation moves on it is clear he is avoiding my gaze.

My body stiffens and a thread of ice travels down my spine. The Verax is responsible for truth. I assumed this meant working with the justice system, the courts and security. How could I have been so naive? I look at him, my back to the King, but his face is half cloaked in shadow, still avoiding my eyes. My mind flashes back to the dungeon. A stranger hidden in the darkness, doing the bidding of the old Almanac. Phantom pain lances through my muscles in memory of the excruciating spasms. Our eyes meet and I see regret before a hot rush floods my cheeks at his betrayal.

My heart thunders. My body frozen in place holds me in my seat. The conversation continues on; Concord members contribute their thoughts but I take nothing in. Their words wash over me and I focus on steadying my breathing. Haelyn nudges me with her shoulder, trying to get my attention. When I don't respond, she reaches under the table, holding my hand tightly. The feel of her palm in mine helps me smothering the panic that threatens to overcome me as I sit next to my torturer.

The man who openly admitted to not trusting *me*. The man who is now apparently concerned for my safety. The man who laughed with me in the rain. This man who can be sour and grumpy and who claims to resent the position he's been put in at court. This man who claims he has little freedom, yet does nothing to prevent people from being tortured.

The meeting draws to a close and I'm still shaking. From what I can tell, despite Dervla's attempts at drawing consensus, nothing has been decided or agreed. Throughout it all, my stomach roiled and nausea threatened to consume me. It was impossible to focus.

Fleeing the Concord chamber, I ignore Haelyn's calls to wait for her. My legs give out once I secure my door against the rest of the palace. For the whole night, I remain with my back against the door, shaking and trembling, rocking back and forth. Eyes open, the nightmares won't reach me tonight.

Chapter 22

On the first official day of spring, when the danger of flooding has passed and the swollen rivers have receded, the King makes his annual announcement to the kingdom.

It's a tradition heralding back to the formation of Trevesiga, from when the Mordros conquered the land west of the Haag. Aubades and Zephyrs were permitted to continue to remain on the condition they served the Mordros and sacrificed using their magic for the greater benefit of the kingdom. Farms were required to donate a portion of their crops, the fisherman to share their catch and everyone to pay taxes. Over time, the Mordros have conceded a little, restoring some rights back to the Zephyrs, permitting them professional roles and allowing them to join the navy but traction is slow and, with the last King, static. However, the sentiment behind the laws remains the same: using our magic is forbidden.

Each year, in an effort to connect to the people and recognise compliance, the King makes his address, praising the successes of the kingdom, highlighting new laws or changes, conveying new punishments or deterrents. Growing up in Pentargon meant I often witnessed the live announcement; for others it was transcribed by the librarians and heralded in every city, town, and hamlet by the start of summer.

In the city it was treated as a day of celebration. A carnival. Pentargon consists mainly of wealthy Mordros families where food and entertainment are in abundance and the King's address marks the start of the social calendar. The contents of the announcement make no difference to the Mordros; they purely enjoy the benefits of this national holiday.

As a child, displays from the travelling fairs provided respite from the bitterly cold winds that still blew through the city's streets. We would often detour home from school to see the performers, clad in colourful silks and leotards trying to disguise their shivers between performances. I remember the condensing breath of singing bands and musicians puffing vapour as they played. One year, after the carnivals finished and the address was over, my father returned home from work with some discarded bunting. My brother and I cleaned it and hung it about our small house, enjoying the beautiful patterns and colours until the sun bleached the cotton white that summer.

When I grew older, I found the atmosphere of the day jarring, the joyful abundance clashing with poverty. Half the population were celebrating and the others working twice as hard to compensate. Often, we would huddle on the edge of the central street as the royal procession passed by, straining to glimpse the old king and his court, half hiding in the shelter of a shop's awning. He never acknowledged his subjects, preferring to remain cloistered in the palace, venturing out on Address Day only out of duty and tradition.

I've refused to acknowledge Eskar for weeks. Our tentative friendship crumbled after the revelation that he was the shadow in my nightmares. He drops by my rooms regularly but I refuse to answer the door. I can bring myself to be civil for the Concord meetings, when Haelyn is by my side but I cannot bear to be alone with him. I've been arriving later and later, so he is already seated and I can select a seat as far away as possible. More often than not, in order to avoid him, I've taken to hiding in Dervla's suite. As the Almanac, her time is precious, and everyone clamours for her attention, but she always makes an effort to help me with the Gallos at the end of her day.

Today though is the day of the address and Dervla will expect me to attend with her and the other Concord members, as we take our place on the dais next to the King. Avoiding Eskar will be impossible so I've made a plan to escape before anyone notices. The address will be delivered in the city centre and every inch of the palace has been polished and prepped until it sparkles. Servants dash around, catering to the needs of the influx of guests and visitors. Every member of the Mordros ruling class and their families have descended on the palace, desperate to be part of the action, no matter that they have fine houses in the city.

No one questions me as I sneak onto the ferry leaving the palace as the sun rises. It's already packed and, with my hood raised, the ferryman doesn't give me a second glance. Cedar is waiting for me at the city quay. I cast my eyes at his ill-fitting coat. His belongings are still in our family home; hopefully they've survived the winter floods. He should be able to leave the temporary accommodation provided by the King's new ruling and return home now the floods have passed through. That is, if the damage isn't too bad. This was the first year no one perished but the architecture wasn't as fortunate: homes and businesses were washed away. Still, replacing buildings is easy – replacing lives is not.

Cedar and I linger at some of the carnival stages, eating an early lunch from street vendors before the crowds get too intense. The choice is overwhelming. Aromatic spices linger as we pass the barbeque stalls, grills crackling and flashes of flames popping from fats and juices dripping off the meat. For once I don't miss the fresh fish and vegetables from the palace, and indulge in strips of meat wrapped in flatbreads covered in yoghurt and sesame seeds. One vendor sells hot drinks and we choose different concoctions. Cedar opts for a frothy milk foam that towers over the top of his cup, threatening to spill onto the floor. Mine is a sour apple cider which clashes with the honey syrup I add – heavenly.

Before food comas send us soporific, Cedar and I find a spot in the central square to watch the pageantry. The area is already lined with revellers, more interested in getting drunk and causing disruption than in watching the King's address. Perhaps this spot was not such a good idea.

Cedar is in his element, accepting drinks from a stranger and joining in with the celebrations. I linger, pressing my back into the solid Guildhall wall and try not to panic. I don't mind crowds but this is a cacophony and there's nowhere to hear the address without descending into the melee. The reason why the crowd is celebrating is lost on me; the rebels are still at large; winter has been long and cruel with many suffering from a poor harvest and being locked down after the attack. But then, today signifies a change in seasons. So maybe a change in mood is coming? Or perhaps the alcohol is just about strong enough to ward off the winter chill.

"Can I escort you back to the palace?" In shock I spin at Eskar's soft voice behind me. He's not dressed in his ceremonial robes; his black overcoat allows him to blend into the crowd.

Cedar's forgotten my existence, happily dancing with a group of men. I brace myself, still avoiding Eskar's direct gaze.

"I've been looking for you all day. Your absence will be noticed." Eskar's voice is gentle, as if he's trying not to spook me.

I look over his shoulder. "There are plenty of other members of the Concord – the King won't miss me today."

"Sage, you didn't tell me you were meant to be part of the procession," Cedar whines from behind me and I jump in surprise, causing him to spill his drink over himself. Not that he's bothered.

"She was. And the King will not be pleased if she

misses it." Eskar's tone is full of reproach.

"Doesn't he have more pressing things to concern himself with?" I counter, angry at being exposed.

"Sage, think of all the people that will see you up there." Cedar sounds regretful, pleading.

"Precisely why I want to avoid it." I've spent months learning how the Concord operates. I have no desire to join them in the pointless pageantry.

Huffing at my irritation, Cedar flounces back into the crowd in search of anther drink, leaving me staring into Eskar's eyes. This is the last place I want to have this conversation. I turn and run.

Chapter 23

He follows me. It shouldn't surprise me but it does annoy me. I twist and turn through the streets to lose him in the crowds but he catches on to my tactics and I feel a firm hand on my shoulder pulling me back.

"Sage, we need to talk. Just one conversation." His face is anguished.

I'm sorry but one conversation is not going to justify the hours I spent trapped in the dungeon, writhing in agony at his hands. One conversation is not going to cure my fear of small, dark spaces or the panic I feel when a shadow moves in the corner of my eye and my muscles lock, anticipating pain.

"The whole of the Concord is speculating about what happened. They know we're not speaking now you refuse to sit near me in the meetings. I don't know how else to stop their gossip. Please," he whispers, stepping closer, shielding me from curious onlookers who might otherwise notice my eyes filling with tears. I brush them aside and nod quickly; anything to get away from being spectated on.

He pulls me behind him, weaving expertly through

the crowds, guiding us on to one of the quieter side streets. Satisfied there are no prying eyes or ears, he tugs me into an alley between a bank and a neglected haberdashers and waits for my tears to stop.

"The pain, the torture. It ate me up for days afterwards. You were innocent and I didn't question the Almanac." He rushes to get the words out, as if the conversation has a sand timer against it and the grains are falling too quickly. "I know Trevesiga requires an enforcer, an interrogator, but I didn't choose this position. The old king mandated it once my attitude manifested." I force myself to hold his gaze, shoving my trembling hands deep into my pockets.

"It's a special affinity with magic, found in only one Mordros family. Mine. The old king was always interested in me as a child, hoping I would develop the ability. As soon as it manifested, my parents handed me over to him, thrilled to have a child with such a *prestigious* attitude. I became his personal torturer from the age of thirteen." His face is blank, no emotion apart from his eyes.

"No one knew. They thought I was chosen to be a companion for Cado. We grew up together, the perfect cover for the King to abuse his position and force me to practise my attitude. Now the whole Concord knows what I can do as the Verax but they have no idea how I became so skilled." Those beautiful caramel eyes are red-rimmed and full of pain. To be abandoned by your family and forced to hurt others as a child. I try to cling to my anger but it seeps away.

"What does your attitude do?" I whisper, afraid.

"I can stop water on a minuscule level." He runs a hand through his long hair and continues. "It meant I could be used to stop the blood flowing in people's veins, horrifically painful. The old king had me practise on myself and no one ever knew." His shoulders drop, and a large cloud of air condenses as he exhales.

"Lord Bal and the old king relished using it to root out traitors or to make a point against anyone who stood against them. They kept the details of my attitude secret, hoping to inspire fear and help them keep control."

"Cado promised me I'd never have to use it once he became king, but… old habits die hard I suppose. He's promised once the rebel threat is dealt with then I won't be needed any longer…" His voice reeks of bitterness, of a man who's practically given up hope of seeing his own freedom, but also of something else. Perhaps he's a little intimidated by the power he wields.

I feel for him. He feels as if he's cornered and doesn't have a choice. But there were plenty of opportunities to come clean to me about what happened in the dungeons and his role and he never did. Even now, there's no apology. Just an explanation and it doesn't feel like enough.

"Come on. We might be able to find a good view." I see the effort he's making to smooth things over. To move past this. But I don't think it will be that easy. He's resigned to his position. He isn't fighting back.

We wander towards the city centre in silence. I reluctantly follow, unwilling to return to the palace and with no other options. All hopes of getting a good view of the King's address disappear when we see the crowds. People queue along the streets, lining the pavements, slowing our progress. Eventually, he settles on a position he deems safe in the midst of so many people. It's a good vantage point on the edge of a stone monument and he moves the surly teenagers out of their seats with a fierce glare. I try to apologise for his rudeness but it's undermined by his unrepentant stare. Arms folded, he towers over my shoulder before pulling me up to join him.

I may not approve of his methods, but we undoubtedly have a good view. I can see clearly from the river crossing and the palace all the way up to the spires of Pentargon Library in the east of the city. We won't be able to hear much of the speech but Dervla is sitting on the dais with the other Mordros dignitaries and I'm sure she will be able to give me a recap.

Given the affluence of the majority of the spectators, I imagine most of them are also Mordros or possibly Zephyrs. I wonder if I'll ever learn to stop automatically scanning a crowd for people like me. Perhaps one day, it won't be possible to tell the difference on the outside.

The King lands on the banks of the river and a ripple of excitement extends through the city, and we can catch glimpses of the procession as it passes by. Enthusiasm for the King himself is sporadic at best, so there isn't a copious amount of cheering. The crowd are there to gawk, as if he is an exotic animal in a zoo. He duly waves as the procession makes its way through the street. I try to point out familiar faces to Eskar as I recognise them but he's not paying me any attention; he's focused on scanning the crowds, assessing movement, watching people's behaviour and looking for anything out of place. I feel a little guilty at the risk I'm taking and anything that could impact me puts him at risk too.

The lacklustre spectacle finishes, the King's words were lost on the wind before they made it to our position, we make our way back to the palace. Everyone else is heading the other way, to find taverns or restaurants for the evening. I lose sight of Eskar several times, and call him to slow down. People are parting to let him through but I'm being pushed further and further back. I assume he'll wait at the quay for me before crossing back, so I take a moment to get my breath, away from the crowds before pushing on. A couple, older than me, pull me towards a spot in the crossroads where we wait for the melée to pass. Grateful for their help, I let them tug me out of the crowds and on to a side street.

They don't let go once we're in the street. As I straighten up to reassure them I'll be fine now, the woman twists my arm behind my back, keeping me bent over and helpless. The man stuffs a sweet-smelling rag in my mouth and my eyes begin to water. I wait for them to empty my pockets, panicking now as I have nothing of value to offer them in exchange for my safety. I realise they aren't trying to steal from me and fear rises in my throat, my vision swimming. Instead, they manhandle me aggressively down the street, hissing at each other to go faster, work quicker.

Instinct kicks in and I let myself go limp to make their lives harder, letting my weight drag me to the floor. If they aren't mugging me, then they have a different reason for targeting me. My feet struggle to find purchase on the cobbles and, wriggling and squirming, my shoulder wrenches and I scream into the rag. My head is pounding. The more I breathe through my mouth as I struggle, the harder I find it to focus. Desperate, I reach into my magic, thinking to summon a small ball of light to blind them. It's a last-ditch attempt; this street is quieter but I hope someone will see before it's too late.

Two unearthly screams pierce the air and I hit the cobbles hard. Blackness envelops me.

Chapter 24

Sounds register: running water, light conversation – words indecipherable. I can smell antiseptic and an underlying scent of lilacs that the palace uses to fragrance their bed linens. I open one eye; morning light sears into my skull and I quickly shut it. My head pounds. I scan through my body, assessing my limbs and cataloguing where else I feel pain. Other than my head and shoulder, I think I am relatively unscathed. A few aches and bruises. Bracing myself, I open my eyes again. Nausea rushes up and I vomit violently over the side of the bed. From the look of the considerately placed bedpan, conspicuously not empty, this is not the first time I've been sick. The conversation in the other room pauses as my vomit clatters off the metallic pan. It resumes a few minutes later when I make no further noise.

Flopping back on the bed, I drift off again.

When I wake the sky is darker outside and my head is more agreeable. I shuffle to the edge of the bed, eyes firmly closed until I'm upright. No dizziness so far. Cracking open my eyes in the dim light, my head thumps harder but it's not unbearable and my unsettled stomach craves food.

Haelyn has taken up residence on one of the sofas in my lounge – food and drink detritus from several meals surround her and books are strewn across her lap. Her face floods with relief when I appear, leaning heavily on the doorframe from my bedroom.

"How're you feeling?" Her voice rings loudly and the words take their time to form into coherent order. My eyebrows furrow and I relax my face to combat a stabbing pain that shoots across my forehead.

Haelyn guides me to the sofa. "What do you remember?"

"Being dragged away from the crowds. Then a loud scream. My head?"

She nods. "Eskar found you being taken by two rebels. He said you put up quite a fight." Haelyn smiles ruefully. "He managed to rescue you but you got injured. When you lost consciousness, he panicked and rushed you straight back to the palace."

I look round the room again, expecting to see him lurking.

"He's not here. He let one of your kidnappers escape because he chose to protect you first. The King is furious," Haelyn continues, "and Dervla is incensed; apparently some of the Concord decided to let you act as bait for rebel sympathisers. They told the ferrymen to let you into the city unescorted. They were unsure of your allegiance but I guess being nearly kidnapped proves that at least. Eskar is being punished for killing one of your attackers and letting the other get away;

the court wanted to question them. I haven't seen him for a couple of days, but Dervla says she's working on his release."

"Killing?"

"Err yes..." She coughs awkwardly. "He said he had no choice."

After a time, the silence I've created becomes oppressive. Haelyn shifts in her seat but I can't even bring myself to acknowledge her. My thoughts are jumbled and I'm struggling to reconcile what Eskar has done alongside the fact that I was attacked in my own hometown. I've walked through the city so many times. It's a weird thing to be grateful to the magic that saved me but also fearful of it.

When Haelyn leaves, I remain on the sofa. My heads throbs. Drifting in and out of sleep, I watch the candle's flames flicker and the wax trickle down the sides, until a sharp knock on my door startles me. The candle flames dance across the walls as I open the door.

Eskar's tall frame fills the doorway. We stare at each other. His stubble is darker than usual, his eyes hollow and bruised. He flinches as his eyes pass over my forehead and I raise my hand to the source of my headache. As my fingers test a lump above my right eye, my vision sways and nausea rushes up my throat. I crumple towards the floor but he catches me.

Grey stars swim in front of my face as he lays me on the sofa and holds my hand. Satisfied I'm not going to throw up, I open my eyes.

"Can I get you anything? Water, a compress?"

"No, thank you. I'm fine." My cheeks redden at his

persistence.

Undeterred, Eskar continues to hold my hand tightly.

"Dervla said you were healing well. That you needed time. But I bumped into Haelyn on the stairs and she said you were awake… So…"

"Like I said, I'm fine. Processing but fine." I fix my eyes on the ceiling, watching it swim.

"The rebels should never have been able to get that close. I'm so sorry."

"What do you think they wanted with me?"

"I don't know and, unfortunately, I didn't keep one alive for us to ask."

"I heard." I can't meet his eyes.

"Sage, I'm sorry. I should have said I'm sorry the second I laid eyes on you outside the Concord room after the torture. I've had so many opportunities to explain and apologise but I kept pushing it down, pretending it didn't matter, that we weren't friends or that you already knew and didn't care. I was a coward. I hope you can forgive me."

I can't bring myself to look at him. "You killed someone to save me."

"Yes." His voice catches, stretching the single word over two syllables.

"You torture people, regularly."

"Yes. In exchange for my freedom one day. Under the pretence of working towards a better kingdom."

"You tortured me." I hate how my voice fractures.

"Yes. I'm so sorry." The hand that's not holding mine claws at his dishevelled hair, tugging at the roots. I focus on the action, avoiding his caramel eyes.

"I think I need some space. Please don't come by my rooms again." He drops my hand and the cold night air has me crossing my arms tight against my chest.

His footsteps are unsure on the tiles as he leaves. The candle light flickers a little as the last of the wax burns out and then extinguishes. I sit in the silence, in total darkness, focusing on my breath. The shadow in the corner was Eskar: nothing to fear anymore.

Chapter 25

I'm on strict bedrest whilst my concussion heals. There's a limit to my patience until I snap. Only so many days I can spend pacing my rooms or reading the books Haelyn brings me from the palace library. Every day I'm not in my lab, is another day when I'm not making progress. It gives the rebels another day to plan their next move. After my abduction attempt, I'm certain somehow that they've found out what I'm working on. Found out and decided to take it and weaponise it for their cause.

"I brought your letters and correspondence, as well as some more texts on minerals and geological deposits." Haelyn bustles through the doorway and drops the dusty tomes on the table. "If you could give me more information, I would be able to give you better recommendations. It will take you years to work through everything I have on rocks. Literal years."

My laugh is brittle; noise still causes a slight ring in my ear. I take the letters and the thick cream parchment with Howl's curling script stands out. I pull open his message. Before I can read past the first few words, the man himself barges into my rooms.

"Good morning! I hope you're feeling up to some good news?" His hair is in total disarray, as if someone has been running their hands through it all night and his face certainly looks as if he could do with a good night's sleep. I hope Haelyn might take the hint and excuse herself but she's smiling warmly at Howl and settles deeper into the sofa.

"Hello, Haelyn," he smiles back. "We've become well acquainted since our visit to Pentargon Academy and your accident. She's been kind enough to keep Cedar and I updated." A slight blush spreads across his cheekbones at the mention of my brother and I make a note to question him about Cedar later. Howl takes a seat next to Haelyn and leans forward eagerly. "We think we've cracked it."

"We?" I look between them and Haelyn has the grace to look sheepish.

"Sage, you can't do everything on your own," Howl chastises.

"I thought you were only doing this as payment for a favour you owed?" I fix him in place with a glare.

"I am, but Haelyn is your friend. Why shouldn't she help? Even if you won't tell us why this is so important, the more people researching the better. We wouldn't have made this discovery without her." Reproach seeps into his voice, as he leans back, mirroring Haelyn's crossed legs. One abduction attempt and I'm the odd one out it seems. I sigh. There's little I can do about it right now, other than pray Haelyn doesn't put the pieces together.

"So, where were we?" He turns to Haelyn who picks up the story with ease.

"Howl mentioned you were looking for something when he came by to check on you after the incident. We got talking about our visit to Pentargon Library and your search."

Howl jumps in. "The books in Pentargon Library confirmed there may be one group of minerals to match your expectations. The problem is, they're outlawed. Have been for years. And all records of their existence are held in the palace library."

"So that's where I could help," Haelyn chimes in.

"We've been searching through old alchemist records this morning and… I found it!"

"Why didn't you mention it before?" I turn to Haelyn angrily.

"I didn't want to get your hopes up… I also thought you might want to discover it for yourself. The details are in the books I've been giving you but…"

Clearly my brain still isn't working properly if I've missed her hints. She pats my knee awkwardly. "What have you found then?" I ask Howl, trying to ignore my flaming cheeks.

"It was there all along; we just needed to confirm its properties."

Haelyn and I lean in expectantly.

"Serpentine," he announces triumphantly.

I sag in disappointment and Haelyn blanches. Serpentine is the reason behind Trevesiga's isolationist tendencies. It was mined extensively, decades ago, in mines that sit on the borders between us and Aiche. It was only found in the Haag and shipped extensively to the rest of the continent. However, when the mists descended and mining became impossible, other kingdoms abandoned us and refused to trade. It's rare and rumoured to be a critical conduit in amplifying magic, not storing it. The continent blames us for withholding serpentine from them and think we are intentionally stamping out any magic that is not Mordros. I tend to agree with them.

The old kings of Trevesiga forbade anyone from using it. Even having it in your possession is a criminal offence, so that's another law we're going to have to bend if we want to get our hands on it. I point out as much to Howl but he is undeterred.

"You just need a sample. There should be some lingering in the old mines. They were evacuated pretty quickly. Bounty hunters couldn't have taken it all. Plus, if it works, there's an incentive to try to eradicate the mists and reopen the mines. We'd be able to travel to the continent again." His gaze travels to the distance, no doubt envisioning the riches he would make if travel to the continent became possible.

It's a long, long shot. But right now, I've got no other avenues to turn down and limited time to solve this before the rebels incite a civil war.

Chapter 26

"It's a terrible idea. Absolutely awful! You don't know what you're getting yourself into." Haelyn shuts down the plan. She's incensed, standing in front of the window in my sitting area, the fading sunlight turning her into an avenging angel. After the Concord meeting, she followed me, espousing the reasons why my expedition trip to the Haag is the worst idea she's ever heard. I wasn't expecting so strong an objection in front of the Concord though. It took me by surprise when she voiced her concerns, even going so far as to vote against it.

We've been arguing all the way back to my room where I found Dervla lounging on my sofa in her travelling cloak. Clearly, she is so desperate for good news on my research that she couldn't wait, despite not making it in time for the Concord meeting.

"I'm not convinced, but what other choice does she have?" Pensive, and taking her time to digest my idea, Dervla is contemplative. "It does carry some risk; you obviously couldn't go alone. But if this is the missing piece, then we could have this wrapped up in a matter of weeks."

Haelyn is not deterred. "It's not worth it. The Haag is dangerous and you'll get lost in the mists. There's no food or water. It's not completely uninhabited – who knows what's lurking there." She is full of conviction and desperately looking to Dervla for support.

"What do you mean it's not uninhabited?" Dervla asks sharply, fixing Haelyn with an acidic stare.

"Well, they're rumours from growing up in Tanwen." She deflates, flopping to the sofa beside me. "Sometimes bounty miners braved the mists in the hope of digging up treasure. Not just serpentine, mind you. Rare stones... precious gems, but those that came back were changed, different."

The room is silent. Dervla and I sit, heavy with anticipation, waiting for her. "They talked of being stalked, herded deeper into the moorland, of eerie noises in the fog and things mysteriously being lost or going wrong. None could ever describe what human or animal they thought they'd encountered but they all had similar stories."

A slow crawl of goosebumps develops up my arms, an icy breeze brushing past.

"Ridiculous. Superstitious nonsense, then; stories to keep children in line and well behaved." Dervla regains her confidence and Haelyn's concern has swayed her in the opposite direction.

"I'm telling you, there's something out there," Haelyn pleads, capturing my gaze, eyes full of worry.

"Anyway, the decision has been made." Dervla turns to me haughtily, "and don't think I'm not annoyed about that either, Sage. You could have waited until my return to petition the Concord." The dressing down is gentle compared to what I expected. I knew this would be breaking her trust in me a little but I don't need her approval for every decision. She gave me more autonomy when I was working in Athnavar and this project means as much to me as it does to her.

It was a calculated gamble to raise my proposal at the Concord and risky without speaking to Dervla or the King first. I thought about it at length, and given how nothing ever gets decided by vote if the King brings it to the table, I wondered what would happen if I brought something up unprompted. I was sure it would also help that no one is interested in the proclivities of the eccentric King's Alchemist.

My gamble paid off. It turns out the Concord's dislike of me sitting at their table outweighs their need to vote conflictingly. I'm well aware the majority of them voted in favour of my expedition in the hope I wouldn't return.

The King, however, is unlikely to forgive me as easily as Dervla. His anger simmered at the surface at being caught unawares and his green eyes raged with a vicious stare throughout my proposal. I think my refusal to baulk at his displeasure also won me a few votes.

Dervla is staring me down expectantly, as if she anticipates an apology. It might have been her initial idea but this project has taken over the last few years of my life. While the King and Concord don't understand the true purpose of my research, she does and that's why I had to make a move without her. No one else in the room would obstruct my expedition on the grounds of keeping me safe and I've seen her work the room a little too well. If she wanted me to stay, she would have got her way.

"I needed to do this on my own," I shrug. I don't owe her any more of an explanation.

Later that week, a tentative knock at my door interrupts my pathetic attempts at packing. I shout for them to come in as I survey the disarray across my suite of rooms. Haelyn sticks her head round the door and, seeing I'm alone, picks her way through the mess and perches on the arm of the sofa.

"Look, I'm not going to try to persuade you not to go. I can tell you're set on leaving, despite my reservations. I didn't know when I volunteered to help you that it would put you in danger." A rueful smile spreads over her face and she appears older. "But I want to give you some advice about Tanwen and the people who live there."

I stop what I'm doing and put down the heavy winter overcoat I'd been deliberating on. Bringing up Tanwen gives her face a painful twist. Her hands are clenched in her lap, fingernails bitten to the quick. Whatever she has to say, it's more important than the pain she's reliving from bringing it up.

"It's a brutal place to live; the forests are unforgiving and those that thrive there… well, they do not operate on the same code the rest of us do. Everyone has one priority: to survive in the wilderness."

I grow uncomfortable at the thought of her and other children, having to endure such a place.

"You can't trust anyone; their price for selling you out to others will not be as high as you think." She sees my look of confusion at the term and laughs hollowly. "Oh, they may appear friendly, or even disinterested on the surface, but there'll be another game afoot that is designed to trap you down the line. They will tell you misinformation and lie in wait to rob you. People don't get caught, because no witnesses are ever left alive. I was lucky to get out, but I can never go back and, if you upset anyone there, neither will you."

What must it have been like, to grow up in such a lawless community, closed off from the rest of the kingdom, remote and lacking the protections and civility found elsewhere? Knowing the setbacks she faced whilst growing up far exceed anything I dealt with, I marvel at Haelyn's rise to King's Archivist.

This conversation has drained her; her face is unusually pale and there are dark smudges under her eyes.

"Don't linger – get to the Haag as soon as you can. You'll be safer there, despite what is lurking in the mists. Take this with you." Having relieved her conscience, she hands me a book. It's heavy and old, pages crumbling at its well-thumbed edges. On closer study I recognise it from our conversation in the palace library. It's the book on attitudes.

Suitably warned, I ruminate on Haelyn's words late into the night, opting to pack an extra dagger despite being clueless about how to use it.

Chapter 27

I've nearly finished packing the next day, uneasy about Haelyn's confession when an unexpected visitor knocks on my door. The King, accompanied by two guards, stands in the hallway. He strides into the room as if this is a completely normal occurrence. Looking well-polished and suave, he surveys the tidy piles of equipment and clothes I'm deciding upon. Thankfully, the guards remain outside. My lounge, that felt so spacious moments before, now feels cramped.

We face each other for a moment as I struggle to find the words to ask what he's doing here. His presence in my personal space is jarring and I try not to focus on how well his shirt fits. Try to stop myself from noticing how, when his sleeves are rolled up, I can see his forearm muscles tense as he crosses his arms.

"So, it seems the knock to your head has given you permanent brain damage," he announces ostentatiously to the room.

"Well, I suppose I have you to thank for that then, since being used as bait was your idea."

"Technically not my idea and, for the record, I trust

you. I wasn't aware of the plan and I've spoken to the guards who let you leave unescorted; they've been reassigned. As for the Concord members who bribed them to do it, I'm still waiting for one of them to crack." He relaxes into my sofa, flinging his arms wide and leaning into the cushions. "If you did more than just attend the Concord sessions, and actually tried to integrate with the other members, then perhaps they wouldn't be so suspicious of you..."

"So, it's my fault that I got attacked by rebels and kidnapped then?" An insufferable smile dances across his lips and makes me want to smack it right off him. Where has this violence come from?

He looks round the room and notices the disarray. "You really are going then?"

"Of course. I need serpentine for my research. It's essential."

"Are you going to tell me what the research is about? I noticed you were rather light on specifics in the meeting..."

I stand mutely. This is why I didn't ask him for his approval beforehand.

"You'll know if I lie; it's better I don't say anything at all."

His head tilts in surprise and his body tenses.

"You said you trust me. When I have something to share, I will." I hope the benefits outweigh the fact that I've broken the Difan right under his nose. Although, the reaction from the other Mordros is what I fear most; they won't all be as accepting as Dervla. With the magic imbalance removed, their hold on power might become more tenuous, not less, and all I will have done is incite a civil war. A shudder runs through me before the King interrupts my train of thought.

"You could send someone else." He flicks a piece of dust off his shirt, both of us avoiding each other's gaze.

"And stay holed up in the palace for the foreseeable future? I accepted the escorts into the city before but now I'm not permitted to go into Pentargon in case of another abduction attempt. I'm useless here."

"You're in more danger outside of the city, unprotected."

"I'll be another traveller; no one will recognise or notice me. Besides, you said it was a democracy and the Concord voted. You can't stop me."

He sighs dramatically, emerald eyes darting about the room.

If it was anyone other than the King, I'd say he was looking for another reason to stay…

"I wanted to ask what you thought of my address this year. I assumed that even if you couldn't be bothered to attend the parade with the other members of the Concord, you would be in the crowd. I was certain you'd seek me out afterwards." He sounds hurt, as if my opinion matters to him. He's a good actor then – I'll give him that.

"Your address? I was there but I couldn't hear a word you said. No one in the crowd could. Then I was slightly preoccupied. Trying to recover from a concussion and attempted abduction." I slam closed the books I'm taking and stuff them into my bulging rucksack.

"But you're recovered now. Aren't you the least bit interested in what was said?" I notice a bit of anger slipping through his diplomatic mask.

"Absolutely not," I snap. "This might come as a bit of a surprise to you but no ordinary people actually give a damn about your address. It's always been irrelevant to our daily lives and is just an excuse for the Mordros to throw another party." It's a small exaggeration but it gets my point across.

"What on earth are you talking about? I'm the King."

This frustrating man! I throw my final pieces of clothing into a bag, turning to face him. "You may be king in name but you are as cut off as possible from your subjects. You have no interest in their lives. Their troubles. Their heartbreak. You surround yourself with advisors as privileged as you are and let them lead on all the decisions, even when they go round and round in circles with nothing ever decided upon or any change committed to. You may consider yourself above politics but nobody else is. Influence is traded every night over dinner and you are conspicuously absent. You're a figurehead at best and an ignorant, conceited aristocrat at worst."

The colour drains from the king's face as I finish my tirade and his mouth is set in a firm line as he stands to leave.

"I see. Thank you for sharing your perspective so eloquently. I shall leave you be." He strides purposefully to the door, no sign of anger but it's clear from the waves of displeasure rolling off him that I've overstepped, massively.

As he opens the door to leave, Eskar appears in the doorway, hand raised and about to knock. The two men face off.

The King breaks the silence first. "If you've come to try and dissuade her from leaving, you'll be wasting your time. She's quite determined." I glare intimidatingly at his back but he refuses to turn around.

Eskar responds, "Actually, given the importance of this journey, and the risk to Sage's life, I'm volunteering as her escort." His gaze passes by the King and his caramel eyes hold me in place.

A staring match begins between the King and Eskar, with the rest of us observing awkwardly, guards shuffling their feet. When I'm about to interrupt to break the tension, the King laughs cruelly and says, "Very well then. Enjoy gallivanting about my kingdom."

He walks down the corridor, guards following like shadows.

"I'd planned to speak to you about the expedition beforehand but it took longer than I planned to get my affairs in order. I've booked a ticket on the same ferry to Cathair in the morning, if that's alright with you?"

I huff; travelling alone had felt daunting but I'm still too rattled from losing my temper with the King to thank Eskar for volunteering. His magic and training will provide protection and, as long as we aren't recognised, it should make my journey easier.

The next morning, I make my goodbyes, leaving Dervla until last. We stand by the ferry, sprayed by water from the ocean, blown in on a strong gale. Kaens takes her usual place on Dervla's shoulder, her head tucked under a wing to stay dry. I'm consciously ignoring the rocking of the boat which is packed with provisions to last until Cathair. Every cabin is booked and the ferry sits lower in the water than I would like. Compared to the vast sea beyond the archipelago, the vessel feels rickety and small. Before I board, I ask Dervla about the address and she grimaces; apparently the King made a change from tradition after all.

He spoke about a changed Trevesiga, a new Trevesiga where the laws and culture are changing. She said he was vague on the details but he's been steamrolling Concord members behind the scenes for weeks on the contents. Challenging them on their committee agendas and getting into the weeds of what they're doing and achieving. Apparently, he's taken a proactive stance since his announcement to protect the city from the spring floods.

More than a few feathers have been severely ruffled and he is gathering momentum amongst the younger members of the Mordros at least. Her approval is clear: she's never been one to let her political leanings show but the pride in her voice increases the guilt I feel for my treatment of the King. I'll sit with that guilt over the next few weeks.

Eskar joins us late, jumping onto the ferry as it departs. He's travelling light with one rucksack and disappears into his cabin before we set sail. Dervla remains on the quay until we sail out of sight past the first islet.

Chapter 28

The ferry ride up the coast feels endless and my stomach fights against every moment at sea. The crew check on me frequently, laughing at my dishevelled state, curled round a bucket. I'm well aware that we are sailing under flat conditions but my body reacts to the perpetual rocking. By the time we reach the estuary up river to Cathair, I've not even opened a page of the book Haelyn gifted me before we left.

When we finally turn inwards from the coast, I can see land on either side of the ferry and the rocking subsides to a gentle sway. Braving the ever-present nausea, I leave my room to seek daylight and find an unoccupied wooden bench on the upper deck. Wrapped up tight in a scratchy woollen blanket, I try to ignore the pervading smell of sea salt that lingers in the air and watch the countryside pass by.

Growing up in Pentargon and then living in Athnavar, these wide-open landscapes are strange to me. Fields stretch for miles, a mix of red-brown and yellow with the barest hint of green peeking through. There's a quiet here. My ears struggle to adjust to the lack of city bustle and I don't see any other boats for days.

The river we sail is now blue and clear, with bright reflections that make my eyes ache as the sun rises higher in the sky each day. Across the water, a large bird circles above the treeline. As we progress inland the landscape changes, so do the trees: endless shades of green, some dotted with blossom and flowers and others, the evergreens, with a variety of leaves. The colour contrast between the pale blue sky, the dark blue water and the vegetation makes my eyes feel like they've been hibernating for my whole life. Taking in these views makes me feel truly alive.

When I'm certain none of the other passengers have noticed me, I take out the book Haelyn gave me. It's an encyclopaedia of attitudes. Compiled before living memory, it's fascinating. For the author to have been able to capture the nuances between Zephyrs who can make waves with wind, and Mordros who can manipulate water suggests there was once a time where magic was more openly accepted, more integral to our society and not reduced to tools of warfare and conquest, where Zephyrs and Aubades didn't have to hide in the shadows, suppressing their magic.

The author's clinical, overly detailed description of magical traits slows my progress. Daylight dims before I make a dent in the large tome, each page covered entirely with a fine, cramped scrawl. As darkness settles, the air chills and I stretch my stiff limbs. There's movement in the corner of my eye.

A few benches along sits Eskar. I don't know how

long he's been there but when he sees me looking, he moves closer and passes me a blanket to curl under. It's soft and warm from his body heat. He retreats back to his bench in silence. I tuck my book into the folds of the blanket, hiding it from his view.

I refuse to go through the next few weeks barely speaking, even if I don't understand where we stand now. "I'm feeling much better now." My voice struggles with speaking after so long, my throat sore from retching.

"I can see." He drags his eyes from the invisible horizon to survey what little there is of me poking through the blanket.

"Why did you volunteer to come with me?" I whisper quietly, conscious we should be discreet.

He leans closer as if checking he's heard me correctly. I look over expectantly and he sighs heavily, comes over and sits next to me, our blankets touching.

"The chance to escape the city, to see my hometown, to make amends with you – I have many reasons..." His voice cracks, painful and tired but his eyes are lighter as they scan my face.

"Your hometown?"

His voice softens, unlike anything I've heard from him before. "I grew up in Cathair. It's the most beautiful city in the whole of Trevesiga. I'm not able to return as often as I'd like, particularly since I was appointed the King's Verax. Even if it's a brief stop, I couldn't miss that opportunity."

"Tell me about it."

"You'll see for yourself soon enough." His smirk

unfolds at this and my mouth smiles in response.

I have to restrain myself from quizzing him more and satisfy myself with savouring the contentment that falls between us. I sink further into my blanket, "Thank you for coming."

He tucks the ends of my blanket under my feet and lets out a huge sigh, a half-smile on his face, "You're welcome."

Sitting together and watching the occasional pinpricks of light on the shoreline puncturing the darkness and sharing body warmth, my mind quietens. For once I'm not thinking about the travel ahead, my research or what we've left behind.

Chapter 29

Cathair looms ahead of us, blazing white as we turn the final bend in the river. I hadn't spent much time contemplating what the city would be like but, even if I had, nothing could have prepared me for the vast expanse of white limestone buildings covering the valley floor and stretching into the green foothills on both sides of the river. Up close, many of the buildings are covered with winding vines of budding wisteria, about to flower. The grey finger-like buds droop over every doorway and windowsill, looking like petrified worms crawling from the brickwork. The ferry takes us into the heart of the city and the sunshine bounces off the white stone, bleaching my eyes and causing my head to ache.

Eskar was reluctant to give me much detail on Cathair and says he wants me to discover it for myself. We won't be staying long, but there is time for me to pay my respects to the Principal at the Academy and to restock our supplies. I hope we'll have sufficient time for Eskar to keep his promise to take me to one of the cafes in the city which sells the best stewed apple pastries. From the way he described them, I get a sense of its being an almost religious experience and one I want to share with him. Growing up, he would sneak from his family home and visit every patisserie in the city. Even if it's been years, he knows his way around.

The Academy is perched in the foothills and I see its domed roofs as we sail by them. As with all the academies in Trevesiga, this has its own pragmatic specialism, focusing on agriculture and farming with research on drainage and harvests. I'm told this was where the complex aqueduct that feeds all of Trevesiga was first designed.

Our plan is to keep a low profile politically, other than meeting with the Principal. Even agreeing to that took some convincing from Eskar. After the attack in Pentargon, he's taking no chances. We wait on the ferry long after the other passengers have departed and skulk quietly on to the shore.

Barely a few steps onto dry land, a pompous-looking city official steps directly into our path.

"The Governor is thrilled you are making a visit to our beautiful city. He has graciously extended a dinner invitation this evening."

"Excuse us – you have the wrong people." Eskar attempts to pass the official but he's surprisingly nimble and side-steps him. Eskar turns, furious to see the official has weaselled his way between us. I look at him in alarm. How did the Governor find out about our visit? The expedition is meant to be secret. I haven't even reached out to the Academy's Principal yet.

"I'm certain, I don't. The Governor was quite specific:

The King's Verax and the King's Alchemist will be travelling together and will be the last passengers to disembark. I've been waiting a while."

Eskar tenses, looking to see if anyone else is paying attention to the official's loud voice.

There goes keeping a low profile.

"If you'll kindly follow me, I'll take you to the Governor's house now. There's a long list of people who are looking forward to meeting you." Anxiety tightens my throat, as any of these people could be a threat. I don't want to play any political game with more entitled Mordros when I need to get to the Haag. I don't have the time.

He offers his arm and, before I can accept it, I find Eskar at my side, linking us firmly together.

"Lead on then." Eskar's disinterested tone perfectly plays the bored aristocratic member of the Concord, dismissing the official as not worth his notice. I attempt to copy his expression, mimicking the look of haughty distain I've seen Dervla adopt when she doesn't get her way.

The official huffs and reluctantly walks ahead, turning back every few steps to check we are following. I risk a glance at Eskar whilst the official's back is turned and recognise the steely set of his jaw, eyes darting back and forth, assessing our path.

Even so close to the harbour the streets are immaculately clean, and every house has window boxes with neatly pruned and well-watered flowers. I scrape my fingers through my windswept hair as we pass, feeling out of place. Despite it being close to the end of the day, a time where I would expect a city to be busy and bustling with people jostling to get home quickly, it's quiet and serene. No one rushes, voices are muted and people take the time to point out a newly flowering plant or interesting shop display to their companions. The affluence in this city is clear: children are well-dressed for the spring winds, hats neatly tied under their chins and, unlike me, not a hair out of place.

We leave the harbour, climbing the valley slopes and the houses become larger, each building secluded in its own private plot, ice-white stone walls and wrought iron railings separate each from its neighbours. Eskar pauses in front of one and I note the large brass nameplate on the gate front which says Devath. The sheer scale and opulence of it puts even Howl's mansion in Pentargon to shame.

"The Governor must allow us time to freshen up after such a long journey. We will attend his dinner once we have settled in."

I tense, expecting the official to argue, but he is at ease with the suggestion, smiling obsequiously and attempting a half bow towards Eskar.

"Of course, Verax. A carriage will be sent to collect you."

"No need, I prefer to travel in my own."

"Very well, I look forward to seeing you both later." He backs away awkwardly and, once at a respectable distance, turns and scuttles up the hill.

Eskar watches until he is safely out of sight before steering me away.

"Quick. We don't have much time." He tugs my

hood farther over my head so my face is obscured. He does the same to himself and takes my hand, leading me back into the city.

In confusion, I follow without question as we twist and turn through the quiet streets, I assume the reason we double back several times is to make sure we're not being followed. By now, the bright moonlight illuminates the stone; soft reflections cast off the buildings, chasing away the shadows. I try to count the turns but the feel of his strong hand covering mine and taking charge has my brain faltering.

Between a closed music shop and what looks to be a patisserie is a narrow, bland doorway. No adornments or name plate. Eskar checks the street, confirming we are alone. He slips a small silver key from his pocket, opens the door on creaky hinges and ushers me inside.

In the crowded hallway I can smell the salty ocean clinging to his coat. I resist climbing the dusty stairs in front of me until I know what I'm walking into.

"Welcome to my home." He shrugs off his coat and leaves his bag by the doorway, gesturing for me to go upstairs.

Chapter 30

"We can't stay in my family townhouse. It will be the first place they will look when we don't show up to dinner," Eskar explains as we climb the stairs, my bag banging my shins as I heave it up with me. "Someone at Chi An Mor told the Governor we were coming. And that is not a good thing. No one should even know we are here." He tugs hard at the wind-tangled strands of his hair. "We'll stay here tonight and leave first thing tomorrow morning."

At the top of the stairs, I open a second door to find a cosy, bookcase-filled front room, dusty from lack of use.

"I need to keep you safe. Nobody knows I own this place. If the traitor is part of the Concord, then they will be relying on their connections here. Staying here tonight means they can't find us."

"Part of the Concord?" My throat catches and my back stiffens. I'm alarmed one of the most powerful people in Trevesiga could be working to destabilise the court right under the King's nose.

"We're not ruling anything out at the moment." He

walks around the open-plan apartment, pulling back curtains and adjusting shutters to let in what little light remains.

"Who's we?" I'm on edge; it occurs to me perhaps I've trusted the wrong person. None of my friends or family back in Pentargon will know where I am either. If something happens to me, Eskar is my sole connection. Panic rises and sweat collects on the back of my neck.

"None of your business." He's rooting through the cupboards, assessing their contents.

I edge back towards the staircase. "Well, it is my business if I'm going to trust you here. Who's to say you're not the traitor?" If I make a run for it now, I'd have my rucksack and very little money. I don't even know how much the passage back to Pentargon will cost, let alone food on top. What if I'm not safe there either? I have nowhere to go, nowhere to stay.

Turning round and seeing me scared and flustered he rolls his eyes. "If I am the traitor, then I'm not being a good one. I would have let you get kidnapped at the King's address."

I release a long breath and try to regulate my breathing; instead of letting me get kidnapped, he murdered one of my attackers. My panic subsides but my chest aches with pressure. I've been in denial about the precariousness of my situation, fully dependent on the benevolence of the King. A man I angered as I left. Everything I own currently has been given to me as a result of my position on the Concord. This new position and the home that comes with it is temporary while I complete my research and the thought of losing another position shakes me. I can't go through that again. As soon as I get home and solve this mess, I'm moving out of the palace and setting myself up independently.

Interrupting my train of thought, Eskar announces he's going out to get us some food.

"While I'm gone, there's a cupboard through there – go and change your hair ready for tomorrow." He gestures to what I presume is one of the bedrooms.

"Cut it, colour it, I don't care, just change it. Do something so if anyone is looking for us then they won't immediately spot us in a crowd." The implication of a repeat of the attack in Pentargon is a stark reminder of how serious the threat is against me.

"After that, leave everything you can here. We're travelling much lighter from now on."

I resign myself to an unpleasant evening. My hair is one of the features I'm quite attached to. I can hide behind the long, light gold strands like a curtain and the heavy weight of a ponytail grounds me when I'm working.

"Trust me, Sage. This is my job." He's right, when he's not being forced to torture suspected rebels, he's a captain in the king's guard. He leaves with a wink and an attempt at a reassuring smile.

I venture into the cupboard like he said, trying desperately not to notice the personal details in the room: a painting above the bed of a shaded woodland glen, the books beside it – all fiction, even the clothes spilling from the wardrobe.

The cupboard is a treasure trove of disguises, rows of hats, glasses and other accoutrements. I wonder how much use he's actually made of any of these things and why he might feel he needs to hide in his hometown.

I select a small brick of dark dye and grab a pair of shears. After some time, my new inky black hair swings above my shoulders. Satisfied with the unfamiliar light breeze across the bottom of my neck, it feels pleasant to shake my new style back and forward, letting the shorter strands graze my skin as they pass. Looking in the mirror, I don't recognise myself.

My stomach grumbles waiting for Eskar to return and the cupboards are bare so I turn to the book from Haelyn. It's a slow read but I'm finally rewarded by a chapter on Aubades. I jump ahead to that section, doubting I'll want to carry the whole book through the Haag: hopefully, Haelyn will forgive me.

The book details how Aubades used to fall into two categories. Some people could focus their magic into a thin beam that burns and others could build some sort of reflective shield that others' magic couldn't penetrate: both incredibly useful and powerful attitudes that have been lost to time.

Chapter 31

Thoroughly absorbed, Eskar's return takes me by surprise. When the door opens, I flinch and drop the book to the floor. He looks different too: his hair is much shorter, face clean shaven. I don't recognise him and clearly from the look on his face the feeling is mutual.

"Nice work." He stares intently at me. I blush at the unexpected compliment before helping him unpack the food he's carrying. It's still hot – heat seeps through the brown paper.

"Anything of interest?" he gestures at Haelyn's book as I start to eat the pasty, not bothering to find cutlery or a plate.

"Actually, yes. Did you know Aubades once had attitudes too?"

"No, I didn't, but then… I guess it never occurred to me what anyone else's attitudes were. Mine was enough to handle on its own." There it is again, a trace of bitterness mixed with something I can't place.

"Do you know anyone else's attitudes at court?" I pause mid-bite.

"No, I don't make a habit of sticking my nose where it doesn't belong; it's very personal." Conversation closed then, he opens his parcel and eats. After a few mouthfuls, he adds, "You should ask Dervla, though, when we get back; she knows what everybody's is."

"Hmm, maybe I will. In the meantime, I want to learn more about my magic. Perhaps I have a previously undiscovered attitude. Something that will make up for my limited capacity."

He smirks a little at my statement and the usual irritation I feel at seeing that half-smile doesn't materialise.

"How do you know if you have an attitude?" I ask.

"Nowadays, once you've mastered controlling your magic, the Gallos we call it, your attitude comes forward as the way your magic is most inclined to behave. Your attitude is central to your being; it's as easy as breathing and requires pretty much none of your capacity. Attitudes are generally limitless."

So, in theory he could torture thousands upon thousands of people. My stomach turns.

"So that's another incentive for you to keep working on it then." He must have heard from Dervla how I'm struggling with mastering the Gallos and he's laughing at me. Strange, I didn't realise they discussed me behind my back but I push that thought to one side for now. Huffing, I sag back into the sofa, my newly cut hair tickling my neck as it swings around. "I just can't visualise it properly. Every time I create one strand perfectly, it slithers away as soon as I focus on creating the second."

"Will it help to see mine?" He leans forward from the sofa opposite.

"I'll try anything at this point." He raises one of his eyebrows and his nostrils flare slightly, teasing me.

I roll my eyes at his insinuation; he laughs and sits back. A crease appears between his eyes as he centres himself. Taking a deep breath and moving his hands purposefully, he summons a pulsing, woven ball of magic through his palms and allows it to hover in front of his chest. It's smaller than Dervla's but from what I can tell the colour of the water is mostly the same.

Frowning a little now, a single strand separates and floats through the air, as if pulled by an invisible needle. It reaches towards me and I let it rest on my open palm, sizzling where it touches. It doesn't hurt but my magic takes over my conscious thoughts with an instinct to draw the power inside me. As it disappears under my skin, the connection drops. Eskar looks at me in alarm and the ball of power dissipates back into his hands.

"How did you do that?" He's stricken, face chalky, eyes wide in panic.

"I'm not sure," I answer and I feel different: my magic dances and writhes in my chest. There! I can see it! A single thread slithering across the surface of my usual sphere, different from the rest. "I think I just absorbed some of your magic." From the look on his face, that's not what he intended.

"But how?" The crease between his eyebrows deepens. "I was just trying to show you how to separate your magic."

I take a moment to examine the new magic within

me. Given what he's told me, I can feel the new thread of magic has become fuzzy on the edges, trying but failing to blend with the rest of my magic, like oil and water.

"Honestly, I have no idea. It was instinctive. As if my magic summoned it." My stomach rolls at the strange sensation and I suck air in through my nose to counter the rising nausea.

He pauses, the fragile trust we'd established on the ferry ride fracturing. "Well, what do we do now?"

"I don't know. I was going to try and send it back. But since I don't know how to control my magic like you do then maybe I'll just hurl it all at your head and hope for the best." It's petty, I know, but I pride myself on my intellect, my knowledge of the world and this has floored me. How have I stolen his magic? Yet it happened so naturally.

He rolls his sleeves up to his forearms and braces his hands on his knees. "If it'll make you feel better to try and incinerate me magically then let me have it." His teasing fails to cover his unease and I don't know how to take it. "Come on, I dare you."

This is a ridiculously stupid idea. I could hurt him. And I don't know how I feel about showing him my magic either.

"Don't you want to see what happens?" His overconfidence is needling me just in the right place. I glance at the sky through the window; there's just enough evening light left that I'll be able to recharge if needed. Inhaling deeply, I draw my magic to the surface. This time I can see how to shape it, to mould it to my will.

It goes gladly, as if the strand I took from him is pulling back towards its original owner, taking the rest with it and leaving me with a familiar void in my chest.

He opens his hands to catch the ball of light and hisses when it touches him. Red welts appear on his palms as if he's placed his hand on a hot stove. I rush forwards, cradling his hands in mine, examining the damage before I pull him to the sink and run cool water. His shoulders sag in relief as the water splashes over them and I shudder.

The water dances across the back of my hand where I'm still holding Eskar's. It hums and I flinch. The void in my chest feels a little smaller. A little less empty. There's a single thread of magic inside my chest, but it's not mine. It's a strand of Mordros magic.

The last rays of sunlight flicker across the city rooftops and in through the high windows. My hands reach out towards the fading light and I draw it to me as darkness falls. I did it! I started to master the Gallos, but at what cost?

"There's still a piece of your magic linked with mine," I whisper, as the redness on Eskar's hands fades. The magic from him is deep in my chest, hiding behind my own.

"I can feel its loss – a part of me is missing." He rubs his chest as if it aches and his face is twisted tight, tension drawing his eyebrows together.

"What have I done?" Shame flushes my face red as I stare down at my hands, turning them over, looking for a clue. "I'll return it as soon as I work out how. I'll need to keeping working on the Gallos first because it's pretty tightly woven in there. I can't separate it." My magic is shielding it, becoming intangible and slipping away when I try to extract the rogue strand. I grunt with frustration as he points out it normally takes a few weeks to fully master the concept.

"A few weeks? I'm supposed to live with this piece of magic inside me like a parasite for a few weeks?" I've never hyperventilated before but I expect this is what it feels like.

"I've got to live with it missing. I'd say that's arguably harder."

"Well, what do we do now?"

"You practise weaving your magic into separate strands. You work on mastering the Gallos quicker than any Mordros has ever done. And you do not leave this apartment." He peers out of the window. "I'm going to get us supplies so we can leave this city before we cause another disaster." He's rattled, really rattled.

Chapter 32

The sun rises and I wake alone. I avoided sleep for as long as I could, wanting to understand Eskar's magic. It is tricky and uncooperative, not unlike its owner. I've tried using it, thinking I could wield it and it would dissipate on its own but every time I attempted to call it forward, my magic intruded and surfaced instead, protective of this new strand. That being said, practise has paid off for my magic: I am improving at visualising my magic now that I can feel the differences between Eskar's and my own. The Gallos feels within my reach.

My bag has been packed and repacked and my stomach is deafeningly loud by the time Eskar returns. I've seen him in a grim mood before but that pales in comparison to the thundercloud he's under now. As he makes his breakfast, every drawer, door and cupboard is slammed.

"Everything okay?" I stand in the doorway, unsure how to manage his mood at such close proximity.

"Nope. Thanks to your little stunt yesterday, I've had to change our plans. I can't recover that last bit of magic: it's missing. Completely gone. I was going to propose we sneak up to the aqueducts and travel that way to Tanwen, but I'm not risking ferrying you when my magic isn't at full capacity." He softens and turns to me, "It's another boat trip I'm afraid."

I couldn't give a damn about another boat trip. I'm processing the incredible thing I achieved with my magic yesterday. My mind spins with the possibilities. Not being limited to one type of magic, channelling or wielding. What if this removes constraints on capacity too? What if this is the real answer to giving Aubades equal opportunities in Trevesiga?

Eskar must see the thoughts tumbling through my head, my excitement building. "Don't go there, Sage, it's too dangerous. It doesn't matter who your connections are or what you are. People… the Mordros, will kill you for this discovery without a doubt. It's incendiary." His hands land on my shoulders, forcing me to acknowledge him. "The best thing you can do now is act like nothing happened. We don't discuss this outside my apartment. We continue as planned and as soon as we're back in Pentargon, in the safety of your laboratory, we'll explore it more."

He holds me firmly in place until he's sure I'll stay quiet. It kills me not to ask more questions. But he's right; not here, not now.

We return to packing our essential belongings, for me that means leaving behind the book Haelyn lent me, carefully placing it on Eskar's bookshelves. I'm loath to leave it but now I know how valuable it is, I can't afford to take it into the Haag and risk it getting damaged. For Eskar, it apparently means making the critical decision on which weapon to leave behind; for every dagger and knife that he deliberates over, I open my eyes wider. I'm not sure how we're meant to pass as travellers when he's armed to the teeth.

I roll my eyes deliberately when he staggers a little under the weight of his rucksack – I thought we were packing light.

Downstairs and in the street, the morning light is more intense than I'm used to and as my eyes adjust to the bright ivory reflections, Eskar tenses in front of me.

We're surrounded by city guards, with the slimy official standing in the centre.

"What is this?" Eskar spits, hands balling at his side.

"When you failed to show up for dinner last night, the Governor was concerned. We are simply here to escort you to his house for the duration of your visit."

"That won't be necessary." Eskar's voice is low, his tone commanding. "As you can see, we are both fine and require no assistance. Send our regards to the Governor. We will not be coming with you." He steps closer to me but stops short of letting our arms brush.

"I'm relieved to hear it. Now, please, come this way." The official disregards the second part of Eskar's protest and the guards close in.

"I said no!" The guards falter but the official smiles greasily at us.

"I'm to convey from the Governor, that this isn't a request and to remind you that while you reside in his city, you will abide by his rules."

The guards take another step forward, closing in around us. A shiver passes through my spine and I pull back into a shadow of the doorway. Eskar stops me.

His face is grave; he surveys the guards surrounding us and the citizens peering from their doorways at the commotion, before nodding curtly to the official, allowing the guards to shepherd us deeper into the city.

"How did they find us?" I hiss.

Eskar doesn't respond, just fixes his gaze ahead, remaining silent.

We weave through the city, bustling with morning fervour. The unit of guards causes a murmuring behind us.

Unnoticed by our entourage, Eskar coughs quietly and I look up to recognise his furtive assessment of the streets. He's making a plan: he has no intention of going peacefully to the Governor's house. Faintly relieved at his reticence to engage with the Mordros in charge of Cathair and ready to follow his lead, I shift my pack more comfortably on my shoulders.

Under his breath, he whispers, "If we enter the Governor's house, we're not coming out alive. In two streets time, I'm going to make a distraction and we're going to run. Be ready."

I hate running. Nothing in my life requires athleticism of any kind so this is not ideal. But there's no opportunity to discuss, to argue and I value my life more than making a fool of myself with my lack of fitness. Thankfully, none of the guards closest to me exude health and vitality either. Clearly working for the Governor is a choice assignment.

Time slows as we walk towards the crossroad Eskar has chosen. There's a rhythmic hubbub ahead – it's market day. Chequered awnings over busy stalls are being laid out and crates unloaded. There is a subtle aroma of cooked apple floating through the breeze and my mouth waters, masking my nerves for a moment.

The official and guards turn right as we enter the market, their uniformed credentials opening a path through the organised melee. As they turn, Eskar shoots a jet of water into the middle of the market, capsizing the nearest stalls and knocking over the official. Eskar reaches for my hand, engulfing it with his own and we run.

The market traders don't part as easily for us, but perhaps that is a blessing in disguise as we're more difficult for the guards to place in the crowds. Distantly now, the official hollers for us to stop and for people to apprehend us. Thankfully it turns out the people of Cathair, privileged as they are, have little love for authority. No one tries to stop us. In fact, a few step out of our way before closing the path behind us.

We weave uphill through the stalls, until my breath feels as if it's being torn from my lungs. Eskar's height and long strides make it tough to keep pace but adrenaline pushes me on.

At the top of the market, the protection of the stalls and crowds dissipates and the outraged chatter thins out. Eskar pulls me into a side street and slows. I'm gasping now, legs burning and drenched in sweat under my winter cloak. This quarter of the city is sleeping and the homes, while not dishevelled, are definitely older and in need of some repair. Broken, leaning fences threaten to trip us as we pound up the road. The polished stone pavements change to an uneven dusty brown and cracks open where tree roots protrude through the soil. A quick glance back reveals no pursuers. Eskar pushes on relentless.

We reach the end of the road, the very edge of the city and slip behind the tree line, into the shadows. Legs cramping, I rest, panting against the broad trunk of an oak tree while Eskar peers down into the city we've left behind. Gulping air and inhaling the fresh scent of the trees, damp from this week's rain, I slowly regain my breath.

"We've lost them for now." Eskar's voice is ominous. Sweat also coats his face and soaks his hair. He motions for us to continue deeper into the trees. Legs wobbling, I stagger after him.

"There's a small river source ahead; we can follow it to the other side of the city and hire a boat to Tanwen from there. If we hurry, we can be well clear of Cathair by sunset."

I grunt an agreement, unable to form words as we trudge deeper into the forest.

Chapter 33

The whole day we hiked through the forest outside Cathair, I stressed. What started as a simple stop in Eskar's hometown snowballed into two back-to-back escapes, the second making us run for our lives. Trekking through a lush forest which was just showing the first signs of welcoming spring should have given me time to ruminate on what happened in Cathair but the crunch of branches from animals and the frantic cries of hungry baby birds kept me on edge. My jaw is tense and aching by the time the skies darken, my nerves fraying at every interruption or possible sound of our pursuers.

Whatever Eskar learnt about the Governor while replenishing his magic overnight, and while I slept unawares, he's shaken. I refuse to be kept in the dark any further but he won't relent. He promises to tell me as soon as we're safely on a boat out of the city but as we press on I'm grumbling to myself and stewing in nightmares.

The river we're following widens dramatically during the afternoon and by the time we leave the forest again, it's a slow-moving tranquil ribbon. Ahead, I can see the Thair River from the city – the one we used to travel inland from Porth. It meanders in front of us. A single bird of prey flies overhead, calling out to the setting sun slipping out of the sky. Dusk has fallen by the time Eskar steers us towards a wooden boathouse where the two rivers meet and flow back to sea.

The small boathouse is abandoned and dark shadows obscure its corners. Eskar sets about releasing one of the small skiffs from its moorings. Feeling useless, I have to wait and watch as he expertly unwinds the knots and prepares the boat. Nerves jangling, I scout the treeline for movement through the glassless windows.

Satisfied our boat is ready, Eskar holds out a hand to help me climb on board. I stare at the boat, conscious of how easily we've become fugitives and now thieves.

"Can we leave some money? As payment…" I mutter, ignoring his outstretched hand and climbing in.

"For the love of…"

I don't exactly clamber in gracefully and the boat is tiny, barely enough for two. My foot catches where he's stowed his rucksack under the seat and I tumble on to his chest. His arms wrap protectively round me as he twists, shielding me from the hard wooden side and preventing us both from falling overboard. We collapse into the bottom of the boat, invading each other's space, our faces so close I can feel his breath on my cheek.

I gaze into his caramel eyes to find them swirling with anxiety and his face wincing from the fall and apologise quietly.

He softens, mouth curling into a smile as he rolls me to the side and releases me from his embrace, tracing his hands down to my waist before lifting me up into the seat.

We both startle and separate at a loud bird cry overhead. The cry is a warning; it's found its prey and is closing in.

Tossing a coin into the next boat, Eskar pushes us away from the small dock and into the river. We wobble precariously as the current carries us towards Cathair. I flinch and resist turning to Eskar in panic.

"Don't move. You'll make this harder than it needs to be." I freeze at the strain in his voice, turning my head slowly to see him shift until he's wrapped a leg either side of my hips. He reclines in the boat, far enough to dip his hands in the water and sure enough, our little boat fights the current. We turn incrementally until we're battling to stay in place, Eskar wielding his magic to counter the flow of water. We start to move upstream.

At night, the river is empty of human activity and water sloshes against our little boat, reminding me of my escape from Athnavar with Dervla. However, here we aren't suspended high above the countryside but floating within it. Creatures scurry along the banks, calling to one another and the river reeds rustle, swaying as we pass. I soon cool as the exhaustion from the day settles in and my aching limbs tighten, seizing. Eskar is behind me, pressed firmly into my back. The faint scent of beeswax from candles and woodsmoke lingers on his clothes, wrapping around me like his muscled legs, blocking the odours drifting from the riverbanks.

Once the stars fully settle in the sky I break our uneasy silence. "What did you mean when you said we wouldn't make it out alive from the Governor's house?"

He sighs and our boat slows a little, swaying in the current.

"When we arrived and I saw the official on the quay, it was clear someone had already tipped the Governor off about our arrival. Then when they insisted we came to dinner, it felt like more than a political power play. I did some digging when I was getting supplies but didn't hear anything amiss." He pauses.

"But then when they found my apartment… I knew he would be behind it."

"Who's he?" Before Eskar can respond, a shadow darts in front of our boat, startling me before Eskar can respond. My heart thunders in my chest.

"Lord Bal."

"The old Almanac?" I can't help terror from invading my voice.

"Yes. He was always close with the Governor and his wife. With his assets frozen and the King unsteady on the throne, I think he has sought sanctuary here, biding his time, rallying support."

"Support to overthrow the King? And what? Put himself on the throne?" The thought of that cruel calculating man wearing the crown, having unlimited power chills me.

"To overthrow yes, but he wouldn't want to rule. Power is more easily gained when you are not bound by position. He'll be waiting for the right figurehead to manipulate and eliminating threats in the meantime."

"We're threats?"

"Worse, we're personal. You, for causing the King to exile him and me for failing to leave with him. He would have delighted in trapping us."

"And the Governor is on his side."

"The Governor has always chosen him over me." Bitterness leeches unexpectedly into Eskar's voice and I turn to catch his eye, widening my eyes in a silent question.

"He's my father. But he owes his position as Governor to the old Almanac. And never lets me forget it. They have both controlled me for years. With Lord Bal exiled, the King could remove my father from the position at any point, but he hasn't bothered to yet. The position is everything to my father," he mutters dejectedly, turning his face from mine in the darkness. I sink back into him, offering what little comfort I can in the face of his despair.

We continue on and I sit, useless, at the front of the boat, tasked with shouting if there are unexpected obstacles or debris we need to avoid, struggling to see in the dark, only stopping when Eskar, shaking with exhaustion cannot carry on any longer and daylight creeps over the horizon.

I flatten some of the water reeds, making a small gap for us to lay down once he finishes channelling from the edge of the river. It's going to be rough travelling from here: no fire and nothing to protect us from the elements. I hope it doesn't rain.

Eskar finishes replenishing his magic and joins me. "We'll travel at night and take turns sleeping in the day. It'll be harder to sneak up on us in daylight." Conscious that still leaves Eskar to do most of the work, I settle in to take the first watch as dawn breaks, resolving to let him sleep as long as possible.

The boat trip to Tanwen is significantly less pleasant than our ferry to Cathair. It's small and cramped. Eskar is silent as we travel inland the next night, focusing on overcoming the current as he wields. Unlike yesterday, the weather is dark and gloomy and, when dawn comes, it is miserable. Visibility is limited, trees block most of the light on each side and the sun is too weak to penetrate. The trees have changed since we left Cathair. On the first night they were varied, with berries and blossom and had plenty of space in between. Now they are pine: uniform, densely packed and towering. My body protests from a lack of rest and the cramped conditions but I don't say a word; this is my expedition after all.

We stop to make camp again in the morning, Eskar drenched in sweat and sickly pale. I sit by the small fire he's permitted while he sits in the cold river to replenish his magic. Judging by his gritted teeth, he's not mastered warming the water. He returns, skin wan and shaking and I offer him my cloak and hat to help him warm up since we will be in shade until the sun rises fully. The next three days are the same, starting at dusk, stopping at dawn. We don't see a soul as we battle the current upstream, lit by a waning moon.

On my watch, during the day, I don't see anyone on the river either. The lonely landscape is packed with wildlife, the river teeming with fish. At one point I see a raft of otters with pups diving around them. They regard me curiously as I peep through the reeds.

Every so often, we come across a tributary where another river joins ours and runs back to Cathair. These must produce stronger currents because Eskar flinches and plunges his hands deeper into the water. With every tributary we pass, our river channel gets smaller, the banks closing in. Through the trees, I often find eyes looking back at me, unblinking. I tell myself they belong to deer, but when I mention it, Eskar's face becomes more drawn with worry. We stop lighting fires after that and I don't get much sleep.

Chapter 34

The following night, the river narrows to a stream where I can nearly touch both sides of the bank. Without warning, Eskar pulls over and declares this is the furthest we can go by boat before climbing out and collapsing on the ground, exhausted. I agree. Each night the impact of constantly wielding his magic and draining himself to the verge of burn out before sleeping on a cold floor, has taken its toll on him. And now he's reached his limit. We've been rationing portions so we're also low on food: the little we have won't last much longer.

We hide the little boat a short way inland and mark the trunk of the closest tree by gouging into the bark so we can find it again if the villagers are as unfriendly as Haelyn warned. Eskar sleeps until dawn. I keep watch in the darkness, twitching at the snapping of branches and the rustling of needles on the tall pines but we're left alone.

The walk to Tanwen takes all day and our feet ache by the time we approach the town gates. The small town is bleak, barely distinguishable through the wooded pines and disappearing into the blackness. A high wall wraps round it, the sides made from rough wooden vertical planks, their tips uneven and pointed. It couldn't look less welcoming. I almost consider risking another night in the forest.

Thankfully, darkness cloaks us as we wander towards the inn Haelyn described. Every road we walk down is deserted; every crossroad bare. The wooden houses and buildings have small windows and closed curtains, discouraging unwanted callers. The revolting smell of rotting hay, or actually mould, permeates my hair, my clothing, everything we are carrying. It turns my stomach. The air is damp and I suspect the thatched roofs are the source of the odour. No part of me wants to stay long in this awful place. The only familiarity is the stone aqueduct high above the wooden ramparts, holding judgement over the town. I've never been to the end of an aqueduct before. This one has a watchtower protecting the underground bore that feeds the water source, the creaking algae-covered metal pipe reaching out of the ground.

With little signage, we walk past the inn twice before finally identifying it. It's quiet inside; a lone barmaid polishes glassware behind the bar. She looks up, surprised. "We're closed." A sharp, suspicious tone and an unwelcome stance. I doubt we look like patrons they would welcome here. The inn is shabby at best but we look considerably worse.

Even with the empty tables and wonky chairs, it looks serviceable enough. Cleaner and dryer than camping. I'd come to regret not making the most of the bed at Eskar's apartment in Cathair and this will be a brief respite before we venture out to the Haag.

Eskar steps forward into the light from candles swinging in glass holders above, keeping some of his features slightly in shadow. "We're looking for rooms." I tense at this. Given our reception in Cathair, perhaps the Governor or the traitor at court has influence here too.

She freezes and looks at us a second time, taking stock of what's underneath the grime. Putting the glass down, she comes round the bar. "You're not from around here."

"Is that going to be a problem?" Eskar crosses his arms.

She huffs. I've never seen anyone less thrilled to do business. My body sags with relief. She isn't keen to house us. I doubt she'd be so reluctant if she was working on someone else's orders.

"Wait here," she gestures to an empty table by the unlit fireplace.

Eskar gestures not to talk; he's tense and wary too.

Finally, when the rooms are ready, he does a thorough search of mine, checks out of the window, up and down the street, before deeming the room safe enough. His room is across the corridor.

Once we've settled in, we make a plan. Eskar is keen to leave tomorrow, before word of our arrival spreads through the town.

We'll stock up on food from the market in the

morning before travelling into the Haag. Until then, I sink into the lumpy mattress with scratchy sheets and breathe a sigh of relief. We are somewhat safe at last.

The market is bleak. A cluster of broken, barren stalls and the people manning them don't look much better. They line the street unspeaking and unwelcoming. The childrens' drawn faces hint at a hard winter that has taken its toll. Spring hasn't arrived here yet.

Eyes follow our progress from stall to stall, hungry for information and our money. With no other customers and the majority of stands empty, we pick our way through the slim offerings. There's one baker's stall; the bread looks stale and flat. The townsperson manning it seems more like a guard, silently challenging us to comment on the selection, arms crossed. Tension is thick in the air, as if the people of Tanwen are spoiling for a fight and will relish the violence, exactly as Haelyn warned.

We pay for some loaves, not even trying to haggle. This was a bad move; the baker's forearm flexes menacingly, not moving to package our purchases. Mouth dry, I try to apologise but Eskar interrupts, explaining we are not trying to patronise but have questions about the Haag that maybe he can answer.

Mollified, but by no means forgiving, the baker takes our money, counting the coins twice before acknowledging us again. Eskar changes tack, asking about the market, how often it meets, whether we're the only strangers in town. Patience running thin, the surly man points down the road with a rough grunt. "Speak to Sal, don't go asking more questions round here."

He points to the least dilapidated building in the town and I nod in thanks and start to walk away. Eskar stops me from making my way there and pulls me back to the inn, his hand gripping my forearm tightly.

As we leave the market I turn back, seeing a crowd congregating round the baker's stall.

"Why aren't we going to speak to this Sal person now?"

"We're being set up. See how the baker was unsurprised by my questions, despite the barmaid being unprepared for our arrival. Word's got out." He's increased his pace and I hurry to match it. "We need to leave now."

"How can you be so sure?"

He stops and turns, looking down at me with stormy eyes, fixing me to the spot. "Because I've been here before, I know how this works." He glances over to the alley as if he senses movement. "You have everything with you?"

"Yes, I left nothing behind, like you said."

"Good. Keep walking behind me and be ready to run."

More running. My heart pounds and I double-check the straps on my rucksack, pulling it more securely round my shoulders.

Everything is calm and deserted until we pass the inn. The breeze, previously unobtrusive other than pushing the stench round the town, becomes stronger, gusting debris and rubbish along the road, trapping it in doorways. The further east through the town we head, the stronger it becomes. I struggle to hear anything other than the roaring as it becomes a strong gale. Eskar ploughs forward, not giving in to the temptation to see if we are being followed until we hit the town wall.

Two men appear from the stone archway protecting the town from the mists beyond. No uniform or insignia to indicate who they work for, but both are armed with long, shining silver daggers. From the scars littering their hands, I guess they are familiar with using them. I risk turning my head to see if less danger is behind us. Four people stride purposely towards us from that direction, drawing intricate movements with their hands. They are unencumbered by the gusts and are easily gaining ground. Zephyrs. Powerful ones with no regard for breaking the Difan. If this is the people of Tanwen caught unawares, then they've done a good job of springing a trap with no preparation. Eskar sees the threat from both directions.

"Run!"

The word rips sharply from his lips and hits me as fiercely as the wind. I ignore the madness of heading towards our potential attackers and break into a sprint. Legs pumping and arms pounding we charge towards the town wall, no weapons between us. We battle the wind, which feels like running through treacle.

With feet to spare, the smallest of hand gestures by Eskar, so minuscule and precise I nearly miss them, causes the two attackers to drop their knives. A moment later, they screech, falling to the ground, writhing in agony. My body runs cold as I absorb their screams, and I force my eyes open, my body to keep running, to remember I'm not back in the dungeons and the pain is not mine. There are no visible marks on their skin as we pass them by. Then their screams stop. No footsteps follow us.

We emerge through the gap in the wall and cross to a barren field where a dark grey mist hangs over the ground, obscuring it from view. We run until the damp air falls over us, cloaking us from the town, the rest of the world disappearing into nothing.

Slowing to a walk and coming to a stop before we get too disoriented in the thickening mists, we wait to see if we have been followed. My harsh, rasping breath rings through the air as I struggle to recover but we don't hear another sound. Eskar's breathing is shallow, his face white and taut with regret. Another part of him damaged at causing pain to others, even in our own defence.

Chapter 35

I raise my eyes to his, searching for a sign he's okay. That he's still in this with me.

"I don't like using my attitude." He spits the words out angrily, as if any confession of regret is a weakness but his hands tremble.

"So, you're saying you'd feel this wretched if you attacked the people in Tanwen or the guards with a blade?" My tone is accusing but I don't know how else to make him understand. Without his attitude, we'd be prisoners.

He starts, caught off guard.

"Well no. That would have been self-defence."

"And using your attitude wasn't?"

"It wasn't a fair fight."

I can't help rolling my eyes at the ridiculous set of principles he's determined to beat himself up with. "Ah, so it's perfectly acceptable to skewer someone with a sword, provided they are precisely the same skill level, same ability and have the same experience as you then?"

"That's not what I mean and you know it."

"I know you're being ridiculous. You saved our lives. What's your problem?" I peer closely at him; his dark eyes are guarded and glint vulnerably. There's something more, something else is going on.

Stepping closer, he steels himself for another verbal attack, holding his body rigid. What is driving him to abuse himself every time he uses his attitude? I think back to the segments of the book Haelyn gave me, and like a piece of a puzzle that's finally spun round to fit in the right way, it clicks. "It feels good, doesn't it?"

What little colour remained in his cheeks vanishes. He freezes and shame floods in as the moment passes and he sinks to his knees, face in his hands. I watch curiously, not alarmed at his silent admission. His hands scratch at his arms, leaving shallow red grooves. Avoiding my eyes, he looks listlessly at the smooth dirt floor.

I sit next to him, providing what little comfort I can, letting him know I'm not judging him. As the minutes trickle by, I separate my magic from the strand I took from him and pull it outside of my body and into my hands. It glows faintly, sputtering in the damp mists before extinguishing. "I'm grateful to your magic – it saved us." I choke out those words, knowing it's what he needs to hear but suppress the dread that rises when I think about what his magic did to me in the dungeons of Chi An Mor.

Sitting in the dirt, Eskar watches my display closely, chin resting on his hands, which lie on his knees. Rising and extending a hand to pull me up, I see he's avoiding my gaze.

Pulling his face to mine, I feel the pressure of making sure my words come out right, to ease the pain and shame in his caramel eyes and try again. "It's okay, it's natural to enjoy using your attitude, to get satisfaction from how the magic sings. That doesn't mean you enjoy the outcome or the pain." I chew my lip. "Restraining yourself and then beating yourself up afterwards when you're forced to use it for work clearly isn't working anymore. Let me in so I can help you. Perhaps we can negotiate with the King when we're back?"

"It's no use – I've tried."

"It's a question of finding the right angle, the right leverage. The King boasts about not being a dictator – not being like his father – yet he forces this on you? He needs to face up to his hypocrisy."

A fleck of light passes through his eyes, but his brows stay furrowed. Humouring me but not daring to hope? We will get this fixed when we return. I can't bear to see him broken again and again. "What would you do if you weren't the King's Verax? Who would you like to be?"

His answer is instant, as if he pictures the details of this dream often. "I'd return to Cathair, to be a teacher." He looks off to where I imagine a window would be in the classroom he dreams of. "I'd live in my apartment, teach children at school. All children. I wouldn't separate them because of their magic and I'd go fishing on my days off." He huffs out a laugh, almost a chuckle, "I'd be a scandal among the Mordros."

"What about you? Did you always want to be an academic?" He turns the question back to me.

I pause. Being an academic was the most success I was permitted to ask for, even then many would say I've pushed too far. I should retreat into the background, quietly move on with my life and settle somewhere out of the spotlight. I'm tempted to be honest with him, to tell him that being an academic is a means to an end; it doesn't fulfil or satisfy me the way teaching would him. I have bigger, grander dreams and more ambition than I know what to do with. I'm not wholesome and selfless. I want power and I think our world could be so much better if I had more of it.

But that's not what Eskar wants to hear right now. Not what he needs. So, I tuck that private, ambitious part of me away, no longer smothering it but not letting it grow and respond, "It was always my dream growing up but I suppose sometimes we outgrow our dreams."

Chapter 36

The Haag. An inscrutable moor obscured by heavy fog, which forms the boundary between Trevesiga and our neighbour, Aiche. Practically impossible to navigate, it extends from coast to coast cutting off all contact between our kingdoms. The mists are dank and murky, visibility non-existent and we now stand on its edge. Leaving the security of civilisation behind so suddenly was a wrench, despite how unwelcome we were in Tanwen. Already I can feel a soupy dampness in my clothes as the mist envelops us.

Historically, the mists used to be less opaque and more transitory, appearing and disappearing on a whim, likely tied to the properties of the minerals and precious gemstones running through the land. The Haag was mined for rare earth metals providing the clans that occupied them with a small fortune from trading. But some years ago, they became a permanent fixture, severing ties with Aiche and forcing the people of the moor to relocate to border towns and villages. The deposits are now lost: mining is impossible when working nearly blind.

Despite the lengthening days, not enough sunlight penetrates the fog to allow me to channel. Not that I would be much use if we ran into trouble but I hate feeling vulnerable. I clutch my remaining magic close; it is my last resort. I can tell Eskar feels the same. I warned him about the Haag's barren lands when he insisted on coming with me.

There's plenty of water but it is putrid and stagnant. We stumble across a few ponds in the first few days, but learn to avoid them once we realise they turn into dangerously deep bogs. The quick-mud pulls you in deeper if you tread in the wrong place; it's caught both of us out a few times. I lost one of my overboots, sunk under the surface with no hope of retrieving it. Several times we accidentally disturb the noxious bubbles of bog-gas floating on the surface. The first time the smell turned my stomach so violently I vomited, wasting a meal.

Our original plan was to stick to the mining tracks; however, the undergrowth means the old maps I spent so long scrutinising back in the capital are redundant. We struggle on, using the method of orientation Haelyn taught us. Locals in Tanwen rely on it when the mists come crawling towards the town's boundaries. One of us can move at a time, directed by the other's compass bearing. Provided the one with the compass remains in place and waits, we should be okay. It's not perfect but should enable us a semblance of awareness of our location and prevent us from getting too lost. We're aiming for one of the largest mines, the name long forgotten, but it should be a three-day walk north-east of Tanwen. With the detours round the bogs and slow progress through the fog though, I think we'll be here for longer.

We keep quiet at first, as the mist does strange things to sounds. Every squelching footstep in the mud echoes and the scraping of bracken sets my teeth on edge. We could be alone or we could be being watched – we have no way of knowing.

We walk further than planned on the first night because there is nowhere dry enough to stop. Finally, under the relative shelter of an old, mouldy elder tree we give up and try to rest.

It's not cold which I'm thankful for as no fire would stay lit here, but the dampness pervades every fibre of our clothes and leaves our skin slick. I crave the salty ocean breeze on a warm, summer's day, or the crackle of a fire in my cosy lounge back at Chi An Mor. – anything but the muggy swamp we find ourselves in. Wary of animals or people lurking out of sight, we set up shifts but sleep doesn't come easily.

The next morning and the one after are more of the same.

On the fourth day, in the late morning, the fog darkens. An eerie splattering and howling builds behind us. Fear lances me. I look back towards Eskar who's holding the compass. He's blurry and indistinct; this visibility is worse than we've experienced so far. He shouts my name. At least I think it's my name – the mists reflect the noise back at him before I can make it out.

Now I can't see his eyes, or the rest of his face as

the fog descends, separating us. The roaring increases and I run back towards him. Every part of me protests at running towards the sound of danger. My lungs fight to extract air from the thick mist around us. I trip, stumbling to the ground and a flash of pain radiates through my shin.

Eskar's given up holding his position and crashes through boggy water. The sound of him gets nearer though I can barely make him out until he thuds down in front of me and pulls me against his chest. Adrenaline pulses through me and the pain in my leg dulls. I peer over his shoulder to see a black fog coming closer, cloaking the ground and turning day into night, bellowing and hissing. I huddle tight into Eskar, clinging to him and close my eyes.

The darkness is complete. I sense it enveloping us, even with my eyes squeezed shut. I gasp as it hits, ice cold pellets raining down on us. Hail – that was the noise. The stinging balls of frigid ice pepper any exposed skin and Eskar takes the brunt of it, encircling me and tucking me under his coat.

We ride out the hailstorm, clinging together, ears overwhelmed with the racket. Eventually, a dim grey light returns and the hail changes to a fizzing drizzle, raindrops sibilating on the icy ground cover, hissing as they hit the balls of hail. The bogland is white and blends indeterminate from the sky. All bracken, tree stumps, boulders are erased beneath an undulating, monochrome landscape.

Eskar's face is stricken, shards of ice cluster on his furrowed eyebrows and his eyes swirl with regret.

"I'm so sorry," he pulls me tighter. "I dropped the compass."

Chapter 37

Losing the compass is a bitter blow. Without it, we have no way of finding the mines, or even our way out of the thick fog that remains after the hailstorm. I smother my rising panic, pushing it down from my throat into my stomach. Eskar's eyes are wide, his grip on my forearms is like a vice.

"We'll retrace our steps, you didn't run far. We might be lucky…" I venture hopefully, voice echoing. Staying together, arms linked, we walk blindly into the fog. After a couple of minutes, it's clear the further we walk, the more adrift we're becoming. I pull us to a halt and grab the map Howl sourced from Pentargon library to help us. His neat annotations litter the paper but I work out we should have seen some sign of the old mines by now – we must be nearly on top of them. I refuse to come all this way to abandon the expedition empty-handed. Tucking the map away, we decide to keep walking onwards with what we think ought to be sunlight on our backs. This will keep us heading roughly east and we should find the mine eventually. From there, and once we have the serpentine, I reason that we'll walk into the sun as it sets and find our way home. It's far from perfect but having a plan helps keep our panic under control.

Eskar hears it first – a loud slurp of a boot being heaved from a bog, too loud to be an animal. He looks down at our feet, currently standing on thick moss. Heavy silence follows. More wary, we continue, adrenaline rushing through my veins.

A few hours later, it happens again, closer this time. Eskar's hand rests subtly on the hilt of his jagged hunting knife; there's someone out there. We can't rely on our magic in the mist. If we burn out, neither of us will be able to channel again. His weapons are our only option. We regroup, neither wanting to stray far from the other as we make our way through the moorland. There's little daylight left and we take care when finding shelter, trying our best to ensure it's somewhat defensible.

The noises continue sporadically through the night. We're being stalked. Hunted down. And now we're sitting prey. Neither of us sleeps. Sitting with our backs to each other, we keep vigilant watch, flinching at every shadow and wisp of mist.

The cool morning dew provides a slim chance at finding out more information about our trackers. Wet footprints are scattered round our camp, some coming within a few feet of us but for now we're alone. We press on, blindly looking for a marker, anything we can use to find ourselves again on the map.

There's no sign of the old mines, just endless empty moorland. I'm beginning to doubt our bearings; we should have seen signs of excavation by yesterday at the latest.

When I mention this to Eskar, we pull out the map and lose focus of our surroundings for a moment. It's long enough for us to be surrounded.

A group of at least ten appear through the mist. Their faces, murky at this distance, but their weapons are clear.

"Release your weapons." The command comes from a voice younger than I expected.

Eskar looks round, calculating our meagre odds. There's one of him and they have the advantage of knowing the terrain. Resigned, he drops his hunting knife, balancing it on the rough granite boulders at our feet. I raise my hands above my head to show I'm unarmed.

Their faces are now visible through the mist. They look like a hunting party in their heavy outdoor clothes with an assortment of bows and arrows and long, curved blades.

"Who are you?" I sound braver than I feel. These lands are meant to be unoccupied, there's no animals to hunt and we're too far from Tanwen to stumble on anyone else.

"We are the Kevren Gwir."

Chapter 38

Our hands are bound and we are corralled into following the leader of the group across the moor. We're prisoners. We pass small gashes in the sloping hillside that are concealed entrances to mining tunnels. Invisible from the summit and the bottom of the tor, I look carefully to spot the depressions in the land which house them. We pass several and I shudder at the thought of being forced underground. Our captors lead us into a large tunnel which is big enough for us to be escorted side by side. We're swallowed by the darkness. I prepare to be smothered in panic at the blackness, forced to relive captivity under Chi An Mor.

However, the moment we enter the tunnels, the mist abates and candles flicker from within, sheltered in glass cylinders and fixed to the rough clay walls. I can breathe deeply again, a small relief in such a dire situation. The clear air sharpens and stills my mind. The irony of being in more danger but able to keep my head isn't lost on me.

The tunnels are made from cracked mud, well-trodden and the colour of dried blood. I've read that the dark red clay is a positive sign of mineral deposits. Roughly hewn wooden arches bracket the tunnel every few feet, providing a semblance of support and reminding me how much weight is above our heads.

Our captors hushed conversations echo, ricocheting away down side tunnels, words jumbling and indecipherable as we march deeper underground. The ropes tying my wrists chafe and burn each time I stumble. Eskar tugs at his restraints as I struggle to stand, his face a violent storm of barely contained rage. The path ahead is blocked: a landslide of mud and rock fill the space. The captor in front swears colourfully, wrenching us back on ourselves, winding further through the labyrinthine maze.

We stop in a large central cavern, a meeting place. Small, smokeless fires flicker in the corners, providing scant light and dancing shadows. A group of similarly dressed men are gathered round a table with a detailed map in the middle, deep in discussion. A small woman stands in the middle, not contributing. She sees us and raises her hand; the discussion halts immediately. Our captors bow their heads in muted respect, waiting for her to speak.

"Are they the ones we were expecting?" Her accented voice is clear, a sleek black bob swings across her shoulders.

The leader of the group that captured us falters. I'm interested to see the deference given to this tiny woman. She's about my age, maybe a few years older. Her skin looks awkwardly pale, as if she's spent too much time in the mists and caves and it's not where she belongs.

"They matched the descriptions; we've tracked them for days," the leader mutters petulantly.

Her nostrils flare in annoyance. The group leader seems oblivious to the knife edge of her patience which he appears to be treading along.

"Names, please." Her whisper is softly venomous. She comes round the table, hand resting on an intricately detailed dagger at her waist.

I'm more afraid for the captain than for myself. I'm nobody important, but he would be a huge prize for the rebellion.

Eskar's eyes search mine, his eyebrows raised in regret. "I'm Eskar Devath and this is Sage Dewnam. I'm her escort on a scientific research expedition." The storm in his face rages, defiant against her cold enquiry.

Recognition glitters in her eyes as she all but purrs in satisfaction, grinning greedily. "Thank you Verax." She turns to our guards. "Take him away."

I don't get a chance to react, to grab him and keep us together. They try to drag Eskar roughly out of the room by the rope restraints. It takes several men to subdue him, even as he fights to crawl back to me, dragging his knees against the clay. In contrast it only takes one guard to hold me back but I'm fighting with everything I have. My magic fizzles pathetically, my hands too tightly bound behind my back. Eskar slips one hand free. The guards around him freeze in agony, more of them affected than the two in Tanwen. The blood flow stopping in their bodies has them screaming and twisting in agony. More guards drop to their knees, clutching their limbs. But he missed the true threat.

Sighing impatiently, the tiny woman is suddenly in his eyeline. I barely saw her move; her hands flick towards me and there's a solid wall of air preventing me from making a noise. I feel my eyes straining in panic and scratch at my throat, looking to Eskar for help as my legs buckle.

"Go peacefully with the guards and she will not be harmed."

The guards drop simultaneously, all unconscious. Air rushes back down my throat and I'm kneeling on the ground retching. The man leading the expedition rushes to restrain Eskar.

The tiny woman turns to him. "Clearly you misunderstood me. You are our prisoner but she is our guest. And we are not in the habit of harming our guests – unless provoked." Her statement cows Eskar and his shoulders slump.

"You just blow innocent citizens up instead." I retort.

"Ah yes, I will not deny that we can be ruthless." She appears blase about the loss of life, face rendered ugly by a wolfish, barbaric grin.

"But you," she tips my chin up with her knife. "You are quite the prize." Close up, fine lines are faintly etched in waves across her forehead, the kind caused by heavy responsibility. She wears them well though.

With a wave of her arm, new guards escort Eskar from the chamber and I'm left alone with the rebels.

"Leave us!" her imperious tone jangles through the cavern. It empties quickly but the unconscious guards Eskar felled still carpet the floor.

She picks her way through the bodies, not checking whether they're breathing and stands in front of the map.

"I'm Kitto, leader of the Kevren Gwir and of the rebellion." All pretence of formality, leadership and prestige evaporates as she finishes her introduction and I'm left with the impression she somewhat begrudgingly wants my approval. Confused, I remain silent.

"I've wanted to meet you for some time, Sage. Come, I have something you need to see." She gestures for me to follow. Torn, I glance down the tunnel where Eskar was dragged moments before.

"Where have you taken Eskar?" I stand firm.

"To the cells. His treatment will depend on your cooperation." She doesn't turn to see if I'm following and her words are swallowed ominously by the mud walls. Against my better judgement, I follow her deeper underground.

Chapter 39

These tunnels are bustling and I have to press myself into the red walls to let people pass. Kitto leads me through the warren and the trickle of rebels parts before her. She doesn't pause but nods and greets those she passes in the dim light. All incline their heads in deference and peer at me in suspicion. I try to count the turnings, twists and switchbacks until I'm dizzy. I've not eaten or drunk in hours and the dry air scorches my throat. The monotonous corridors press towards me and the panic of claustrophobia returns.

My breathing quickens and I clench my fists, nails digging into my palms to ground me. Eventually, the rush of people peters out until we're alone but my body continues to shake. The tunnel we are in slopes upwards towards a spark of daylight. Already accustomed to the gloom underground, my eyes ache by the time we venture into the open air. Kitto strides ahead, eyes impervious to the changing light, leaving me to stumble behind until I can see properly.

She stops on the precipice of a natural stone balcony, jutting from the side of the tor. The mud has given way to rock around me. The floor tilts from the mouth of the tunnel, worn smooth by exposure to the elements and I hesitate to step too close to the edge. Even the weak daylight tempts me to channel but my hands are bound too tightly.

Ahead of us is a formidable cavity cleaved into the rock below, a horrible wound of a quarry. Fog floats menacingly at the top of the hole but below our feet, threatening to drop at any point, bulging with rain. Above and all around us are sheer cliffs reaching up to the low clouds. We're trapped in this artificial valley. Below, through gaps in the fog, on the surface of the rock, veins of minerals run through the red clay and granite. A tempting, glittering river of wealth. I assume some of those veins are serpentine but I don't comment or ask. Plumes of smoke rise at intervals deep within the quarry and I realise this mine is operational.

If there are sufficient rebels to run a mining operation, then they are better funded, and better organised than we knew. The Mordros back in Pentargon have no clue this is how the Kevren Gwir must be able to organise and fund the attacks and bombings. With access to rare minerals, gemstones and potentially serpentine, they have everything they need to re-establish trade with Aiche, right under the King's nose.

Kitto gestures for me to join her on the edge of a rock ledge, where we can examine the activity. "All these people are willing to risk their lives in the mists to help our cause. They're mining a critical mineral to help with my experiments." Her gaze fixes on me knowingly. Somehow, she knows what the serpentine can do.

I hope I school my features into a bland expression. Dervla's worst fear was the rebels would manage to democratise magic using crystals before we would. Perhaps they've already achieved it; maybe the attacks were a demonstration. But why retreat back here? There must be a flaw in their design.

"Fascinating. From the frown on your face, I can see you putting the story together," Kitto jeers, jolting my attention back towards her.

"I don't know what you're talking about." I regret the tremor that slips past my guard.

"This will be a lot easier on Captain Devath if we can be frank." Her smile turns my stomach. The thought of punishing Eskar is clearly pleasing to her.

"What do you mean?"

"The Captain has a certain reputation amongst the rebels… Many of them have family or loved ones that have suffered under his *interrogations*. Most never returned. Those that did…" She watches my face closely for a reaction and I fight the panic in my chest as my mind takes me back to my interrogation at Eskar's hands.

"The guards are under instruction to keep him breathing, but that's all."

"What do you want from me?" I grit out a response.

"Everything you know about serpentine and how to store magic in it."

I can't help but widen my eyes. All my hours of research, everything we've worked for to make Trevesiga a better place. And she wants me to hand it over to her, to be used against the King. No, I can't let that happen.

"I thought that might be your response." Kitto's smile widens at my silent refusal and it chills my blood. "Shall we visit the cells then?"

Chapter 40

"Your lack of cooperation has caused this. If you intervene, I will make it worse for him." Kitto's voice is flat and emotionless as she leads the way through the maze of tunnels.

We round the last corner. The walls are a honeycomb of holes, each the size of a coffin and dug out of the red earth around us. Cells are too generous a term.

In the centre of the floor, surrounded by rebels, Eskar lies bleeding into the clay floor. The rebels take turns, kicking and spitting on him.

"Stop!" I shriek when the violence finally registers, disbelieving that in this short time he's been beaten so savagely.

Eyes bruised shut, hands whipped and bleeding, he raises his head. Hot tears spill over my cheeks as Kitto steps in front of me, preventing me from rushing to his side.

The guards pause their assault and Eskar's bloodshot eyes crack open, finding mine.

"I'm not going to make apologies for how the rebels choose to settle their quarrels with your captain. He's handled worse before, I'm sure." Kitto sounds bored. She waves away the other guards, leaving the three of us alone.

Eskar groans and tries to pull himself towards me. He nearly makes it when Kitto lashes out, landing a kick to his stomach. I catch her eye when I go to help him: it reminds me not to intervene, not to break the tentative bargain we've made for his life. She ties his hands to two separate stakes, tight enough to prevent him from wielding.

Her manic laughter smothers his rasping coughs. Every fibre of me wants to pull him close, to protect him from her vengeance but I continue to hold myself still, even though his eyes are pained, confused about my silence.

"A quick demonstration, Sage." She leans in, whispering, "A kind of retribution for your lack of transparency earlier."

The little blood remaining in my face drains as I realise she's not going to explain my refusal to defend him. The cloying, sweet aroma of Eskar's blood splits my vision. A trickle runs towards my feet and I shrink from it. Across the room, Kitto removes the leather bracelets covering her forearms, revealing a chaotic mess of thin scars, new and fading. Rolling up her sleeves, her mouth curves in a wicked smile. "Let's begin then."

My gaze is locked on Eskar, desperately trying to let him know I don't want this. I don't agree with this. It starts.

Kitto's attitude is obvious now it's not being used on

me. She can suck the air out of your lungs, keeping them empty. Eskar rolls on the floor, smearing blood. His eyes bulge and roll back into his skull, face reddening.

When I can't take the silence and am about to scream at Kitto to release him, she does. He's permitted one, huge, gasping lungful of air before it's squeezed out of him and he's brought to the edge of unconsciousness again.

A soft smile creeps across her face as she leads him to the brink of asphyxiation, threatening to push him over the edge. Each time, the suffocation lasts a little longer. Despite the cramping starvation from lack of oxygen, Eskar thrashes violently, desperate for relief.

Again and again, she pushes him. I'm fighting against the memories of my torture, trying to stay present in the tiny room. Eskar's and my gaze lock tight. Every part of me hoping, praying he can see I'm not complicit. Not here willingly.

As the torture wears on he stops noticing me. When his eyes open for a fraction of a second, they stare blearily over my shoulder, unseeing, before screwing up in agony again.

Satisfied she's made her point, Kitto stops. I sag against the mud wall and fix my eyes on Eskar until I'm certain his breathing, although ragged, is stable.

The guards return and stuff him into one of the honeycomb cell holes and Kitto ushers me away.

We cannot stay here. She'll kill him.

Chapter 41

Kitto collects me the next morning, to show me the laboratory. I've not slept all night, despite having a bed for the first time in weeks. My thoughts are on Eskar, imprisoned in the cells and suffering. Nonetheless, I make sure to be more agreeable.

We make our way through the tunnels, taking another route and discreetly I try to map our journey by scuffing my heel at every corner, creating a shallow mark in the well-trodden mud. It's not much but it's a start. Our escape will depend on me.

I'm hopeful the journey to the laboratory will mean a trip outside so I can channel before we arrive but, to my dismay, Kitto opens a thick wooden door embedded in a nondescript corridor and ushers me in.

The setup is rudimentary at best: a few workbenches, some scales and other odd pieces of equipment I don't recognise. It's simpler than my first shared laboratory at Athnavar Academy.

Reading into my surprise, Kitto says, "I hope you weren't expecting top of the line equipment and fancy measurement tools? It's probably the worst laboratory

I've ever worked in too but it gets the job done."

Interesting, I wonder aloud where she worked.

"Nowhere you'd recognise. Let's say I'm a long way from home."

Ambiguous. I peer closely at her, searching for clues. Her twisted smile shows she's enjoying the joke. The lack of daylight has drained her skin of colour which contrasts with eyes so black I can't see her pupils. Given the propensity for rain and cloud here, I wonder if she's alluding to studying much further afield. If she has connections outside Trevesiga.

"Let me show you where we are now." Her pride is evident; she plans to impress. A nasty thread of insecurity pulls at me. What if she's better, smarter than me?

Deft hands assemble seven crystals on the closest workbench in order of size. Serpentine crystal. I recognise the vivid green colour with navy veining from Howl's description. Starting with the smallest crystal, the air quiets in the room as she wields. The crystals look ordinary: no polishing or cleaning, just roughly hewn lumps of rock. When the first begins to glow, she moves on. With all seven glowing, getting brighter in intensity the longer they are left on the workbench, I back away to the door, looking for shelter, anticipating an explosion.

Laughing, Kitto pulls a lever and a bell rings. Four men run into the room, grab the crystals with thick leather mitts and run out again. Gesturing for me to follow, Kitto jogs down the tunnels. A couple of turns and we're in daylight; the men run several feet to the edge of the mist which looms overhead, blocking the sun. They place the crystals down and retreat to the tunnel entrance behind us. Smugly I realise why the lab is based there: it's got easy access to outside. I'm not the only one with incendiary issues.

We wait a few moments, watching the glowing crystals as they glow brighter and I begin to think she might have nailed it. Then she throws a hand over my eyes and pulls me urgently to her chest. Seven booms ring out across the landscape and echo through the mists, each louder than the previous. Between the bangs, Kitto laughs gleefully, revelling in the destruction. My neck strains as she holds me to her chest. Ears ringing, I push away to survey the damage. Seven concentric burn marks overlap in front of us, deep scores into the earth, the nearest alarmingly close to our feet.

She's done it though – the magic was stored there temporarily. It's closer than what I've achieved. The only difference I can see is her access to the right material. Based on Dervla's theory that if I can fully master the Gallos, if I can gently feed my magic into the crystals, then it might actually work.

Her laughter subsides. "I love the bangs." Hand on chest, catching her breath, her eyes sparkle. "So, this is where we've been stuck for the last few months. But now you're here, we can finally make some real progress. We need to delay the detonation as long as possible. Ideally, I want to be able to pull the trigger whenever I want." She reels her objectives off like a shopping list.

Bombs. That's all she's interested in. Making bigger

and more deadly weapons to cause more damage to ordinary people caught in the crossfire.

Her wolfish grin returns, canines catching on her bottom lip.

My hackles rise. "Well, I don't know what to tell you. Clearly you know all my experiments end the same way at the moment. We know the same as each other." I fold my arms over my chest angrily, disgusted at her bloodlust.

"No, that's not right. Our intelligence said something had changed, that you'd made huge progress. You need to show me what you can do. Or do we need to make another visit to your captain?"

I wonder if she means using the Gallos principals to imbue the magic, but Dervla suggested that weeks ago.

I scrabble to think of something to buy time; I need to stall. I survey the landscape. The mist is too thick and I don't fancy our chances down a rocky cliff edge leading to nowhere. I need another way out.

"I'll need to channel first. I'm spent." Getting her to show me another way out of the tunnels might be my best option.

Her jubilant grin returns. "Fine, come with me."

Chapter 42

We return through the tunnels, climbing this time. There's no chance to scuff my shoe on the intersections to help with my mental map, as Kitto is practically running ahead in excitement. We reach the top and I'm out of breath. A tall metal ladder is hammered into the rock ahead of us, each rung slanted and uneven. Kitto goes first, wrapping her arm through a rung and hanging on at the top while unlocking a trap door at her head.

Pure, brilliant daylight streams in and I turn my head, blinded as the trapdoor opens. I haven't seen sunshine since we left Cathair and my heart lightens as the warm light bathes the tunnel walls above me. I go to climb up the ladder behind her.

"Oh no! You haven't earned that privilege. I'll let you see the view when you've impressed me. You can channel from down there."

Irritatingly smart woman. Quietly seething, I settle for raising my hands into the small rays above me and summon the light to me. My magic revels in the light, expanding and filling my chest. How I've missed this.

The flood of warmth spreads from my fingers through my whole body, rejuvenating me and soothing any lingering exhaustion.

The trapdoor snaps shut, hurtling us into darkness and Kitto leads us back to the laboratory. I stay silent, meticulously cataloguing the twists and turns. Right now, the trapdoor is my best option for escape. If it's high enough for sunlight, I might even be able to see Tanwen or the edge of the Haag from the top of the tor.

Kitto takes a set of keys from her pocket and unlocks the door to a small antechamber connected to the main laboratory. In it are shelves of serpentine, neatly categorised by size. She selects a small crystal, closes and locks the antechamber door, and places the serpentine on the bench.

"Now I want to see you try." She waves me forward, crossing her arms.

My mind races and my eyes dart round the room, looking for a way to buy more time to think. In the cells with Eskar yesterday, I would have done anything to stop his torture. But last night, I was haunted by the screams of terror I witnessed when Dervla and I escaped from Athnavar. How can I be complicit in helping the rebels to injure more innocent people?

"I know what you're thinking," Kitto's sneer makes my skin crawl. "You don't want to help us. You'd rather sit back and let the Mordros continue to exploit and restrict us. You'd rather be their pet, praised for your research and living a comfortable life of luxury in the palace while the Concord continue to vote against the rights of everyday people."

My attempt at protest dies and thin tendrils of shame clutch at my throat. She's wrong. My research will make the Concord listen. Dervla and I will make a difference and no one needs to get hurt. I reject the tiny seed of doubt Kitto is trying to plant in my brain. Diplomacy is better than violence. I just need to get us out of here and back to Pentargon in one piece.

Bracing as far from the crystal as possible, anticipating another explosion, I start. She watches the magic flow from my hands with interest. I can't help noticing the change in my wielding since practising the Gallos. It's no longer possible for me to hurl my magic out at once. Despite not fully mastering all the principles, I can control the flow so I don't overwhelm this new material. Even so, I pray that Kitto hasn't seen an Aubade wield before and that she attributes the slower flow of magic as an Aubade weakness, not a show of control.

The crystal emits a different, softer glow when I'm done. It's hard to explain but I can sense when the crystal is *full* and I know not to push it further. My magic feels more at home with the serpentine compared to the experiments in my laboratory. I sense it settling in within the crystal, making itself at home. The thread of Mordros magic still writhes in my chest, reluctant to come out and play.

Kitto rings the same bell again and we follow the assistants back out to the platform to wait for the explosion. The previous scorch marks have been scrubbed clean and Kitto produces a small, sand hourglass from her pocket, making a note of the time until detonation. I hope the hourglass shatters from the impact.

We wait. My body cracks with tension as I anticipate the explosion, flinching at every noise and rustle. Kitto is the opposite: each time she turns over the hourglass to reset the timer she becomes more gleeful. An hour passes and she declares it a success and gestures for us to leave. Was it that simple? Does it have to be Aubade magic and serpentine together? What about properly mastering the Gallos? I have so many questions.

"Let's seal up now. One of the guards will remain on the other side of the door and will hear when it detonates. I'm satisfied with the progress today."

Her voice shakes me from my reverie. Now I know serpentine is the missing piece, it complicates our escape. I can't return empty-handed. I have to get Eskar, myself and a bag of those crystals out of this place.

I count the turns back to the laboratory, noting the turning that leads to the trapdoor and the way out. I add another scuff to that junction, just to be sure.

Chapter 43

The next morning does not go as well. The guards that escort me back to the laboratory inform me that my attempts exploded sometime overnight.

When I reach Kitto's laboratory, she is already there and waiting, anger radiating from her.

"Why aren't my experiments working?" she shouts. I hedge, evading her question which infuriates her further.

"I copied everything you did yesterday, I even used less magic like you did. The crystals didn't last anywhere near as long as yours did before they exploded!" Her normally pale face is blotched and red, mouth thinned in a tight line. I blink through her rage and make a stark realisation: when Kitto gets what she wants from me, I'll be put in a cell next to Eskar. Both of us trapped underground and at the mercy of the rebels. Adrenaline courses my body as she stalks menacingly towards me.

"Do we need to visit Captain Devath again? I know there's something you're not telling me."

"Perhaps it's because I'm an Aubade; my magic is

different from yours," I shrink from her pointing finger.

"I'm not stupid." Gripping my wrist, she drags me from the laboratory, back into the tunnels. Her pace is brutal, my shoulder wrenches as I stumble behind her.

The guards outside Eskar's cell-like coffin react at our appearance.

"We were expecting you later…" one bravely ventures.

"Get out of my way!" Kitto shoves past the much larger guard, releasing my arm and proceeds to pull Eskar out of the horizontal cell by his wrists. The guards rush to the muddy coffin to assist her and I notice fresh wounds covering him. I feel sick. The rebels have no shortage of vengeance. If those wounds are left, weeping into the mud, it won't be long until he succumbs to a serious infection.

As soon as he's lying crumpled on the floor, I see they've forgotten to bind his wrists.

Kitto either doesn't notice or doesn't care. She uses her attitude to smother him, bringing him to the brink of unconsciousness again and again.

A tear rolls down my cheek and falls to the floor in front of me, quickly absorbed by the clay. Eskar's struggle stops. He summons his remaining strength and his bruised eyes flick from the damp spot on the floor to the streaks on my cheeks. Suspicious, Kitto glares at me threateningly. The next suffocation lasts until he passes out completely.

At the sight of his limp body, I lurch forward to check he's alive. There's a pulse; it's weak but steady and I relax when I finally see his chest rise and fall.

"As I said, your lack of cooperation is detrimental to the Captain's wellbeing." My heart aches to see him so broken. She kicks his legs before striding from the room.

"Come on. You have work to do."

I hover, desperately wanting to stay. I need to tell Eskar I'm going to get us out of here; he needs to hold on a little longer. I haven't abandoned him. He doesn't wake. The guards return and manhandle him back into the cell hole, hands still unbound.

That day and over the weeks that follow, I infuse more crystals than I can count, burning my magic out again and again. Each time, Kitto lurks over my shoulder examining my magic as it flows into the serpentine. She meticulously times how long it takes until detonation, comparing it to her own efforts. The rebel mining operation must be extensive at the rate we use serpentine but Kitto never shows any concern. Only a maniacal focus on cataloguing the detonation time and impact of each explosion, ink staining her hands as she completes chart after chart and scours the results for a pattern, a trend – anything that could give her more information. My only reprieve is the walk back from the trapdoor to the laboratory when my replenished magic hums, reviving me. Each evening, when I've summoned the last rays to me, Kitto drains me dry. She selects large crystals and forces me to empty my magic into them, stopping only when my aching hands curl towards my chest and my legs give out.

Her scoff of disdain at my limited amount of magic provokes my anger but I am too weak to even voice it. The only strand that always remains, is the little piece of Mordros magic I'd taken from Eskar. It curls deep inside my chest; I can't access it even if I needed to. Then, on shaking legs, she escorts me to the cells where I am forced to watch her and the other guards take turns to torture Eskar.

Kitto has made it evident Eskar's treatment is wholly dependent on my cooperation. And so, each day I get up, go to her laboratory and pretend I'm doing everything I possibly can to improve the process, quietly cataloguing the differences between our attempts. We stabilise the magic for longer periods of time, mainly by slowing down how we put magic in and using larger quantities of serpentine. I'm distracted by why my magic seems to always last longer in the serpentine than hers; it's not much of a change but I don't understand it. Given her glee at each explosion, Kitto doesn't seem to care. I worry bombs are her only interest. If the day's experiments go well, the torture sessions are mercifully shorter.

Tonight, however, something is different. When the guards extract Eskar from the cell, his eyes stay closed, bruised shut, his skin flushed red. I'm no medic but I recognise the signs of infection. The session doesn't last long. Kitto grows bored as he is too weak to scream and she turns to me.

"I know you're keeping something from me. Is it worth letting him die for?" She kicks his ribs as we leave. His ruined body haunts me.

Chapter 44

The next morning, I wake with depressing clarity. I've failed and time has run out. When I'm escorted to the laboratory, I resolve to tell her something, to do what I can to save Eskar. Even if it puts the rest of Trevesiga at risk, I can't lose him. Not after the sacrifices he made to keep me alive and protected.

I stare at the back of Kitto's head as she works and make my decision.

"Have you heard of the Gallos?" Her head whips round. It's the first time I've initiated conversation. A grin envelops her face when she sees I'm about to crack, that I can't bear Eskar's suffering anymore.

"No, I haven't. Is this the missing piece you've been keeping from me?"

I fix my gaze directly at her, refusing to answer her question. "Eskar needs medicine; he has a fever and will die without help."

"Most likely." She shrugs and leans back on the workbench surveying me.

"If you guarantee he gets the help he needs and a reprieve from the torture while he recovers, I'll tell you everything I know."

She cocks her head, regarding me closely. "Everything. Otherwise, I will kill him."

I believe her completely. She would enjoy it too. I nod tentatively, aware I am handing over the last fragment of my power to her. Once she's mastered the Gallos, she won't need me. My theory is only valuable if you want to safely store the magic indefinitely; she just wants to control the pyrotechnics.

"I'm all ears," she waves me towards the workbench.

"Tell the guards to treat him first. He needs help now."

Her eyes roll as she opens the door and calls out instructions to the guards waiting outside.

Satisfied she plans to hold up her end of the bargain for now, I talk her through the Gallos principles. Her eyes widen, glittering menacingly at the Mordros' secret.

"So, it's not what you use, it's how you put the magic in there?" she clarifies.

"Yes." She is a quick student. But it should take her at least a few days to learn the principles. That will have to be long enough for Eskar to recover. We have no other choice.

"Then why did you travel all this way for serpentine?"

"Because it's the only material we believe could contain magic."

"Hmm. Nothing else works?" she waits for me to shake my head before walking back to the fresh crystals laid out on the bench, bigger than the ones we used before.

"Show me."

It takes all day and involves more trips to the trapdoor to replenish my magic before Kitto deems she's seen enough and wants to try it herself. Throughout the day, she's been rocking on her heels in anticipation every time I wield, incessantly asking more questions than I can answer. Exhausted, I collapse in a chair, resting my head in my hands while the crystal is carried outside to detonate safely. "Can I see Eskar?"

"No. I think some time apart would be good for your motivation. Consider it your punishment for lying to me. You're going to have to trust that he's being well looked after." A nasty grin slides across her mouth before she turns to count the remaining crystals before returning them to the antechamber. I watch her distractedly throw the antechamber keys in a drawer. If I can smuggle a crystal from her watchful eyes, then I can charge it and use it as a diversion. When it explodes, I can run for the cells, release Eskar and make a break for it.

It feels unachievable. There are so many opportunities for it to go wrong but, honestly, I'm out of options. Eskar won't withstand any more torture and my use expires as soon as Kitto masters the Gallos.

That night and several more, when I finally am released from Kitto's laboratory, I use the time in my room to rehearse the routes from the lab to the trapdoor, from the lab to the cells. I find I can't visualise anything and my scuffs on the mud are getting worn away so I can't depend on them either. I'm determined not to be foiled by my lack of navigation skills so I practise until I can recite the number of turns and junctions. Anything to distract myself from the knowledge that if we break free, we'll have no belongings, no food and no obvious way of getting out of the mists. These are problems I'll need to solve once we escape.

With no torture to oversee after a day in the labs whilst Eskar supposedly recovers, Kitto takes to bringing me with her to dinner. We sit on long tables, without rank or hierarchy. I endeavour to eavesdrop as different rebels approach Kitto for her decisions on everything from supply runs to food distribution.

The rebel at our table who led the expedition to capture us, is lazily causing his knife to spin in circles while he absent-mindedly waits for dinner to be served. His dark auburn hair matches the mud walls behind us, blending into the background. I haven't seen him around much since we were captured; he's never been one of my guards or one of Eskar's. He sees my interest and laughs teasingly.

"Finally cottoned on then?"

"What do you mean?"

He glances round to make sure Kitto and the rest of the table aren't paying attention.

"How you managed to do so much walking only to be found half a day from Tanwen."

I flinch and fumble to grab my glass before it falls. Even with the mists, we're only half a day from Tanwen? So close. A jolt of excitement fizzes through me; if I can trick him into revealing the base's location, then our escape might become possible.

"Half a day? But we were on our feet for days." His

eyes meet mine, a piercing blue.

"Following your compass right," he pauses, "or was it left…" the knife spins in the opposite direction.

Our conversation catches Kitto's attention and she snaps at him to be quiet. His eyes widen in alarm, then he winks slyly at me before digging into his food.

As dinner ends, he sidles past me. "Walk with me, Sage. I could do with some fresh air." The guards nod at him with respect and fade away, leaving us alone.

It could be a trap but my options are slim. He overtakes me as traffic in the corridor thins and we travel along new mud corridors, venturing to a part of the base I've not seen before.

After several minutes of walking, we reach a wooden hatch similar to the trapdoor Kitto keeps me from going through, although this one is at head height and doesn't require a ladder. It swings down and I let the rebel hoist me up, clambering ungracefully through the hole. After I'm through, he jumps and levers himself through as if it's second nature.

I take a moment to appreciate the damp, fresh air. The feel of a breeze on my face and daylight on my skin is something I've sorely missed. The mists linger, obscuring most of the landscape as the last dregs of daylight fade but ahead of me I can see trees and shrubland. Behind me the vast slope of the tor rises into the mist. The tunnels must be carved into its base then. At the peak the craggy silhouettes of dark stone loom. Sleep will not come easily tonight knowing these stone monoliths sit above me.

"It's sturdier than it looks, you know." His rueful

comment pulls me back.

I huff, unconvinced. "Explain what you meant about the compass?"

He pulls a simple compass from his pocket, similar to the one Haelyn gave us. I peer at its needle, juddering under the slight tremor in his hand. "Watch." Gently, he coaxes the needle on the compass away from north. It flickers then points to the tor behind me, towards the setting sun.

"You tricked us!" Though why I'm so affronted I'm not sure.

"Yes, it's not a common Zephyr attitude but they eventually found a use for me."

It would be presumptuous to read resentment from that one comment but it niggles my curiosity. "Why are you telling me this?"

"Call it self-preservation, call it a sense of foresight. Why, I'll call it a conscience if it means I can sleep at night," he continues, pointing north-west. "Tanwen is a half-day hike in that direction. Even if the mist descends, keep travelling that way and you'll reach the boundary of the Haag in no time. You should be able to find your way from there."

"And how am I meant to know which way is north-west without a compass?"

Sighing as if I have the intelligence of a small child, he walks to a small, spiky bush a few feet away. Plucking two small yellow berries, one from each side of the bush, he hands them to me.

Perplexed, I hold them in my hands and stare at him, waiting.

"I don't recommend swallowing them, but you do need to put them in your mouth at least."

As if that is the most obvious thing to do in the world. I go to shove them both in and he grabs my wrist strongly.

"One at a time, one at a time!"

This man is insane. The first berry is bland and earthy and I have the distinct impression it might, at some point, have been pissed on by a wild animal. I spit it out in disgust, retching.

Bracing myself for the next disgusting taste, I pop in the second berry.

A vibrant, nutty flavour explodes in my mouth. A flavour completely at odds with the previous.

"See, the berry that gets the sun produces the oils that make the flavour."

"The sun, here?" Even with the rich taste fading in my mouth, I'm sceptical.

"Not much, but it's enough. The side of the bush with sweet berries faces south. As long as you don't swallow them, you can find your way."

Interesting. It might be a trap, but my gut is telling me to believe him and it's more progress in forming an escape plan than I've managed over the last few weeks. I'm running out of time. Kitto is working frantically to master the Gallos and her behaviour becomes more erratic each day.

"Are you planning to leave?"

A coarse laugh, tinged with regret, I think. "I'm more useful to Kitto here. When you're back in Pentargon, remember not all of us wanted to attack the cities." His fractured sigh breaks free. "Many of us had friends, family there. There's been no news..."

I think of Cedar back in Pentargon and I understand. I don't know how the King will respond when he learns of this place, how aggressive his retribution will be, but we should allow those that want to, an opportunity to surrender if we can.

"I can't promise I'll be able to temper his response, but I will tell the King of your help and regret."

Looking to the distance, towards where Pentargon should be, soaking in the view as if he knows his time is limited, his response is heavy. "I understand – that's all I could hope for." He pauses, then reaches his hand to mine. "I'm Ciaren by the way."

Savouring the fading daylight for a moment more, I take his hand and shake it.

Chapter 45

I spend the next two days rehearsing the route from the dining hall to the trapdoor Ciaren showed me. Since our conversation, I've been left unguarded. Every spare moment in the evenings is spent wandering the tunnels, familiarising myself with the warren of routes and pathways.

Ciaran has conspicuously ignored me since our conversation; he's rarely at dinner again, so I've not had an opportunity to ask for more help. Every time I've made the trip to his trapdoor, there's no lock or barricade preventing me from opening it. Once or twice, I've been tempted to crack open the door, to get a lungful of fresh air. I resist, unsure whether Kitto or one of the other Zephyrs would be able to sense the change in air in the tunnels and become suspicious.

Living in this heightened state of anxiety is exhausting. I've stopped sleeping properly. Balancing Eskar's healing when I'm not permitted to visit him versus Kitto's progress with the Gallos is nerve-wracking. I need him to recover as much as possible, but if I leave it too late his torture will resume or I'll be imprisoned too. Kitto, normally so sharp-eyed and observant, misses my frequent yawns and doesn't mention my brain fog. Nor does she remember to reassign guards to me in the evenings. She's distracted by our progress, honing her visualisation skills and having me infuse bomb after bomb, each one bigger and more powerful than the last.

The next morning, the laboratory is empty. I call out for Kitto but get no response. The air is stale; I'm the first to arrive. I check the drawer and the keys are there. It takes seconds to make my decision. This is it. We're making a run for it. The antechamber is lined with shelves of serpentine crystals. I only have the rucksack I've stashed in the cupboard under my workbench. It will have to do. It doesn't take long to fill. I swing it on my back, staggering under the weight, knocking over several vials of Kitto's other experiments.

I didn't consider this. If I bump into someone, they'll know I'm hiding something and I won't make it far if I run. I'll have to go slowly and trust I won't be seen.

My heartbeat is so loud, it drowns out everything. The route is burnt into my memory, each step towards the wretched cells is a step closer to being free from the rebels. The heavy sack thumps against my back as I creep through the tunnels.

Eskar lies on the dirt floor of the cells, being kicked and spat on by two rebels. I left it too late; they consider him healed enough. My steps falter; I can't take them both on. I swing my heavy rucksack at the one closest, hearing the rocks connect with the back of his head with a sickening crunch. He drops to the floor, blood pooling beneath his head. The other guard shouts for back up, charging at me in a rage, hands reaching for my throat.

My eyes bulge as his grip tightens and my airway crushes. He's so much stronger than me and lifts me clean off the floor, slamming me into the wall.

Black spots interrupt my vision, blotting out his face as he prepares to throw me into the wall again. The rebel guard's hands slacken and release. Then relief – I can breathe. I drop to the floor with his bone-chilling scream deafening me, blood vessels popping in the whites of his eyes.

Eskar kneels, panting, his unbound hands contorting and twisting. There's silence after the guard dies.

"Are you okay?" I whisper as I help him stand, taking in the blood pouring from a head wound and black, green and yellow bruises merging across his ribcage. He staggers a little, legs buckling and winces. "Likewise."

"I'm not the one who's been tortured."

"Not today at least." His eyes are full of relief as they sweep across my body. Guilt at my silent observation of his treatment eats at me and I struggle to find the words to explain I never left him there intentionally. That I was never on their side. My words taste like dirt on my tongue.

"I'm so sorry," I choke out, pulling him close.

His clothes are covered in the red mud from the tunnel floor and it's smudged into his skin. Bruises and old lacerations interrupt the smoky red staining of the clay. The time in the tunnels has weakened him. I don't understand how he's even able to stand.

My hands claw his clothes, trying to get closer. The strand of Mordros magic I've been harbouring, lights up and dances. His chin presses into the top of my head before he pulls back.

"Here, give me that," he rasps and I shift the rucksack off my shoulders and he swings it onto his back with more ease than I managed. Despite his treatment, Kitto kept her word about curing his infection: his eyes are focused and clear.

"Follow me, I promise I can get us out of here." My voice cracks, neck throbbing from the rebel's hands. I hope that's what Eskar puts the tremble down to. I push the nerves back into my stomach, ignoring my clammy hands and we leave the cells.

He leans on me for support as I start to lead him through the tunnels. Our hands grip each other's tightly, knuckles glowing white in the dim light. Turning back, I flinch when I see spatters of fresh blood leaving their damning trail behind us. We need to hurry.

We walk, shoulders tense and too afraid to speak. The corridors are barren lengths, no room to hide and nowhere to run if we are spotted. No one appears. Our luck holds. I don't think I breathe until we finally reach the trap door Ciaran showed me.

It's locked, a shiny new padlock hangs above our heads and I swear viciously.

Eskar turns, what little colour in his cheeks vanishing along with the hope in his eyes. I can't bear it. Then I hear footsteps.

The hatch where Kitto permits me to channel from is

our last option. Pulling away from the padlock and the footsteps, we break into a slow run until we're safely round another corner and hidden from view. I worry that even that short jog might be too much for Eskar but he simply shifts the rucksack to his other shoulder. We have to keep moving; the hatch is back past the laboratory. An invisible noose feels as if it tightens round us as I lead us back to the laboratory.

Kitto never let me see what lay outside this trapdoor. I don't even know which side of the tor it comes out on, or whether it's another exit into the quarry where we'll be easily discovered. It's a risk we'll have to take; there's no going back now.

In my panic, I take several wrong turns and am sprinting when I get to the hatch. It's unlocked but the ladder is missing. I look to Eskar, unable to hide the fear that's threatening to take over. He doesn't falter, lifting me above his shoulders to open it. My face flushes as I scrabble with the catch, fingers slow and conscious of his hands so easily gripping my waist, despite weeks of being held prisoner. How does he have the strength?

I pull myself through the hatch, arms straining and breathe in the cold damp air, my lungs struggling from the underground run. Eskar passes through the heavy rucksack and as I'm hanging through the hatch to lift it out, we freeze at the sound of footsteps. Our luck has run out.

An unfamiliar face rounds the corner; he shouts at us to stop. Thankfully, the guard is slow to progress down the tunnel and unarmed.

Conflict over whether to incapacitate them or to

escape flits across Eskar's face, anguish in his caramel eyes.

"Leave him, let's go!" I make the decision, extending my hand to help pull him up. He ignores it, launching himself and grabbing the sides of the hatch, pulling himself through in one swift motion. He lands less elegantly, stumbling and getting tangled in my legs. We stop to close the hatch, throwing as many loose stones and boulders on top as we can reach, hoping it buys us precious seconds to escape, then we take off at a run downhill.

Chapter 46

The mist is thinner here. The outline of a tor towers above us but I can't make out if it's the same view as Ciaran showed me. If it's not and we're heading deeper into the Haag, then we're as good as dead. With no food or supplies, I was banking on being able to make it through the moorland to Tanwen. The view of the tor fades as we tumble down the hill.

Even in his weakened state, I struggle to keep up with Eskar until the ground flattens. He pauses in a hollow at the base of the tor and we stare over the boggy quick mud vanishing into the fog. As the stagnant, fetid air of the swamp washes over us, my stomach turns. Each step is a risk; we cannot afford to get stuck.

At the first gorse bush we find, I dive upon the berries, pulling one from the nearest side. Luck is not on my side – I heave. My heart sinks as I calculate our direction. We've travelled down the tor away from Tanwen and now need to circle the base before we can make it out of here.

That's more time to be caught in the open, more time for the rebels to send out scouts to find us.

I barely allow myself to think as we pick our way round the base of the tor, keeping the slope on our right. Large boulders interrupt our path and I have the strongest sense we're not going quickly enough. Neither of us is prepared for this terrain and the rucksack of serpentine is bulky and unyielding.

Our slow pace raises my anxiety. The rebels are familiar with this terrain. If Ciaran is leading the hunting party then there might be a chance he can put them off our tracks, but if he's not…

Every few minutes, we stop to test a berry and alter our trajectory. Before long I'm sick of the taste of both types, the noise of retching accompanies our heavy breathing as we continue our blind escape.

Several times I think I hear shouts and cries from rebels chasing us but I tell myself if we can't see them then we're hidden as well. Neither of us speak, not wanting to risk our voices carrying through the mists and revealing our location.

Finally, the berries lead us away from the tor. I'm facing towards Tanwen when I notice parallel lines of grey stone laid into the ground. Each slab is as wide as my hand and as long as Eskar is tall, laid next to one another, pointing towards the town – an old mining track we can follow. This is how they must transport the serpentine into Tanwen. It's a risk, the rebels will know this route but, without food or water, we won't last long in the fog. Exposure will kill us just as easily as the rebels will.

As we leave the rebel base behind, the mists are dense. Several times I nearly lose Eskar ahead of me, his longer strides covering the ground more easily on the stone path. My breath is loud and I'm convinced it will lead the rebels to us.

We press on, running now the ground is firmer, despite exhaustion settling into my aching muscles. Something tall and dark rises out of the mists, on either side of us – a dense tangle of thorns over ten feet high. We're being funnelled towards Tanwen. We've no choice now but to hope this will lead us safely there.

The mist abruptly lifts when we nearly stumble upon the town gates. That's it – the boundary of the Haag. I try to keep running, but Eskar pulls me back. With the mists lifting, we're exposed. He pushes me to one side, pressing us into the bracken. Thorny spines poke through my clothes, scratching my skin.

"Follow my lead. Head straight for the boat. No stopping for food or water until we're clear of the town. We can survive in the forest but I don't trust anyone in Tanwen." I nod, aware of my dry lips and thirst.

We approach the gates, keeping close to the barbed walls. Some of the tension slips away when I see they're open and unmanned.

"Keep your head down; we need to make it through to the other side, find our boat and get out of here." Eskar mumbles as we pass, hoods drawn tight. I follow suit, wincing as I notice the red mud spattered to our thighs, a clear calling card to where we've been.

It's late afternoon, the streets are quiet and long shadows help hide us as we creep into the town.

We're halfway along the first street when a strong hand on my shoulder pulls me away from Eskar. I stumble, and being off balance, my pursuer wrestles my arm behind my back, pinning me to their chest and pressing a knife to my throat. I freeze.

"You're coming with us. Kitto warned us about you."

"Not going to happen." Eskar unleashes his magic on my captor and his accomplice. They scream, high-pitched noises ripping from their throats. This is different from before: their shrieks are short and brutal before both drop to the ground, dead.

Eskar is vibrating with the release of power and I run to him, to prove I'm okay, we're okay. A thin film of sweat covers his forehead.

"There'll be more." He's wound tight, pulling me close for a moment, furtively looking through alleys and side streets, before grabbing a dagger off the dead townsperson at our feet.

"Where are we going?" I call as he pulls us away from the main street, all pretence of hiding disappearing now the screams will have alerted the whole town.

"To the watchtower. They'll catch up too quickly if we go by river." The watchtower leads to the aqueduct. He's going to try and transport us out, like Dervla did. She is the most powerful Mordros I know, and it nearly killed her.

"Can you do it?" He hasn't been able to channel in weeks. I have no idea how much magic he has left and I'm intimately aware of the single strand buried in my chest, depleting him further.

"I'll have to." His mouth sets in a grim line, but if he burns out all the determination in the kingdom won't make a difference.

He pulls me towards the watchtower; we break into a sprint as a band of rebels turns the corner behind us. Our change in direction confuses them for a second but it won't be long until they reach us. All of them are armed.

The bottom of the watchtower is guarded by two rebels with swords out ready to attack as we hurtle round the corner towards them. I push Eskar behind me, shouting at him to close his eyes as I launch what little magic I have. Blinded, they swing at us but luck is on our side. I pull us to the wooden doorway and up into the staircase. Grunts of pain at the bottom tell me I don't think they'll be following. I hope they managed to stab each other. Hands finding purchase on the rough steps, we climb frantically, desperately trying to extend our lead.

The open doorway to the quayside is blocked by another pair of guards and the commotion below means we've lost the element of surprise. They see us climbing and are ready. It's too narrow for Eskar to fight them without injuring one of us – not that the townspeople have the same concerns.

The first guard raises his sword above his head and swings it to meet me. I realise Eskar's pre-empted him as the spasm ricochets through his body. He loses his grip seconds before injuring me. His sword tumbles, impaled between floors and Eskar grabs it. Both guards follow suit, disoriented and in agony. We avoid being knocked down with them, squeezing tightly against the wall as they tumble past. I don't have time to see if Eskar's okay after using his powers again. I push forward, pulling him behind me.

We reach the top. Thankfully the quay is empty and I bolt the door behind us.

"Please Sage, go. I need to get you out of here." Eskar's hands cup my face, tilting it unbelievably gently so I can look directly at him. His caramel eyes swirl with regret and for a moment we breathe each other's air before a crack at the door jolts us apart. The door buckles and he pushes me towards the water with the bag of serpentine.

I'm standing waist deep before I realise he's not following. At my shout, he turns back with a sad smile and his magic wraps round me, buoying me into the current.

Grasping the bag of serpentine tightly, the magic takes me. I manage to twist to look back at the quay to see the door has broken and it is being overrun with guards, dark shadows against the approaching dusk. Eskar stands in the water, channelling and ready to fight.

Chapter 47

With nothing else to focus on, no stars to watch over me, the gentle lap of water against the stone walls of the aqueduct is deafening. My eyes remain closed and my forehead feels permanently wrinkled from the deep creases I've imprinted between my brows. I cling to the heavy rucksack as I'm swept along, knuckles aching from fighting to balance it on my stomach as it threatens to tip into the current and sink me with it. My legs are stretched out in front of me, often hitting the stone walls of the aqueduct as the current buffets me.

As long as I'm suspended, Eskar is alive. Alive and fighting.

Several times I feel the cushioning impact falter and I drop lower in the water; each time the movement jostles my stomach and my muscles tense even further. Breathe in. Breathe out. Don't let go of the bag. Hours pass and dawn breaks, grey light shining through my closed eyelids.

A strange, metallic smell invades my nostrils. It's subtle at first but becomes all encompassing, as if I've walked into the meat market in Pentargon after the abattoir has finished for the day. Frozen in place by Eskar's magic, I dare not open my eyes but it's impossible to ignore the smell. My empty stomach roils but I purse my lips, sucking air in, tensing my jaw.

Another jolt and I inhale abruptly through my nose. My stomach protests at the cloying smell, forcing me to vomit violently to the side. My eyes open on reflex and all I can see is the glassy rose-pink water around me. I'm floating in blood. So much blood.

More heaving and coughing, I fight to keep myself away from the darkening water. Then it hits me: I can move. And I'm getting damper by the second, the diluted blood soaking through my clothes. The rucksack is a dead weight, dragging me lower and lower. I panic.

Eskar's magic has gone. Is he…? The tinted water around me is evidence enough. I can't bring myself to think about it and push my grief down and kick my legs, twisting to keep my head above water.

I can't swim properly with the rucksack of rocks dragging me under. I tell myself it's only water, as it floods my nose and burns my throat. Spluttering and coughing, I refuse to sink, to give up the serpentine we risked so much for. I go under, the cool water closing in over my hair and my wet clothes adding to the weight of the serpentine.

I sink until my toes find firm ground and the lazy current gives me traction. Kicking against the floor, I push my way to the surface to breathe and sink again.

Panic barely under control, I fight my way to the wall of the aqueduct, using my spare hand to feel for purchase, so I can hold myself above the water. It's futile: the walls are old and worn smooth and I'm quickly tiring. Fighting the current to stay in one place feels impossible.

Panic wins the fight and I thrash and kick, mind and limbs jumbled. The burning lack of air confuses me and I lose track of the surface. I'm blind, trapped in a liquid prison, twisting and turning underwater. By sheer, dumb luck, as black dots fill in my vision, I break the surface and gasp a final lungful of air. The black dots recede. I've delayed death for another minute.

The magic in my chest will not give up: it rebels at my hopelessness and my hands burn. Strong light colours my eyelids white as my magic fights desperately to keep us both alive. I wish I'd had more time to explore this wondrous piece of me.

I think of Eskar in Tanwen. Perhaps our bodies will wash up together. I feel my own burnout approaching: my light flickers. The urge to breathe becomes stronger. I hold out for a few moments more but I know as soon as I try to breathe my lungs will fill and it'll be over.

Then a tug, a small boost upwards. Then another. My eyes open in surprise and the water is clearer, the surface not so far. I feel a niggle as the last shred of my magic nudges me to reach for the surface. My hand breaks free, there's another tug and I'm up. I'm suspended again, my face breaks through the water and I suck in a lungful of air, choking as the churning current splashes over my head.

The relief is temporary – Eskar is fighting. I cling to that fact, but his magic is fading in and out; it's not stable and I won't survive if it disappears again.

The niggle inside me draws my attention again. It's the strand of Mordros magic I took from him in Cathair. The strand that refuses to bend to my will. In my desperation to help Eskar, to make it easier on him, I draw that last scrap of magic to me and this time my intent is so strong, the magic obeys. I direct it to the rucksack, winding it round the straps to give it buoyancy, to reduce the load on Eskar. The effect is instant: the stuttering lessens and I begin to hope.

Chapter 48

The sun is about to set when I see a quay appear ahead. I hope it's Cathair but, right now, I'll do anything to get out of this freezing water, still tinged with the faintest pink. I paddle closer and grasp the wooden structure. My fingers are cramping. I crawl onto the dock. White knuckles, arms shivering, I make it out of the water alive.

And I wait.

The cold sets in but I feel nothing. I will not leave until I know if Eskar is alive. The last ray of sunshine flickers over the horizon and through habit I channel. Thank goodness I do because I'm at risk of hypothermia. I send a flash of light upwards, alerting the aqueduct guards to my presence. It occurs to me they could be rebels but I doubt that they will kill me on the spot. Nonetheless, I'll die if I stay here exposed. I don't even care that I've used my magic so openly. Logic has abandoned me and I can only think about the cold... and Eskar.

The guards, taken aback to find a member of the King's Concord stranded at the aqueduct quay, give up attempting to get me to leave after a while. If they think my behaviour bizarre, they don't say. I'm left with heavy blankets and some food but I can't bear to eat right now.

I sit and wait, and think of all the things I haven't said to Eskar – how he's been constantly on my mind, how he kept me sane in the Haag and protected me time and time again. I never got to explain or apologise for his torture.

The water keeps flowing, its rhythmic noise hypnotic. I scold myself when my eyes try to shutter and resume my watch.

My ears are so attuned to the regular pulse of the flow, they catch a slight variation. An irregular splash, then another. All of a sudden, I'm wide awake, peering through the darkness, wishing the moon was brighter.

A silhouette rises from the water. My heart threatens to pound out of my chest at the hope it could be him.

The figure struggles and collapses, too weak to make it to the bank. Without thinking, I jump back in the water, icy in the darkness and make my way over.

I get close enough to recognise his face, his broad shoulders, his height. It's him – it's really him. In the darkness I can't see if he's injured but he's alive.

He's too exhausted to speak but I see a smile once he recognises me and pulls his arm over my shoulder to help him get to dry land. He's too heavy for us to move quickly and when we get to the bank, I use my light to signal the guards below for help.

While we wait, I hold his head against my shoulder, giving his legs a rest. His eyes close, pale face drawn but his hands start to channel under the water. Good, hopefully that will give him something to keep in reserve, since his magic must be thoroughly depleted.

The guards help me carry him out of the water and down the stairs. They must recognise him because a carriage is called.

I refuse to let go of his hand on the journey and every so often he jerks into consciousness and panics. When he sees my face, he relaxes and slips away again.

My heart sinks when we are taken through the streets of Cathair to his family home, a monolith of white stone glowing in the moonlight. The driver opens the carriage door and coughs when I don't move to leave.

Eskar peels open one eye. His attention snaps to the driver when he notices where we are, his gaze narrows.

"Sir, the house is err… quite empty. Ms Dervla Cairbre told us to keep it maintained but your arrival is unanticipated. Your parents have been…" Eskar visibly relaxes as the driver stumbles for the right word.

"Removed?"

"Yes sir. Quite right. You're safe in the city for now."

"Do you happen to know by who?"

"The new Almanac I believe. They've been suspended and asked to retreat to their summer estate outside Restormel."

That's miles away, far from Cathair and I sink into the carriage seat in relief.

Eskar's nod is the full extent of his remaining energy and he all but falls out of the carriage and stumbles up the steps to his family home.

The housekeeper is awake when we arrive, but

the rest of the house is deserted. She leads us to our rooms but gets flustered when I refuse to leave his side, eventually conceding this is an argument she won't win. I'm not going anywhere until I'm certain he's safe.

I curl up tightly against his side, ignoring our damp clothes. My shivers stir me long after I fall asleep.

Chapter 49

In the early hours of the morning, the adrenaline leaves my body. My aching muscles relax into the soft mattress and I'm warm and dry. Distant birdsong draws a faint smile as I doze. At Chi An Mor, the birds soar high. Trilling and calling to each other as they rise on the thermals, where they bathe in the river at the top of the cliff, their songs echoing against the cream sandstone. Deep in the rebel tunnels it was silent. Depressingly so. Hearing their sweet, warbling song soothes me back to sleep.

A hot prickle sweeps across my scalp as sweat beads in my hairline, waking me. Eskar has melded himself to every inch of my body, cocooning me in a hot oven. The heat is overwhelming. My feet touch the floor without disturbing him and a cooler breeze wraps itself around me. Then the bed creaks and he groans loudly. His hands search the bed and I don't move quickly enough before they tug me back towards him. His large body wraps round me, his legs pinning me in place and his chin pressing into my forehead. A sigh of contentment comes from deep within this chest as he settles back to sleep.

"I can't do this. You're boiling me alive." I wriggle away, trying and failing to put some distance between us, avoiding the lure of the hard planes of his muscles. The weeks of torture underground have had an impact but not enough to stop me appreciating his body.

"Is that your only complaint?" His eyes aren't even open but a lazy smirk stretches across his face. His hand draws circles on my lower back and my stomach tightens. I take in his sleepy form and briefly consider giving up and curling back at his side when his caramel eyes open and glint at me.

The noise my hand makes as it whacks off his chest is not as satisfying as I want it to be. He flinches and my cheeks flush when I remember the beatings he's withstood. He relents and shuffles back to his side of the bed.

"I didn't think I'd be able to sleep after yesterday," he admits sheepishly, staring at the ceiling, one arm slung behind his head. I tilt to meet his gaze but he's stubbornly shy and won't let me see his eyes.

"Want to talk about it?" This time I'm the one who leans closer. I cup his cheek, turning his face towards me.

"Not particularly." He burrows his nose in my hair, then recoils sharply.

"You smell revolting. What is that?" Eyes wide open now, he looks as if he's going to be sick.

I stop breathing through my nose because I know I'm going to vomit now too. Somehow I'd got used to the smell overnight but flashes of the red tinged water yesterday swim in front of my vision and I start to hyperventilate.

"Shhh, it's okay. I'm here; we made it." He repeats over and over, stroking my hair from a distance, mouth tense.

"Blood. The smell. From the water. Your magic faded... I thought..." My nails scratch at the skin on my arms to rid myself of the unclean feeling crawling through my body.

"Come here." He holds my hands firmly but gently to his chest and pulls me towards him. "It wasn't mine. I couldn't risk fighting them with magic whilst also wielding to send you away; it took a lot longer and ended up being a lot messier but I'm here."

We lie for a minute and I'm acutely aware of him breathing through his mouth, avoiding the smell which creeps through my nostrils, churning my stomach.

Eventually I can't stand the smell either, or the proximity to him when I smell like an abattoir and I pull away to find a bathroom. I'm conscious of his gaze watching me leave.

When I return, long after the water turned cold, Eskar is gone and a set of clothes is laid on the bed. Gratefully I pull them on. They're oversized, sleeves tangling over my hands and trousers tripping me up. I sit on the bed waiting for Eskar to return.

My fingers can't help but play with the soft cotton of the shirt. Despite its size, I've never worn something so lovely and I start to take in details of the room. It's vast, for a bedroom. Large, relaxed sofas frame the fireplace and I'm tempted to sink into their embrace and sleep some more. The desk is neat and tidy and the morning light reflects off the polished mahogany surface: not a speck of dust can be seen in the air.

"Not quite what I had in mind, but I can't say I'm complaining."

I startle at his return, clearly from a washroom down the hall as he's wearing a towel draped across his lower half. Water runs down his chest, finding a path through an excess of muscles and ageing wounds and causing my mind to go completely blank. His stare is fixed on the loose cotton shirt I'm wearing and he offers me a genuine smile.

I realise the clothes laid out on the bed weren't meant for me and a hot blush races from my chest to my cheeks. Eskar chuckles at my embarrassment and struts to the wardrobe to pull out a fresh shirt.

"Hoping for a show?" He says, one hand on his towel about to untuck it. I can't stand that eyebrow, sardonically rising above the other whenever he teases me.

I gulp, still processing wearing his clothes and that I think he likes it.

"Absolutely not." I make a show of being interested in the books on his nightstand.

He coughs, sounding uncomfortable for once. "I'm going to need you not to be sitting on my bed while I change. In fact, I need you far away from it."

I lean back on one arm and half turn towards the sound of his voice. His eyes travel up and down my body before he shakes himself.

"Sage," he grits out, jaw tense. He drags his hand

through his hair in irritation and the towel slips lower on his hips, "Go and get some breakfast or something." I frown. There's no need to be so rude.

Frustrated, I storm to the bedroom the housekeeper assigned to me, tossing his oversized clothes in a crumpled heap on the floor.

Chapter 50

My relief at our escape is regrettably short-lived. Cathair may be far from Tanwen, but the rebels have contacts everywhere. Every servant in Eskar's family townhouse could be working against us, plotting to stop us returning or to take back the rucksack full of serpentine stashed in my room. We have to get back to Pentargon as quickly as possible, to tell the Concord what we've learnt. I try to convince the housekeeper to send a message to Pentargon and to book our passage home but she resists. She makes it clear that only Eskar's approval matters and I should wait for his instruction. It rankles. Particularly since I can't find him.

After I've meandered through the house, unable to sit and still full of restless energy, the housekeeper sends me to the greenhouse for herbs for dinner. She's a stern old woman and not one to take no for an answer.

Flowers bloom at every turn. The grounds are beautiful. I can't miss the greenhouse, a monstrously large wrought iron structure nestled deep in the garden. It towers over me, the size of a marquee and when the gardens are in full season, then that is nothing compared to the lush green foliage pressed to the glass surface roaring to break free.

The humidity punches me in the face. Breathing is a challenge and my body braces against the increase in temperature. I stroll further into this tropical oasis, lifting the huge, variegated leaves out of the way, noticing hoarse croaking of tree frogs and the gentle hum of insects. Sweat forms at the back of my neck, across my collarbones and down my spine.

Cursing as I trip on an exposed root, no herbs are going to thrive in this heat. I turn to leave and spy Eskar through the dense leaves. I falter, tilting back and forth between leaving him in peace or investigating what he's up to. Curiosity wins and I creep closer.

There's a stream bubbling through the centre of the greenhouse that I hadn't seen before. What wealth his family must have if they have this private sanctuary to ensure they are always able to channel. No need to share the rivers or canals like common Mordros.

The stream explains the humidity. Eskar reclines in it, channelling, a pile of clothes discarded on the bank next to him. I blink twice, taking in the view.

His broad shoulders and back muscles are relaxed and my eyes can't help tracing the pattern of bruises downwards until the water obscures his body. He leans back on his hands, head tilted back to the foggy glass panes above, eyes closed. I'm jealous of his state of relaxation, my mind still jumbled and processing our escape, heart racing and palms sweaty. Instead, I settle for admiring each individual muscle from his neck downwards – there's plenty to appreciate.

After a while, my sanity returns and I realise how creepy I'm being. I go to leave but as I turn, he calls out.

"Finally finished staring then, Sage." His caramel eyes are mischievous and the creases living round their edges have been erased by the damp air. I'm struck by how much younger he looks without the dirt from the Haag coating him. We're so similar in age but have had such different lives.

After all we've been through together, I recognise the pull towards him, the desire to climb into the stream with him and smooth away the bruises lingering on his skin. But after the mixed messages this morning, I'm uncertain whether he feels it too.

"You made it clear touching wasn't allowed. You didn't say anything about looking." To make my point, I strut over to a smooth rock nearby and sit facing him.

He rises to my challenge and leans back in the water.

I gulp – obviously, he is definitely very naked. Fidgeting, I can't get comfortable, nor can I ignore that the sight of him has made my mouth incredibly dry. He's clean-shaven again and he looks like he did when we were in his apartment in Cathair, after we changed our appearance to go into hiding. I wrap my fingers self-consciously around my dark hair, the dye still lingering.

Eskar blatantly stares at me, tempting me to push back, to ask why he kicked me out of his room earlier. To finally address what's been simmering between us now for months.

"Well, I hope you enjoy the view then," he drawls, languidly tilting back and closing his eyes. He shifts down to his elbows, allowing his hands to move. They remain submerged, drawing slow circles as he channels to replenish his magic.

I test my magic while sitting on the rock, ruminating over my confusing companion's behaviour. I'm unable to wield through the glass. It must be specially made then, a safety precaution. Unusual though – normally Aubade magic is overlooked.

I notice his eyes are staring at me hungrily.

"Now who's enjoying the view?"

A drop of perspiration leaves my face, trailing down my neck. I freeze when it pauses between my collarbones and changes path, creeping towards my breast.

Eskar is smiling lightly, hands now static. If he's stopped channelling then he must be working on something else. I narrow my eyes and the bead of water continues its journey south, feeling pleasantly cool against my overheated skin. More droplets join, condensing from the air around me. My nipples respond. If I'm reading the new tension in his shoulders correctly, it's something Eskar has also noticed.

"You have no idea what you do to me, do you?" His voice is low, gravelly and full of something I can't identify.

I'm struggling to process words, let alone full sentences, my concentration focusing on urging on the delicious tickle of the water droplet.

His eyes darken. "I said no earlier because I won't be some trivial, spontaneous escape for you. I won't be temporary." The water caresses my ankles in cool strokes and winds round my arms.

"We won't be short-lived." Liquid shackles pin my ankles in place with his words. "I intend to spend a long, long time with you." In my distraction at the bead of water teasing my breasts, he's restrained my limbs completely. I tug gently, confident he will release me at the slightest indication. But he knows that's not what I want.

"Tell me what you want, Sage."

I want him to get out of the stream and replace the water with his hands.

"Use your words." The ropes of water pulse and tighten at his command.

"I…" I've never had to articulate exactly what I want before. Any trysts I've been involved in happen spontaneously, after plenty of alcohol and I've never lingered. Almost all were disappointing and I've never sought a repeat. But I know with Eskar it would be different. I'd have to be vulnerable and, right now, I don't think I can open up.

There's no trace of disappointment on his face as the silence continues. I can't find the words to explain. I want to forget the rebels, Tanwen, how close he came to death trying to save me. I need to clear my mind for a moment and lose myself in the fact that we miraculously made it out alive.

He senses my frustration but doesn't give in. "I won't do half measures with you, Sage. If I'm in, I'm all in. So, I'll wait until you choose me for the right reasons. Not because you need to forget the rebels or because you pity me for being tortured. I can be patient."

And with that confusing statement, the liquid chains dissolve and flow back into the stream. He leans back and closes his eyes, seemingly relaxed and returns to channelling.

He is quite possibly the most irritatingly handsome man I've ever met. My body is on fire and yet he's content to subject us to this misery. His previous behaviour with other women back in Pentargon led me to think he was never interested in something more serious, but his attitude to me suggests otherwise. I contemplate climbing into the stream and onto his lap but I can't promise him anything more than a temporary distraction and he deserves more.

Chapter 51

We retire to separate rooms that evening. Neither of us mentions the greenhouse over dinner but I catch myself staring at Eskar whenever he's not looking at me. He sent a message to Pentargon via the aqueducts, letting the Concord know we're alive and returning shortly but that was all. Neither of us wanted to risk the message falling into the wrong hands. We have to wait a few days for the next ferry to take us back to the capital and I would be lying if I said I was looking forward to being back at sea. But for now, we can rest.

I wake from my bed to a crashing, thundering noise and the room trembles. Immediately, I'm a child trapped in a nightmare. I've never experienced an earthquake. In Pentargon, they're told as fairy tales, abstract in a way I've never considered before. I grip the bedposts in terror, frozen, as the world ricochets around me.

The trembling finally abates, and I clamber out of bed and head towards the window, head pounding from the noise. Outside, the street is in complete darkness, the moon obscured by thick clouds. The world looks strange, not because it is night-time, or because the city is unfamiliar. As my eyes sweep along the rooftops, I know in my gut something is wrong with this silhouette.

When Eskar bursts into my room, my gaze is fixed on the window, fuzzy brain still trying to understand. "Are you alright?" His hands cup my face, eyes raking my face.

"I'm fine. What's happened? I was asleep and then… was it an earthquake?"

He grabs a cloak from the wardrobe and thrusts it into my arms. "Not an earthquake, Sage, an explosion. The rebels targeted the aqueduct: the city is flooding." Ice-cold dread runs down my body. This beautiful city, the people, the damage will be catastrophic. That's what was wrong with the view: the towering aqueduct framing the city is gone.

"Because of us?" He doesn't answer, grimly pulling the hood up so my face is fully covered.

"We need to leave." His voice is remote, authoritative. I feel him slipping away, back into the role of the King's Verax. He reaches for the heavy rucksack of serpentine I've stored at the foot of my bed and slings it onto his back.

Sensing my need to protest, to stay and try to help people in the city who are vulnerable to the flood water, Eskar interrupts me.

"There are enough Mordros in the city to minimise the damage, to buy them time to escape. The city has evacuation plans for an event like this. People know what to do. My job is to get you out of here safely and back to Chi An Mor. We're leaving now."

The streets are treacherous and becoming lethal. By the time we leave Eskar's home, with instructions to the housekeeper to let in all those needing shelter, the water is trickling over the cobbles. However, at the bottom of the street of family estates, we're hit by rapidly rising flood water, threatening to steal our balance. Its icy fingers curl round my legs to my knees and continue to rise. Eskar navigates the streets ahead, I'm grateful he grew up here as the midnight black sky provides no light to see by. Kitto would have chosen night-time deliberately. It's easier to cause chaos and sow fear in the dark.

We pick our way through the streets, moving as quickly as possible. People shout from home to home, offering sanctuary to those trapped outside. Being in the lowlands, Cathair was always at risk of flooding. But not in summer and not to this extent. There is a frantic energy from the people we pass, but no desperation or panic. I want to shout at them to get out, to get to higher ground, that the Mordros holding back the water will falter eventually and the city will be swept away.

The river quay is deserted. Not even the night security have stayed; they've all gone into the city to help. Finally, the moon breaks free from the clouds and I get one last look at the beautiful stone buildings glowing like pearls. I wonder how many will be standing once the water fully rushes in – how much guilt I'll forever carry at bringing this destruction here.

There's a boat, barely larger than a dinghy, which

Eskar beckons me to. There's no wind for sailing and, although it's downstream to Porth, we won't be able to sail to Pentargon in this tiny boat: the currents will rip it apart in the open sea.

"Get below and, whatever you do, don't come out until sunrise." He pulls me onboard and gestures into the hold. It's tiny and cramped, clearly designed for food and drink storage on a hot summer's day. I won't be able to lie flat but if I curl up tightly then I think I can make it work.

The boat rocks precariously, the current bolstered by the floodwater. I feel the boat moving into the current and my nausea rises. It's a miserable few hours, punctuated by my intermittent vomiting. The rocking of the boat is more intense than the large ferry ride up the river and despite Eskar's best attempts, we hit the bank on several occasions. Each time we make contact, the boat shunts aggressively to one side and I'm thrown against the small, wooden walls. Cramp settles into my legs, and my head is woozy from being hit repeatedly. I drift in and out of sleep or unconsciousness, I'm not sure which until a bright light sears my eyelids.

"Sage? Sage! Can you hear me?" Eskar's voice is far away and muffled. I turn towards him, wincing at my bruises.

"Why didn't you say something?" Anger and concern fight for dominance in his voice as I raise my head.

The brightness recedes as my eyes adjust; it's early morning and I assume we're somewhere outside of Cathair but still far from Porth. My stomach heaves one final time and I must make a pitiful sight, covered in my own vomit, bruised and dazed.

Eskar reaches down and lifts me out of the craft, careful not to jostle me. He cradles me and carries me across the little sandbank where we're moored, and back towards the water.

"This will be cold but I promise it'll be over quickly. You'll feel better afterwards."

He wades into the shallows of the slow-moving river, kneeling so the water rises to his shoulders, fully submerging my aching body. The water is frigid, but the relief of being able to move my arms and legs and being buoyant in the water is bliss. Eskar holds me to his body in one arm, washing away traces of sick with the other. My poor head aches as he runs his fingers through my hair, feeling for lumps and cuts.

I feel pathetic – he endured weeks of torture without complaint, stayed awake overnight twice and I've struggled for a few hours cramped in a boat while being rescued from a city where thousands of people were losing their homes or worse.

We huddle under his cloak on a sandbank while we dry off and I feel anger at the rebels build.

"What was the point of attacking Cathair? Of destroying the aqueduct system? What will people do for drinking water in the remote villages now? Tanwen will be run dry too."

Eskar sighs and looks back towards his hometown in the distance. "Chaos and fear. Because they can. Because they're radicals. Honestly, I don't know why."

The full scale of the destruction is now hitting me:

hundreds of towns will be cut off, right as the spring rains have finished and through summer when other water sources run low. Instead of inciting a riot, Kitto has condemned them to a slow and painful death. "I guess she's angry we escaped."

"Maybe. Although an attack of this scale couldn't have been organised overnight. Clearly, they've been planning this for a while. You can't take all the blame."

I scowl into the distance and he braces his hands on his knees, pushing to his feet. "We've made good distance so far. I'll channel while you dry off and then we'll continue."

Chapter 52

The sun glints off the summit of Chi An Mor as we finally approach Pentargon days later, the palace a proud beacon, welcoming us home. We're beaten and exhausted, dishevelled and weakened. Long days on the tiny boat were followed by catching the first ferry from Porth. No personal cabins this time, as we assume the role of common foot passengers, wanting to blend in. As we step off the quay in the city, I see new fine lines written on Eskar's face; the grief of carrying the news of Cathair's destruction weighs heavy on us both.

Pentargon is unchanged and uninterested in our arrival. Nobody takes any notice of two jaded, haggard entrants at the main city quay. We pass through the harbourside docks and are ignored by the sunburnt fishermen discussing the catch of the morning, fiercely negotiating a price to sell at the market. Fish are abundant in the summer months and yesterday's unwanted catches sit festering in crates next to their boats. The Mordros will only eat fresh fish but the waste turns my stomach, we'll look back on those fish and regret wasting this glut come winter. I peer through the streets, eyes searching as we cross Cedar's rubbish collection route, hoping for a glance of my brother. An eerie calm follows us through the city, languishing in the late haze of a summer afternoon.

The streets are bustling, lively and carefree. I never saw what it was like directly after the attacks last winter but I imagine the reaction now will be worse. Those attacks were remote, the subject of gossip and speculation and incited anger in the citizens but had little impact on their daily lives once the mandatory curfew ended.

Now though, it will be different. Their halcyon days are numbered. The aqueduct systems will have started to drain as soon as the explosion in Cathair occurred. For a coastal city, with a large river feeding the majority of the population, news will spread slowly as dependence on the aqueduct is low. But the news can't be contained forever and, once word spreads, fear will worm its way into people's consciousness and further separate the classes.

I hesitate at the doors to Chi An Mor, finally home and uncertain. Part of me wants to run to the Koes Dowr, to ground myself in the tall trees there. The rational part demands we go straight to the King and petition for retribution for the people of Cathair and for what the rebels did to Eskar but I realise I'm not exactly a neutral party right now.

Eskar lets me make the call, glancing at me as he shifts the heavy bag of serpentine from one shoulder to another. One big breath in and I brace to tackle the never-ending stairs to the Concord chamber.

The guards shuffle back a few steps when they see us, dirty and dishevelled, recognition slowly filtering in when they meet our eyes. Their reactions spur me on; we reflect a fraction of the suffering of the people of Cathair and the Concord must understand the severity of the situation.

I stride into the Concord chamber, happy to interrupt whatever meaningless debate they currently feel is important.

Thick silence spreads through the room at our entrance and nobody moves.

The King is the first to react, rising from his seat, his political mask fading to reveal shock and disbelief.

"You're alive," Dervla's hands rush to her mouth, trembling slightly before she regains her composure. Surveying the room in more detail, the Concord looks as if they've seen a pair of ghosts appear. Haelyn's seat is empty, as are ours, but the rest of the members are assembled.

"Barely," replies Eskar. "We have pressing news."

Chapter 53

The surprise at our return is smothered quickly. Before we can recount our news, we are ushered to our seats and required to wait until the end of the current discussion.

Eskar sits next to me, a mask of professionalism in place, his mouth tightly shut and his face devoid of expression, but his hands fiddle constantly with the strap on the bag of serpentine. I hate seeing him recede into himself like this, smothering his emotions, playing the part of the King's Verax. The reflection pool in the middle was still when we arrived but now churns intensely.

I shift my weight from side to side, frustrated at the delay, but then I tune into what one of the Concord members is saying.

"All rebel activity in the city has ceased. None of the suspected rebels has been seen in days; they've gone underground."

"Do we know why?" the King responds. I'm about to jump in when Eskar puts a firm hand on my thigh. I glance at him, mouth set in a firm line and remember what he said when we were back in Cathair about a traitor in the Concord. We need to tread carefully.

"Nothing confirmed," the same Concord member replies.

At this, the King halts the conversation and brings the meeting to a close.

"I would like to speak to my Verax and Alchemist alone. Almanac – you should hear this too." Dervla stiffens, her attention pulled back from the reflection pool in the centre.

The rest of the Concord file out of the room, disgruntled and clearly dallying in the hope of catching a scrap of conversation between the King, Dervla and us.

Once the doors are firmly closed, with no chance of being overheard, the King turns to us sharply. "Explain. The last message we received was from you alerting us that Lord Bal might be in residence in Cathair. I sent Dervla there immediately but you were nowhere to be found. You've been gone for nearly two months."

I share a look with Eskar, unsettled at the cold reaction before I turn to the King.

"We were captured by the rebels. They are using the mining tunnels under the Haag as a base. Eskar was tortured. We escaped and then their leader, Kitto, triggered another explosion in Cathair which drained the aqueducts in retaliation."

Nobody moves or even breathes at my revelation. Dervla's face is frozen, her hands grip the edge of the table and her body sways slightly. The King watches her, looking to her to speak first. When she can't, or won't, he clarifies.

"You've been with Kevren Gwir this whole time?"

"Not willingly. We were their prisoners. We just managed to escape." How dare he assume we didn't take this mission seriously.

Dervla regains her composure enough to interrupt before I argue further with the King and asks in a quiet voice, sounding unlike herself, "The aqueduct. What happened with the aqueduct?"

Eskar's voice holds so much sorrow at the destruction of his home city. "About a week ago, the morning after we arrived, Sage and I woke to an explosion that rocked the whole city. The flooding was underway by the time we reached the city quay to escape."

The King looks at Dervla confused before schooling his features to a nonchalance that makes me want to punch his chiselled jaw. "But surely, we would have heard if there was a problem. The aqueduct levels would have dropped, merchants travelling back from Cathair would have reported the disruption?"

Dervla considers him closely. "Not necessarily… The aqueduct levels always drop in early summer, as the glacier melt recedes. If it's been a week then perhaps the city watch hasn't noticed anything too unusual. And if Sage and Eskar left immediately and sailed straight here, they're the first people out of the city. Anyone travelling by road will be at least a week behind them."

"What does this mean?" The King's impatience cracks through his mask of indifference; he hasn't grasped the consequences fully. Yet the air of desperation from the rest of us is palpable.

"In Cathair, hundreds will have lost their homes, their livelihoods – many even their lives." Eskar's voice is hollow and cracked and I think of his housekeeper and the kind carriage driver we left behind. I hope they made it to safety.

"But we face a bigger problem. The cities and villages inland depend on the aqueducts for fresh water in the summer months, as do the farms. Cathair is the central hub; the whole of Trevesiga will be affected. Without access to fresh water, the crops will die and without a good harvest, we'll all suffer come winter." Dervla's mouth is set in a grim line, her face pale. The impacts of Kitto's treasonous act will be far-reaching. The weight of this revelation seems to finally hit the King; he reaches for his chair and sinks into it before I continue.

"And the rebels are organised. They have weapons, they have serpentine and who knows what their plan is now. We need to act."

Dervla turns to me sharply. "The best thing you can do for Trevesiga, Sage, is to finish your research. If you want to take on the rebels, that is your answer." The King doesn't react to her statement so I presume he finally knows what I've actually been up to in my islet laboratory.

"But we have details about their base, their activities. We know how to find them." My voice is weaker than I'd like, petulant. The King and Dervla share a glance.

"You may leave now. I need to discuss this with my Almanac." Dismissing both Eskar and I, the King's voice is quiet, his focus is on the reflection pool which has gone still.

Outside the Concord chamber, I turn to Eskar, about to vent about the King's lack of action when I see Haelyn lurking in the corridor, out of breath.

She rushes towards me and envelops me in a hug. "I came as soon as I heard. I'm so relieved you're okay. We've been so worried."

I laugh, a brittle sound, but it does feel good to be back home. "We?"

"Cedar. I stopped by a few times to make sure he knew what was going on after we lost track of you in Cathair. When we stopped getting any news, I thought he might have heard something. He's been worried sick about you, we both have. But then…"

She stops, and awkwardly looks at Eskar before continuing.

"It's okay, I trust him." I place my hand on her arm reassuringly.

"Cedar's gone." She bites her lip, eyes wide. "I went to check on him last night and his apartment was empty. Just a bag of what I assume could be serpentine left behind with a note that had your name on it." Her face pulls into a frown as she looks between Eskar and me.

Ice shoots through my veins; Kitto's retribution didn't end at the aqueduct. She stole my brother and left me a calling card so I'd know it was her.

"Where is the serpentine now?" I reach for Haelyn's arm, tugging her towards me.

"I took it to your laboratory on the islet. I thought it would be safest there." She chews her lip, eyes carefully tracking my reaction.

I nod and turn to Eskar. "I need to go to the islet; I'm going to solve this once and for all but I'll need your help." His eyes flash at my slip of the tongue, warning me to watch my words in front of Haelyn.

"What can I do to help?" Haelyn interrupts our conversation.

I regard her closely, the final pieces of a puzzle clicking into place.

"Did you master the Gallos?"

"Yes."

"Then you need to come with us." She nods and I feel Eskar's reproach over my shoulder as we descend the stairs. The truth has to come out at some point and if I'm going to trust anyone in this city, then it would be Haelyn.

Chapter 54

The three of us make a quiet group sailing over to the laboratory. Neither Eskar or Haelyn asks questions in front of Diogel and I focus on keeping the food in my stomach on the bumpy crossing. Other than stopping to change our clothes and eat, we didn't linger at Chi An Mor. Diogel was thrilled to see me. I think he, like everyone in the Concord, had assumed the worst when no news came. His open warmth elicits a small half-smile from me as I look to Eskar; no one has welcomed him back home.

The islet comes into view and I'm distracted by the pit in my stomach as my mind runs through all the cruel ways Kitto could be hurting Cedar. She's vicious but doesn't do anything without a plan. Leaving the rebels may have triggered retribution in destroying the aqueducts but this is more personal: she'll want me to suffer. Even if she plans to use him for leverage, it means he's alive for now, and that's all I can hope for. I know my research is crucial but on the walk up to the laboratory, the guilt I feel at not going out and searching for my brother weighs heavy on my chest.

Inside, the instruments and worktops are covered in a thin layer of dust, the only disturbance being the unmarked sack placed on the other side of the room. I take a deep breath as I read the note placed on top. Kitto's handwriting is recognisable. Reluctantly pushing Cedar's abduction aside, I turn to them.

"I need you both to keep this a secret." They nod without hesitation and I twist my hands behind my back.

"For the last couple of years, Dervla and I have been working on a way to democratise magic. To store it outside of our bodies, so we no longer have to be dependent on sunlight, running water or the wind. Serpentine is one of the missing pieces, but after being forced to work with the rebels, there's something else." I pause, rocking back on my heels before taking a deep breath. "Kitto and I could never get it to work," I look to Eskar, "But I had more success than her. I think all three types of magic are needed." Haelyn looks between the two of us, eyebrows furrowed.

I allow them both to digest what I've just said. The idea that multiple types of magic need to be combined has been brewing in the back of my mind since Kitto couldn't replicate my success. I have that tiny strand of Mordros magic to thank, combining the two together seemed so close to bringing the balance that was missing.

"We need to wield our magic together. If we use the Gallos and gently direct it into the crystals, I think they will store it." I look to them in turn, waiting for their cautious nods. Eskar is in shock but Haelyn radiates a smugness that tells me she already had an inkling of what I'd been doing. I set up one of the crystals from Eskar's backpack, choosing one of the smallest.

"We'd better stand back, just in case. My previous attempts were explosive." The three of us retreat closer to the protective screens and I reach deep into myself, coaxing my magic to the surface.

It comes willingly, gladly and the strand from Eskar waits patiently behind, not needed. I send it through the air and into the waiting crystal. Eskar and Haelyn join me, their magics adding to my own. Aubade, Zephyr and Mordros combined.

A heavy pause – I hold my breath as the crystal glows faintly. Before, the glow brightened, showing us it was only a matter of time before the experiment would detonate. But here, as the minutes pass, the faint pulse-like glow remains constant, the magic hums in contentment. In perfect balance.

The void in my chest tells me my magic is depleted but rather than channel from the daylight, I take a tentative step towards the crystal. Eskar flinches but doesn't move to stop me. I place a hand on the warm crystal and before I can think, I feel an intense rush of magic flood into my system. The returning magic is purely Aubade and it fills the void, the little strand of Mordros happily welcoming it back. The crystal is cold, energy depleted.

I turn to them, tension draining from my body. "I think we did it."

Their mouths fall open before identical grins spread over their faces and Eskar closes the distance between us, pulling me into his arms. Safe in his embrace, I allow myself a scrap of joy at this breakthrough. More tests will be needed, of course. But I can tell, this time it's different. My magic could sense it.

The niggling doubt following me from the Haag, the doubt that took root once I saw Kitto mastering the Gallos and experimenting on serpentine evaporates. This is my win. Years of effort, research and setbacks, all leading to this. Kitto had to resort to torture, abduction and manipulation to make progress. I did this on my own.

"This changes everything," I mutter as Eskar keeps his hands on my shoulders.

"I know." His calm voice steadies my growing excitement. We just need to convince the King and the Concord that this is how we resolve the rebel conflict. To show them there's no need for violence. This might be our way out of this mess. A loud cough interrupts us and we turn sheepishly to see Haelyn smirking. Her grin matches my own as we clasp hands: Zephyrs and Aubades now have a chance of a brighter future.

Chapter 55

We practised all afternoon, only stopping when the light dipped below the horizon, preventing me from continuing. Each experiment was a success, every crystal that we hauled back from the Haag was imbued and drained without any issues. Each of us was able to help drain the magic but Eskar and I share a glance when Haelyn confirms that her magic remains the same. Eskar is still completely Mordros. I'm the only hybrid; his magic still burrows deep in my chest but hasn't been replenished by the serpentine either. I can only access my Aubade magic. Serpentine requires all three magics to imbue it but, when it is drained, the magic only replenishes what is required by the user. My happiness dims a little but I'm familiar enough with research to know that often as soon as one question is answered, more appear. It's a problem for another day.

Now comes the tricky part. Dervla will be ecstatic but the King… I gaze sleepily at Eskar as we sail back to Chi An Mor. Technically, I've been in breach of the Difan for years and Haelyn and Eskar are implicated now too. I don't think he will punish us but the Concord certainly will try. If it comes down to a vote, Dervla will need to use every scrap of political capital to spare us. But once she does, I have hope. With this discovery, Aubades and Zephyrs will be able to access much greater quantities of magic. We won't need to calmly accept the rules that the Mordros force upon us. The King will be able to steer Trevesiga towards equality; we can push for representation on the Concord, we can push for fewer restrictions on the jobs we can hold, the schools our children are permitted to attend. My chest feels lighter, my lungs fuller and all doubts on my abilities evaporate. Years of work have led to this moment and even with Kitto and the Kevren Gwir threatening us, I feel hope.

Behind Haelyn's back, Eskar and I sneak glances at each other as Diogel steers the ferry home. The tension brewing since the greenhouse in Cathair is setting my skin on fire and I would give anything to have a few moments alone with him before we tell the Concord. My reckless hands reach for his, pulling them into mine as the city approaches and his caramel eyes track over my body. I know he wants me and if this is our only chance before Trevesiga is changed forever with our discovery then I want him to give in.

A white flash blinds me. Seconds later, an ear-splitting boom punches into my stomach. The ferry rocks and water splashes us. I get a sickening feeling I've missed something. Something essential. Eskar is staring wide-eyed at the islet behind me, horror written across his face.

I turn and my heart stutters. Black smoke curls over

the highest hill on the islet, silhouetted against the sunset. The hill that conceals my lab from Pentargon. It dawns on me. The serpentine. The bag Haelyn brought from the wreckage of Cedar's house. The one I assumed was a gruesome calling card, a personal note from Kitto to remind me of her reach. I never looked inside to see if the crystals were glowing. It was a trap. Wordlessly, Diogel turns us back round.

We leap off the boat as soon as it reaches the shallows. I wade ashore and sprint to the laboratory. Eskar eclipses me with his long strides.

The building is a shell: a blackened hole remains where the whole eastern side should be. Flames flicker at the edges of the broken roof. She charged the serpentine, knowing it would be brought to me. Knowing I would keep it, she hoped it would incinerate me.

There's no feeling of relief at our close escape, only a chilling reminder of her obsession. My body shivers with the ghost of a near miss. If we'd been a few minutes later leaving the island…

I pick through the wreckage, cataloguing the damage, looking for salvageable equipment and pieces of crystal among the debris. Our supply of serpentine is gone.

She told me she would do anything to get what she wants and now, after Eskar's torture, Cedar's kidnapping and the destroyed serpentine, I believe her.

Chapter 56

The next morning arrives and my anger has cooled to a bitter chill. I pound on the doors of the Concord chamber, demanding entrance. Dervla, Eskar and the King sit round the reflection pool, deep in conversation, the pool churning between them.

"Kitto needs to burn!" I don't bother with niceties or politeness. I'm fuelled by icy rage at the devastation of my laboratory, as we stood on the precipice of changing Trevesiga for the better, for everyone.

Dervla flinches at my violent statement but stands and gestures for me to take the seat next to her. "Sage, join us. We were just getting started." The King's face is back to his well-polished mask of neutrality, while Eskar's is tense.

Dervla continues, "I'm hoping you can shed light on the pyrotechnic display on the islet last night. The King requires an explanation."

I look to Eskar but he stays silent. "It was the Kevren Gwir." Dervla's eyes widen at my statement looking to Eskar for confirmation but I continue before he can interrupt.

"It was retribution for escaping. Kitto, their leader," I turn to the King to check he's keeping up, "is obsessed with bombs. She's working on the same research as me, but with a different objective in mind." I straighten my shoulders, refusing to give into the nerves swirling in my stomach. "My research was focused on imbuing magic into inanimate objects, allowing access to all. Democratising it."

"Was?" Dervla moves to the edge of her seat.

"We succeeded last night. I was coming back to tell you but the explosion happened on our way back from my laboratory on the islet. By the time we got back, I couldn't find either of you." The King and Dervla share a look but don't interrupt. "Cedar, my brother, is missing. Kitto left a bag of serpentine at his house. She wanted me to know she was behind his kidnapping. Haelyn bought it to the laboratory but we didn't realise the crystals in the bag were charged with magic. They exploded. If we'd been there at the time, we'd be dead."

Dervla falls silent and looks at me curiously. She and the King straighten and glance at each other as if my new information answers a question that's been bothering them for some time.

"I think we've found our traitor then, Your Highness," she says gravely, condemning Haelyn completely.

"Haelyn, my Archivist?" The King's condemnation sounds uneasy, as if he's struggling to align Haelyn as a rebel supporter.

"No, she wouldn't." I refuse to believe she would harm anyone. They're missing the point: Kitto is the enemy. Haelyn had no idea what the serpentine could do. But then I think of her reaction yesterday, how quickly she understood my research, and the smallest seed of doubt creeps in. If Haelyn is working with the rebels, then she's caught up in something far bigger than she realises. She would never hurt us or put herself in danger either.

"She's from Tanwen," Dervla mutters.

"But she was with us when the explosion happened! She wouldn't put herself in harm's way."

"Maybe Kitto didn't tell her what would happen. It would be a convenient way to tie up a loose end…" Dervla reaches for my hand and squeezes it gently before I can snatch it away.

Eskar's stubbornly watching the reflection pool simmer.

"Captain Devath, bring her in for questioning. I trust you can get to the bottom of it quickly," the King decrees, oblivious to Eskar's trembling, clenched fists.

"No! You can't torture her. Question her yourself. You can tell if she's lying." I can't bear for my friend to suffer the same fate I did.

The King fixes me with a frigid stare, pinning me in place. "Who told you that?"

"Does it matter?" I keep my gaze on him, steadfastly ignoring Dervla, whose face has paled.

"Fine. Bring her in now. We'll discuss your research later. I haven't forgotten." I tremble a little at his tone. It brokers no argument.

Before Eskar or Dervla can move, I leave and run straight for the library.

Haelyn's assessing the damage to a manuscript, a microscope monocle attached to her forehead, emphasising the lines of concentration. She's absorbed in her work, cataloguing each tiny tear and smudge so they can be repaired and preserved. I watch quietly for a moment, struggling to reconcile my friend with the rebel group who have hurt so many.

"Haelyn, I need to ask you something."

"Sage, how are you feeling after yesterday?" The microscope lens slips off her forehead, magnifying her already big brown eyes, making her look like a bug frozen in the face of a predator.

"The King and the Almanac think you're the traitor, that you've been working with the Kevren Gwir." My voice cracks as I evaluate her reaction. Despite advocating for her in the Concord chamber, that small flicker of doubt persists.

"No!" She stands abruptly, chair scraping the stone floor, making me wince. Covering her mouth, she sways, "I don't understand… I wouldn't…"

"I'm to bring you in for questioning. They've known about a traitor in the palace for some time and with your links to Tanwen and delivering the primed serpentine…" the implication sits heavy in the air.

She shakes, her breathing comes in quick, shallow pants, "They've got it all wrong. It wasn't me. Don't let Captain Devath take me." Her hands clutch my arms, nails scratching deep.

"Not Eskar, the King." I mean this to calm her, but it sends her further into hysteria.

"It's not me, it's not me!" In her desperation, her

breathing gets faster, each word sounds like a physical slice to her throat. Eventually it cracks; she can't speak, her lungs are working overtime, tears tracking down her face.

Her face reddens and swells with the effort of breathing properly; she scratches at her throat, eyes unfocused and fuzzy.

I can't stand seeing my friend so distraught. I shout for help and Eskar appears. Haelyn shrinks at his approach, clawing backwards and twisting desperately to get away from him. Her muscles disobey her, weak from a lack of oxygen; she's too far gone for me to calm her.

Eskar kneels before her and whispers his apologies as he cups her face with his hands, then there's silence. She slumps unconscious, her breathing eases and the redness drains from her face. The tear tracks remain, two rivers drying on her cheeks and down to her throat. He lifts her tiny frame and goes to carry her out of the room. I stop him. "What will the King do to her now?"

"He'll confirm the truth. His attitude can tell when people are lying." His attitude? Dread curdles in my stomach, good company for the heavy weight of grief I carry.

Chapter 57

My legs ache from pacing the antechamber outside the palace dungeons. The guards refuse to let me in, to confirm whether or not she's a traitor. I plan to stay here all night if I have to.

When I turn round for the hundredth time, a familiar silhouette leans against the ancient wood doorways. Dressed in his usual black and face clean-shaven.

"Dusk is coming." Eskar looks at me pointedly, somehow knowing I haven't had a chance to channel today.

I falter, not used to having someone to rely on. A fragile warmth settles in my chest at the secure feeling his presence gives me, temporarily papering over my worry for Haelyn. Despite the scowl on his face, I know he's angry at the King, not with me.

"Hi." I don't know what else to say, too distracted by the feelings he brings to the surface.

He pushes from the doorframe and sees my exhausted face and does something completely unexpected. His arms pull me close, wrapping round me, tucking my head under his chin. I lean close and his arms tighten in response and I feel him release a breath he was holding.

Neither of us is inclined to end the embrace, but eventually I pull away, tilting my head to smile at him.

"The King hasn't even come down to question her yet. Waiting is part of the process, to capitalise on the suspect's fear." His voice is grim, his distaste clear.

"I can't leave her down here alone." My voice echoes feebly down the stone corridor.

"The guards won't let you see her. The best thing you can do for Haelyn right now is to wait and let her prove her innocence." He looks at the guards, still standing to attention. "Come, you need some fresh air."

He keeps an arm over my shoulder, pressing me close to his side as he leads me through the palace in silence. We are both still on edge, Eskar scanning the faces of everyone we pass, looking for threats. I focus on the smooth tiled floor, counting my footsteps until we reach the wrought iron gates leading to the Koes Dowr.

"You don't believe Haelyn's the traitor?" I need to know he's on my side and that he doesn't hold my friend responsible for betraying us to the Kevren Gwir.

"No." The solemn set of his mouth hints at something more, something he doesn't want to share.

"But you have an idea who?"

"I wish I did." I track his features, unconvinced but not willing to press him.

"What do I do now?"

"What do you mean?"

"My brother is missing. The rebels have destroyed the

aqueducts that ensure we can survive and I admitted to the King that my research was illegal. Now I have no way to prove its value."

"Your research will be fine. The King will not punish you for that. It will give him hope."

I ponder his words as we make our way through to the garden, trying to reconcile the King's cold anger with the possibility that he might support our efforts publicly. As we cross the stone bridge, my hand brushes the back of his and I shiver. It may not be the time for distractions, but I can't help admire the dusky light reflecting off his dark hair. He's not mentioned the greenhouse since we arrived back in the city but the memory of that humid afternoon brings out goosebumps on my skin.

"You're cold?" He turns, frowning when he sees me shiver.

I shake my head, warmth creeping into my cheeks and I avoid his gaze. Instead, I focus on making my hands move, summoning magic to me. Eyes closing, I bask in the dying warmth of the day – anything to avoid addressing the kindling heat growing between us.

Night draws in and the songbirds fall quiet. The scent of blooming night phlox creeps around us and, when I open my eyes, Eskar is watching me like a predator from his seat on a smooth boulder near the water.

He stands, muscles moving under his shirt and my mouth dries. I refuse to concede any ground to him as he stalks towards me. His fingertips trace from the inside of my wrist to my shoulder. "Tell me what you want, Sage." His voice is a caress down my spine and I take a shuddering breath.

"I want to forget. About the King, Haelyn, the palace, all of it."

"I thought so." His hand falls alongside the breath I didn't realise I was holding. Wrong answer? I search his gaze, catching a fleeting look of something close to disappointment before he curls his lips into that insufferable smirk that used to drive me wild with irritation. Now it has me wanting to see more of it. After the tunnels in the Haag, I'll take his smirk, his smile, his laughter, anything to erase the lingering memory of his beaten and bloody body.

Something in me cracks at the thought of him enduring any more suffering and tears well beneath my eyelids. I look away, blinking to convince them not to fall. Eskar reaches out and turns my face to his.

"Low blow with the tears." His thumb brushes them away and he pulls me against his chest. I feel the press of his lips against my hair. Hidden in his embrace, I focus on taking deep breaths. We're safe. We escaped. Eskar continues to kiss my hair, my forehead, his hands run up and down my spine. My hands trail up his back, finally exploring the shoulders I've glimpsed the breadth of for months now. He tenses as my hands explore, but his lips continue to press to my temple and progress towards my neck. Without thinking, I turn my head away so as not to interrupt his progress, elongating my neck and baring it towards the gentle pressure of his lips.

Eskar groans and I feel its rumble deep within his

chest. "Tell me what you need." He murmurs, face buried in my hair.

"I need you to make me forget."

"Close enough." He tilts my head, capturing my mouth in a deep kiss. My hands grip his shoulders, eliminating any space between us. His palms cradle my cheeks, angling my face to his while his tongue teases my lips apart. My whole body is enveloped by his larger frame and yet I need more. I need him closer. My fingers wrap round the thick strands of his hair, only just long enough to grasp. Eskar responds by deepening the kiss, teasing my tongue with persistent strokes, increasing in urgency. He pulls us backwards and twists, lowering me slowly to the smooth rock below. Its warmth seeps through my clothes and is mirrored by the heat I feel from his body. My hands move from his hair and slip underneath his shirt, roaming across the hard planes of his stomach and up his chest. He breaks the kiss, nipping my lower lip gently.

"Careful, my restraint only stretches so far." A dangerous glint sparkles in his eyes as he presses against me. I can feel how much he wants this. How much he wants me. My hands curl round his neck, pulling him back into the kiss, losing myself in the feel of his lips on mine.

Eskar's hands tease along the curve of my hip, towards my breasts. He breaks our kiss, eyes questioning. I smile and nod, desperate for him to continue. He doesn't move until my hands tease at the belt on his hips. A feral grin appears and my hands are captured, pinned by rings of water. He backs off, one hand unbuckling his belt while the other pulls his shirt over his head, baring his muscled chest at last. Wrists pinned, my eyes rake over his body, drinking in the dips and hard lines. I like what I see and pull at his restraints, needing to ease the growing heat.

"I hope I'm not interrupting anything… important," a rich, deep voice calls through the wooded glen.

We freeze, ice drips down my spine and the King steps out of the darkness.

Eskar groans loudly into my shoulder, moving so he's shielding me from the King's gaze while I straighten my clothes. The heat that surrounded us both just moments ago extinguishes at the unwelcome interruption.

"Verax, I need you." Eskar straightens at the command and his eyes grow cold and hard, the mask of King's torturer and truth-seeker settles over his face. He turns from me, all passion and tenderness extinguished. Panic closes around me when I remember who the King has locked in the dungeons. The person he plans to command Eskar to extract information from.

"No!" my shout echoes off the leafy canopy, birds scattering, screeching into the night sky. The King can't ask Eskar to hurt Haelyn. "You promised you wouldn't hurt her. You said you would do it yourself."

"Sage, stop. He's the King," Eskar interrupts.

"I need answers; we're running out of time." The King's hands are buried deep in his pockets, his shoulders tense. "If she won't talk then I have no way of knowing what she did." He dismisses me and gestures for Eskar to follow him.

"Then let me speak to her," I plead. "You can listen and no one needs to get hurt." I glare at Eskar to keep quiet; he has to know I'm fighting for him here too.

The pause stretches. The King's face is blurred by the shadows but Eskar's is rigid, mask still in place.

"Very well. You have one chance." We move to follow the King from the garden, but he turns to Eskar, snapping, "It looks like neither of us have need of you right now, Verax. You can remain here." Eskar jolts, the verbal slap ricocheting hard across his body and my eyes are full of regret as I leave him behind in the garden, following the King to help Haelyn.

On the walk back to Chi An Mor my mind seethes, yet my body is still wired from Eskar's kisses. The frustration of unfulfilled promise manifests as rage. The King must sense my growing anger because he pauses before entering the palace and turns, blocking my way forward. We linger outside the large doorway as the cold evening chill steals the heat from my skin. The palace is quiet: we've encountered no one else. The King hesitates briefly, casting his eyes up and down my face before he speaks. "I suppose it would be too much to expect you to be grateful after I spared the Verax on your behalf?"

"How dare you refuse to use his name after everything he's done in yours." I lean towards him but he stands firm.

"Seducing you in my private garden was not done

with my name in mind." His words are measured and cold, callous.

"That's none of your business," my cheeks redden.

"Neither is yours regarding my relationship with other Concord members."

"But you grew up together. You used to be friends."

"Is that what he told you?" he scoffs.

I glare mutely at him.

"Ah. Dervla. Yes well, I'm sure she spun quite the tale." He rakes a hand through his hair and regards me warily. "Perhaps I'll tell you my side of the story one day… Maybe over dinner?"

It takes me several seconds to register the question. Not an order, definitely a request. Or the closest approximation that a royal Mordros could ever manage.

Before I can respond, the King huffs and turns from me. Silently we walk through the palace together, my mind spinning wildly.

Chapter 58

Dungeons have no business being wet. I doubt any other dungeons in Trevesiga or elsewhere are quite this damp. I'm aware I'm fixating on the water droplets trickling down the wall and the slimy residue that clings to my skin, instead of replaying scenes from my nightmares of the old Almanac forcing Eskar to torture me. It nearly works, before my magic perceives the rocky cells as a threat and tries to break out. My heart hammers loudly in my ears as I fight to bring it under control. The last thing Haelyn needs is me spooking the guards with a light show. I'll be thrown in the cell next to hers, King's favourite or not. And there's no denying Cado's favouritism now, not with his invitation lingering over me. As if we're not on the brink of civil war.

I tiptoe round the huge puddles coating the floor, avoiding drips from the ceiling. The cells are built into the rock and we must be underneath the riverbed as water is seeping through the stone roof, its incessant dripping making my skin crawl. It is a bit of an oversight, holding prisoners with so much water around but then I realise the Mordros likely wouldn't ever be imprisoned. They would be allowed to remain under house arrest on their fancy islets, or their summer houses, if they ever stepped out of line.

Huddling in the corner of her cell, Haelyn flinches as the light from the guard's torch illuminates her face. She looks unharmed, but cold and dishevelled. Her normally neat and tidy plait is undone and deep shadows underscore her brown eyes. I'm not allowed to touch her; the guard makes it clear if I step too far inside her cell then the unoccupied one next door will be mine.

"Are you okay?" I whisper, leaning further into the cell, inwardly suppressing my magic as it rebels from being enclosed. Her large eyes stare at me, unblinking.

"Haelyn, I'm so sorry. I need to ask you some questions. If you can answer me truthfully then the King will let you go." I cast a look over my shoulder and meet Cado's eyes. He fixes me with a blunt stare, seeming to ask what I will give him in return for his compassion, for letting me see my friend. I narrow my eyes – we can discuss his terms later but Haelyn will walk out of here with me once she's proved her innocence.

I turn back to her, attempting a weak smile. "Please Haelyn. I need you to talk to me, then this will all be over." I reach for her hand. "Trust me."

It takes only a few answers before I turn back to the King, convinced of Haelyn's innocence. I don't expect an apology but he surprises me by coming into the cell and gesturing to the guards to close the door, sealing us in.

"My apologies to you will have to wait, Archivist. I'm sorry to ask but I need Haelyn to remain here for the time being." I open my mouth to protest, but the King holds up a hand, silencing me before looking directly at Haelyn. "I still believe there's a traitor in the palace. I need time to work out who it is and, right now, the circle of people I trust is small." Haelyn slumps against the wall, the spark of hope in her eyes extinguished as though her torment has just begun.

"I'll make sure the guards treat you well. It will only be for a few weeks at most."

"Weeks!" I exclaim in horror before lowering my voice. "She cannot be expected to remain down here for weeks. She's a member of the Concord!"

"It will be less if she consents to help me." Cado turns back to Haelyn and says, "I need your help understanding Tanwen's layout. Dervla has received news that the Kevren Gwir have moved to a new base there with the locals' support."

"That doesn't surprise me. The locals would be happy to support anyone with money and a reason for them to fight." These are the first words she's willingly spoken to him so far and her voice threatens to crack.

"I need your opinion on where they would have their headquarters. And if there's a route I can use to send in a small group of fighters unnoticed."

I wait patiently, not wanting to influence her thinking anymore.

"Can I have a pen and some paper? It's complicated to describe."

The King is prepared and pulls a sheet and pens from his pocket. I jump forward to hand them to her. We watch silently as she sketches.

Eventually she chews the pen thoughtfully and adds in one more section before spinning it round.

"Here – the town splits in two with the market in the middle." She gestures to the map. "Most houses are here, shops and grain stores here, closer to the Haag. If I was leading the rebels, I'd camp out here." She points to a few grain stores. "Anyone approaching the town will have to go through the residential area first, so the rebels have a wall of civilians to hide behind." I nod. "Remember, strangers are immediately recognised in Tanwen. Even if my knowledge is a little out of date, that fact won't have changed."

"And, if we wanted to get in undetected?" Cado's eyes fix on the crude map, as if committing every street to memory.

"Practically impossible. Originally, I'd have said the aqueduct would have been the best option as it's so rarely used, but now…"

I ponder what she's said, the aqueduct system is drained but not impassable at Tanwen.

"A small group of soldiers could make their way along the empty stone channels if the structure is still intact." My finger traces Haelyn's pen strokes. "The watchtower will likely be manned but is too small a space for a large number of guards."

"Thank you, Archivist." Ignoring my input, Cado

cuts the conversation abruptly before we can discuss tactics any further. "That's all I need. I promise you will be released soon."

"You have a plan?" I question after we've left the dank cells behind and climbed up through the floors of the palace.

"Yes, and I will need your support." With a cryptic expression, the King disappears into his private wing. I stare at his closed door for some time.

Chapter 59

Sleep is impossible with the memory of Eskar's touch in the Koes Dowr and I throw my covers off in frustration. Moonlight illuminates my path through Chi An Mor as I wander the hallways lost in thought. Eskar's rooms tempt me, but their location is a mystery, I don't know what reception I would receive if I asked to pick up where we left off earlier.

He's made it clear that he wants me and not just for a night, whereas I'm reluctant to take that step. Not because I have another option. I laugh as I recall the King's bizarre request for dinner earlier. It feels so wrong to be consumed by thoughts of a relationship when my brother is missing, my good friend is imprisoned and the rebels are plotting to destroy Trevesiga. I have more important things to do than give in to the temptation he brings.

I stop wandering aimlessly and turn sharply to Dervla's rooms. She will be awake at this hour. We need to make a plan.

"Who is it?" Dervla calls from behind her door as I pound on the wood.

"It's me. Let me in!"

"Oh Sage, come in." The door creaks open and I slip inside.

The room is lit by hundreds of small, tapered candles, placed round her desk and on the surrounding shelves. Their flickering glow emphasises Dervla's ashen skin: she's exhausted. Kaens perches on the windowsill, head tucked under one wing. She cracks open one beady eye at my entrance, clicks her beak and retreats under her feathers.

"Ignore her; she's grouchy and tired this evening. Her wings need a rest." Dervla strokes Kaens before turning back and passing me a glass of wine.

"How did the interrogation with Haelyn go earlier? I heard you convinced the King that Eskar wasn't required and I believe you owe the King a private dinner?" She raises her eyebrows archly.

I open my mouth to argue that I haven't agreed to anything with the King but notice her crack a rare smile. We burst out laughing and the tension that's lingered unspoken between us since my return dissipates.

"I missed you," I admit. "We could have done with an extra pair of hands in the Haag."

"You escaped; that's what matters," she counters, reaching to hold my hand. The simple gesture relaxes me, grounding me in the candlelight. The mists of the Haag feel further away.

"But now our stock of serpentine has been destroyed. We need more if we're going to stop the rebels."

"I think the time to stop them without resorting to bloodshed has passed. The Concord are meeting tomorrow to vote on how to handle them. I think it'll be unanimous."

"What will they suggest?" I think of Ciaren and how he helped me escape, how I promised to make his case that not all the rebels wanted to attack the cities or harm anyone.

She sighs, the whole weight of Trevesiga heavy on her shoulders. "The King's Admiral has the most support. He wants to take the Navy up the river as close to Tanwen as possible and wipe the whole town off the map."

"That's barbaric. Children were running between the market stalls when we first arrived. The town is still full of innocent people." Even if some of those, adults and children, are in league with the Kevren Gwir.

"I know, but what other choice do we have? We've underestimated them for the last time. Thousands of people will suffer and die this winter thanks to the destruction of the aqueducts. We don't know what they have planned next."

"I'll vote against it." My hand tightens around my wine glass.

"I know you will. As will Eskar, I'm sure." I don't know that he will. I think of the state of his body after the torture and the townspeople who tried to pass us over to the rebels. What I do know is that he just wants this to be over.

"And how will you vote?" I ask pointedly.

"I will vote in the best interest of the kingdom. And

I will carry out the orders of the majority." Her voice is a cold monotone. She will be complicit in the slaughter of innocents then. White hot rage boils up my throat. I turn and throw my wine glass at the wall. It shatters, staining the sandstone blood red.

"You're a terrible politician, Sage." Dervla regards me with a half-smile, lounging back in her chair. "I didn't say that was the only thing I would do." I freeze at her implication, my fury cooling.

"You have a plan?"

"Of course. I always have a plan. Although, right now the King thinks it's his, thanks to your little visit to the dungeon…" Her dark eyes roll and she pulls the leather gauntlets off her wrists. Settling into the sofa, she pours herself another glass of wine but doesn't offer me a replacement. Fair enough – I won't apologise for the one I wasted.

Before speaking, she surveys me like a panther regarding a worthy opponent that's crossed into its territory. "I will need your complete compliance here, Sage. You've always trusted me before, I need to know that hasn't changed."

I nod; I would follow her anywhere. Without her, I'd still be cleaning the fallout from failed experiments from the floors for Principal Alemond back in Athnavar, unable to secure a permanent research position. With her and my research, we will change Trevesiga for the better.

"We desperately need to send support to Cathair if the flooding and destruction is as bad as you described. The Navy is a formidable force but they can be spoilt and complacent. Over land, they are untested. With the rivers running low after the glacial melt and no aqueducts to use, travel will be slow and arduous after Cathair. I plan to leave at least half of them in the city to help rescue people and secure food and water supplies. The rest, we take to Tanwen as the King's Admiral suggests. Keeping them motivated and battle-ready on the journey should be enough to keep the King and the rest of the Concord occupied."

Swirling her wine glass thoughtfully, she continues. "By the time they reach Tanwen, they will be tired, disorganised and at risk of defeat from a desperate town with nothing to lose and no love for the King. The Admiral is arrogant; he won't see the townspeople, or the rebels as a threat. That arrogance will cost them." Her gaze travels to the window, staring out into the blackness before she continues, "I'm proposing that a small, select group of trained warriors, or perhaps only one, travels ahead to Tanwen, searches out Kitto and assassinates her. The rebels will fall into disarray without their leader and once the King and navy arrive, they will surrender. We can commandeer their supply of serpentine and return to Pentargon. Winter will still be brutal but having access to more magic, specifically Mordros magic via the serpentine crystals, will help the people survive until Spring."

Kaens shifts on her perch, tucking her head further under her wing. Her plan is simple but I sense one flaw.

"How will you explain the disappearance of some of your best fighters? Did you say only one…?" my voice falters.

"That's where you come in, Sage." Her face twists into a dark grin. "I knew you wouldn't like it."

My stomach drops. "You want me to convince Eskar to go back to Tanwen, don't you? He's the best fighter we have."

She nods. "Plus, he can identify Kitto; that is essential."

"And if he fails?" I let the question hang in the air. The pause stretches out. Several candles flicker and drip wax onto the reams of paper and technical drawings on her desk.

"Then, as the King's Admiral declares: the full force of Trevesiga's Navy will annihilate the rebels while they sleep, and the townspeople that helped them." Her voice is grim.

"In return, I want him released from his obligation as the King's torturer. He will no longer be forced to use his attitude."

"You want him to give up his position on the Concord?"

"No, that's his decision to make. I want you and the King to promise he won't be required to use his magic to harm people once this mission is over."

Dervla peers at me. I hold my breath while she deliberates. "Agreed."

Steely resolve fills my body; there will be no more bloodshed than absolutely necessary. After this, Eskar will be free.

"Tell me how to get to his rooms?"

Dervla nods but doesn't smile as she explains.

Chapter 60

I bang loudly on Eskar's door, not caring who hears me.

"Sage, what are you doing here?" Once he sees its me, he pulls the door wide. It's late and I've dragged him from sleep. His chest is bare, hair dishevelled. The urge to run my hands through those soft strands almost distracts me.

"I came to find you. I've…" I'm suddenly ashamed that I negotiated something so critical without his permission or consent.

"I spoke with Dervla and with the King. They have a plan."

He pulls me into his room. "I know," he interrupts. "The King came by earlier; he wanted my opinion on infiltrating Tanwen."

I can't read his face, the political mask is in place. "Oh. What did you say?"

"That the town is impenetrable. The town gates are too high and well-manned. The mists mean you'd lose yourself rather than sneak in through that side. Then he suggested the old aqueduct channels…" He stops and pins me in place with those caramel eyes. "That was your idea, wasn't it? There's no way he could have come up with that on his own."

"Haelyn's, actually."

He scoffs, "So, we're going to take the advice of a prisoner?" He paces back and forth.

"She's innocent. I know it. The King believes her too." He's not convinced, a crack slipping through his normal facade.

"What was so important that you had to tell me now? That you couldn't wait until morning?"

"Dervla has given her word on behalf of the King. They have agreed to free you from using your attitude on condition you complete the mission in Tanwen and assassinate Kitto."

He stills and the temperature in the room drops. I wonder if I've crossed some line, using his attitude as a bargaining chip.

"You made this agreement?"

"They're determined you'll go. You're the best fighter we have. I negotiated something in return." His eyes are wide, focussed on every word, as if struggling to comprehend.

"As soon as you return, you have your freedom."

Something flickers deep in his caramel eyes and he turns sharply. "You could have asked for anything."

"I know." I shrug, then gasp as he closes the distance between us, all pretence of hiding behind his political mask gone. His tall height and broad frame block my vision; he is all I can see. His presence demands my full attention. I'm lost for words. His hands stroke the sides of my face and travel over my shoulders before he leans in to kiss me. It's not the passionate kiss of earlier. This is more. His lips caress mine, worshipping my face, my neck, my shoulders, thanking me in ways he couldn't possibly explain. Relief courses through me and I return the exploration, fingernails digging into his broad shoulders as he pulls me to the large bed behind him.

We tumble onto it, limbs tangling as I press myself against him. Letting our bodies speak for us, we pick up where we left off this afternoon, entangled in each other.

He breaks the kiss, breathing heavily. "I am forever grateful. They would never consider it before."

"You don't know that: you never asked. Either way, they've agreed now. They're desperate." I swallow the pit in my stomach at the thought of him in servitude for so long.

"Regardless, I have you to thank." He tugs me towards him, lying my body along his side so he's free to kiss me, his hands trailing up and down my skin. The gentle caresses across my ribs and back have me squirming. Heat pools in my stomach. I can't think when he's touching me like this. His hands slide round my waistband and dip below but I pull back.

"So, when will you leave? Who will you take with you?"

He chuckles, "Not so easily distracted then." He resumes kissing down my neck. "Tomorrow morning. The sooner the better. I need to finish this."

I pull his face away and silence the groan building in

my stomach. "You'll go alone?"

"I work better alone." A careless shrug, he pulls away from my hands and from the bed as the tension cools between us.

His eyes are the warm caramel I remember from the greenhouse but edged with something darker now. The weight of what he's been asked to attempt has shuttered the light in them.

"You don't have to do this alone."

"I do. I'm not risking anyone else being caught in the crossfire."

I follow him to the window where he stares into the inky blackness. When he doesn't move, I reach to stroke his face. How he can still be so compassionate for others after how the King and the Mordros have treated him is beyond me.

"Let me at least try and return your magic; you can't fight the Kevren Gwir, and Kitto when you're not at full strength."

"No." He pulls me close, pressing me tightly against his warm chest. "I can live without it but I don't trust anyone else. I'll sleep better knowing you have some of my protection, even when I'm gone."

My throat tightens and I struggle to form the words to tell him I understand what he's saying, that again he's putting my life before his. I pull his face towards mine, capturing his lips softly. "I understand. I'll be there as soon as it's done. The King will need my help to retrieve the serpentine."

He kisses me back, wrapping me tightly in his arms. "Then we have tonight."

Chapter 61

His hands trail a path from my shoulders to my waist, gripping tightly when they reach my trousers. His caramel eyes meet mine, questioning. I pull his lips to mine, kissing him soundly in response. If we only have tonight, then I'm done talking.

My hands dive into his thick hair, tugging his head to one side so I have better access to his mouth. His lips are soft but soon lose their gentleness as he deepens the kiss, reigniting the heat from earlier in the Koes Dowr. With no one to interrupt us now, he kisses me leisurely, cupping my face. I press my body into his, wanting to feel every hard line of muscle.

His hands roam under my clothes, tugging and pulling them over my head until I stand completely naked in front of him. A scorching fervour radiates from his bare chest to mine as he walks me backwards to the wall. The cool stone pressing into my back calms me enough to concentrate on removing his clothes. They too hit the floor and the sound causes Eskar to break our kiss, eyes glazed. He tilts my head and works his way along the length of my neck, across my collarbones, to my breasts. My back arches and I press towards his touch, wanting, needing to be closer. He chuckles at my movements; hands gripping my wrists and pinning them to the wall, he sinks to his knees. I have no illusions now about who is in control, despite him kneeling before me. His pace slows, and heat builds in my body; anticipating the next kiss or lick is agonising as he descends down my stomach. His soft hair tickles my ribcage as he worships my skin. I tug at my restrained wrists, wanting to touch him, to run my hands down his muscled back.

A deep chuckle whispers over my skin and my breath catches at the sensation.

"Use your words, Sage," his hands tighten slightly, letting me know he has no intention of letting me go. Not unless I beg him to.

"I want more," my throat is dry, my body flooded with desire. I shift my weight between my feet, desperate to ease the tension inside my stomach as his mouth lowers slightly, tantalisingly close to where I need him, before returning to my breasts. The sensation is frustratingly close to perfect but it's not enough.

"Like this?" his tongue flicks across my nipple and my legs give out. His chest presses me into the wall, refusing to let me sink to the floor.

"More," I don't recognise the husky tone coming from my mouth and feel my cheeks redden. I stumble as he pulls away slightly and gives me a small reprieve before his lips return to my body.

"Like this?" Eskar's lips travel down, pausing briefly at my hipbone before reaching my centre. Everything in the room disappears when I feel his hot breath on my skin; my head falls back, focusing only on remaining standing and the sensations he's creating.

"Yes."

One of his hands frees my wrist and I bury my fingers deep in his hair, guiding his head to where I need to feel his lips the most. He lifts my knee over his shoulder, granting him better access as I feel his tongue part my folds and glance over my clit. He takes his time with me, kissing and licking until I'm so tightly wound that I can't focus on standing. My overheated skin warms the wall behind me and, as my leg trembles, he pulls away briefly, blowing softly on my exposed clit. His gaze rises to meet mine and he smirks. My stomach heats in response. He is so devastatingly gorgeous.

Eskar returns to kissing and sucking, stroking me in a way that causes pressure to build low in my hips. I squirm against the intensity of his touch, not wanting to give in, wanting to savour this moment. His body fixes me in place, demanding I feel everything that he is giving me. The pressure continues to build and his name slips from my lips, again and again. The remaining restraint falls away and I hear him moan deeply, the sensation driving me closer to the edge.

His kisses are relentless. I force my lungs to keep breathing, my focus consumed with the sensation between my thighs. Pressure swells and my hands hold his head in place, desperate for him to continue his ministrations. He doesn't cease and continues to drive me towards the edge, maintaining the rhythm that drives all coherent thought from my head. I tilt my hips a fraction and stars erupt across my vision as I come apart. His tongue expertly guides me through wave after wave of pleasure. The room blackens as my eyes drift closed, lungs fighting for breath.

Eskar carefully lowers my leg to the ground and peels me off the wall, strong hands catching my swaying body before guiding me towards his bed. He lays me down softly and positions himself at my side, his hands running up and down my skin, bringing me down from my climax. I watch his eyes take in my body, spread out next to him, following the trail of his hands over my fevered skin.

My breath back under control, I turn to face him, searching for a glimmer of regret in his eyes. I know he wants more from me, but this is all I can offer right now: my body and a momentary distraction from the precarious chaos around us. Finding none, I lean towards him, placing a kiss above his heart. He lets me push him on to his back, his length still hard and I cast my gaze along his body. The bruises are fading, the lacerations healing, soon all marks from our time together in the Haag will disappear – leaving pure muscled perfection behind. I run my fingers lightly over his flushed skin, goosebumps pebble under my touch. He tucks his hands behind his head, content to let me explore and I feel myself return his smirk. I'm going to return the favour. He's not leaving this bed until he begs me to let him come.

I trail my fingers down his chest, lightly over his stomach and stop just above his cock. Eskar exhales loudly and tenses. "I'm warning you, it's been a while since anyone's touched me like that." Good. I like the thought of having him all to myself.

I wrap my hand around his length, watching his reaction. He fixes his eyes on my hand as it moves up and down, twisting slightly. I catch myself smiling when he hisses through his teeth and lets his head fall back on to the pillow. I pick up the pace, enjoying wringing moans from his lips. Then I stop abruptly.

His eyes pop open, "You cruel woman." I smile innocently, pretending I have no idea what he's talking about and resume my stroking. Each time I feel him approach the edge, I freeze, allow him to catch his breath before continuing. I want him begging.

"Please. Don't stop. I can't… I need…" the words tumble out between moans of ecstasy and I remove my hand entirely. Eskar's eyes snap open, his pupils dilated as I straddle his hips leaving inches between us. I reach down with one hand to touch myself, smearing wetness all over my fingers. His biceps flex, fingers gripping the bedsheet, knuckles white. Unable to keep teasing us both, I lower slightly, positioning his cock at my entrance, using my hips to roll the tip over my clit.

One of us moans loudly, and I feel my eyes roll back in my head, revelling in the sensation.

"Please," he rasps, hands now on my thighs. He doesn't take away my control but there's coiled desperation in his fingertips as they press into my heated skin.

I arch my back, letting my hair graze the tops of my shoulders as I sink down onto him. His cock fills me completely. I take a moment to catch my breath at the most glorious sensation of stretching and adjust. Then I begin to move.

Acting on instinct, my hips roll towards him, angling him deeper inside. Our gazes lock and I feel a light sheen of sweat develop across my chest. His hands don't leave my hips, letting me set the pace. The familiar sense of pressure returns, slowly building in my lower stomach. I move faster, hands steadying myself on his shoulders. Our lips meet briefly, but cannot linger, concentrating on the sensations growing between us. I hear him call my name and feel his legs tense. I freeze, not wanting it to end yet, loving the control.

"Sage!" he shouts, voice hoarse.

"Not yet," I chuckle, leaning back a little. He swears loudly and watches as I take one hand to my clit and circle it gently.

The sensation of touching myself whilst he is buried deep inside me has my body clenching. I rock back and forth, focusing on the pressure building until I can't control myself anymore. I erupt, my vision splintering and I scream. My hips continue to move through the savage waves of pleasure that run through me. Eskar's hands find them, setting the rhythm he needs and pounding inside me until he comes. We both collapse, panting, bodies shaking from our orgasms. I crumple onto to the mattress.

A while later, Eskar's breathing steadies. He turns to me, "You're going to pay for that." We laugh and he rolls on top of me, bracketing me with his arms and capturing my mouth in a deep kiss.

Chapter 62

Dew soaks my shoes and trouser legs and the long grass tickles as I head for the Koes Dowr. What was a beautiful, manicured garden when I arrived has now bloomed into a teeming jungle. I search for my favourite worn stone and set myself up to think. Eskar left early this morning. No goodbye, no ceremony, just a cool indentation in the bed next to me and an unspoken promise that, when he returns, things will be different. He will be able to leave Pentargon. To return to Cathair and become a teacher like he's always wanted. He asked me to come with him last night, in between kisses that wiped away my brain's ability to reason. Even then, something in me resisted. I don't know that I want to leave Pentargon, to leave my research, my position behind.

I pick at the skin round my nails, picturing Eskar sailing to Porth to begin his trek to Tanwen – alone and with assassination on his mind. I wish he didn't have to shoulder that burden alone. From reluctant torturer to begrudging assassin, he's more than earned his freedom once this is over and I won't allow the court to hold him back.

Worried as I am, unable to calm my mind and control my emotions, I settle instead to practising my magic. Now I understand how the little strand from Eskar works, I'm able to call it forward with ease. Even though it saved me in Cathair, it's barely depleted. The vast depth of magic held in one Mordros strand is staggering. I need to feel close to him today and reach for it inside my chest.

I visualise a floating sphere of water and pull the magic forward. When it's clear in front of me, I try to make it spin. It's sloppy work, flecks of water spin out as it turns. Soon, I'm soaked through as if I have rolled in the dew like a child. But the sphere holds.

It helps to focus on something tangible. I draw out my light as well, causing the water to throw rainbows across the clearing and admiring how well they work together.

"Perhaps the King's Thief would be a more appropriate title." Dark humour from a voice that breaks my focus surprises me. My sphere of water absorbs into my lap as I look up at the King, leaning against a tree, arms crossed.

He doesn't look angry but he definitely doesn't look pleased either. "Now, are you going to tell me how you managed to steal Mordros magic?"

"Snooping isn't a very regal trait." I shrug, buying time.

"No need to snoop when an aurora appears in my garden. You need to be more careful there." His mouth is a thin line as he scours the tree-line behind us, checking we are alone.

The rainbows – I can't exactly argue there. I shouldn't have been so foolish. "I was experimenting."

"I can see that. More forbidden research?"

"It's not stealing if I intend to return it. By definition, stealing is permanent deprivation." I summon little balls of light to dance round him, trying to distract him but they flicker as my magic exhausts itself.

"Did the person give it willingly then?" If his right eyebrow goes any higher, it'll be lost under his dark fringe.

"Does it matter if I didn't intend to take it?" A bird call overhead punctuates my response.

Concern flashes through his eyes and he stalks closer to whisper. "Can you control it? I can't have you wielding magic wherever you turn."

Fair point. "Yes, I can control it. The circumstances where I obtained it were unique." I blush. "I've been trying to return it but also learning how to make it respond to me."

"Hmm, well, for now, given everything that's going on, I'd put that aside. I don't think you quite realise the danger you put yourself in practising in the open." His hands ball into fists before he slips them into his pockets.

"Speaking of danger in Chi An Mor, I want to come with you to Tanwen. No one else will be able to identify the serpentine. I'll be an asset."

"I don't doubt that, Sage." His deep green eyes hold mine intently. "Don't you trust me to do the right thing?" His voice is barely a whisper.

I don't. Not even the slightest bit. He might think he's helping or trying to make things better but his perspective is so limited and our situation so fragile. "I want to help." Not technically a lie.

His mouth twists, recognising I've avoided a direct answer.

He's hurt. But then the practised courtier is back and he's a blank canvas again.

"If you insist: be ready to depart in a few days." Turning, he walks off with no further comment.

Chapter 63

Leaving Pentargon to meet the King's Navy off the coast of Porth was simple enough. The King commandeered a ferry for those Concord members travelling with us. There was a significant debate about the King's attendance: most of the Concord preferred he stay safely ensconced in the palace but he refused to call a vote and made his own decision. As we travel along the coast, his face becomes lighter the further we get from the capital, whereas Dervla's becomes more grave. We meet the Navy at Porth and it's clear the fleet will struggle to travel all the way inland. The river is low and boats are scarce.

Dervla calculates supplies, rations, everything that will be required for the long trek to Tanwen and has no problem convincing the King and his Admiral that some of the Navy should remain in Cathair once we arrive. The journey will get harder after that.

Meticulously planted hanging baskets and window flowers that should still be in bloom have been ripped from the walls and swept away. The people we see in Cathair, peering from shattered ground floor windows, have cracked fingernails from digging in the mud for possessions, for family members and treasured animals. Their eyes are hollow and judging. We left them here to suffer the floods alone. I let Eskar convince me that the city had plans for flooding, that the people would be alright, but I think even he miscalculated the raging tsunami that would ravage the city. Up in the clefts of the valley, I make out his family estate. No longer standing in the shadow of the aqueduct, it appears undamaged, walls still glistening pearly white. I wonder how many Mordros families opened their doors to those in need during the devastation? From the looks on the faces of the people we pass, it wasn't enough.

The Navy gets straight to work, setting up search parties and organising shelter for those that are displaced. The hubbub of activity will have to suffice as our only cover as a smaller group leave the city for Tanwen. From here we will have to go on foot, the river will carry our supplies as far as possible but we will need to walk and ride on horseback.

The terrain is tough going, the ground cracked and dusty from lack of rain. Heavy clouds cover the sky, thick enough to depress the feeling of summer but not enough to give us the precipitation we need.

Twice, our horses have to be swapped out en route due to exposed tree roots tripping them. At one point, we are stuck for hours as a wagon wheel comes loose on the gritty stones and the men struggle to refit it. It's clear Dervla was right: the Navy is used to being at sea, not on land.

Signs of the aqueduct failing become more apparent

the further we travel, the roads are quieter and we're told people are beginning to hoard water. There's no longer any guarantee of a welcome reception at the next village.

Our final camp – in the impenetrable forest outside Tanwen – is miserable. The clearing we occupy is bleak. Here, autumn has come early. With little rain and scorched earth, everything smells of overripe berries left to fester. The mood of the Navy is equally sour: days of travelling have given many blisters and sore muscles. It's clear we are a pampered lot by the disgruntled moaning whispered in corners. Our numbers are about a third of those we set off with, the dire need for support in Cathair and demand for discretion whittling down the troops. The King's Admiral remained in Cathair, overseeing the troops; Cado and Dervla continued with us to Tanwen.

An old tree stump is cleared of crispy yellow moss and serves as the table for our makeshift war room. We pin Haelyn's crude map across its surface, disturbing beetles. The tree sap curdles the paper. I'm sure Cado knows this map better than the palace floor plan by now; his thoroughness is reassuring. Arguments ensue as the rest of the Concord are made aware of Eskar's mission. Nothing was discussed until now because we weren't sure who we could trust.

After their initial outrage, they want to march on Tanwen now, trusting that Eskar will be able to escape in the melée. That's not a chance I'm prepared to take, and reassuringly neither is Cado nor Dervla.

A scouting mission is needed before any further

decision can be made. Cado summons one of the sailors to join the Concord around the tree stump.

"Follow the town wall until the mists, then make your way into town through the gates facing the Haag. Try to blend in with the townspeople; they will likely be taking shipments of serpentine into the town daily from the mines, so there will be plenty of rebels around. We just need eyes on Captain Devath," the King instructs the scout who nods, his face burnt from the summer sun and makes to leave camp. Kaens is primed to fly between the scout and our camp to relay their messages.

When she returns late into the night, her haunting cry wakes me from a light sleep. I push back the heavy canvas tent flaps to hear the message.

Cado addresses the group gathered in the tent, his solemn face lit by a flickering table lamp. "The scout's reports are concerning. He described more activity than we expected; the rebels are openly stockpiling the serpentine and preparing to leave the town. We need to find Captain Devath before they abandon their base. I'm sending more scouts now. We should know more in the morning."

I nod and look at Dervla, signalling back to our tent to see if she's going to join me. She shakes her head, forehead creased and her attention goes back to studying the map of Tanwen in front of her, fingers worrying the strap of her leather gauntlet while Kaens rests her head on Dervla's shoulder.

Chapter 64

I wake disoriented. There's a hush outside the tent wall that is unnerving. Not even a bird calls overhead. The canvas tent flaps softly. Dervla has gone. A fleeting panic that I've been abandoned while the Navy marches on Tanwen has me ripping open the tent door. I'm greeted with the backs of sailors, crowded in front of Cado's tent, all standing to attention. A solemn formation, some are in full uniform, most are half-dressed as if they were commanded from their beds.

Not a single person turns or moves as I push my way forward, skirting through the rows.

The scout's voice travels lonely on the air ahead and I make my way towards him.

"No sign at all your Highness, until this morning. Right when we were about to leave, we saw him." His voice is grave and the sailors gathered round the tree stump part to let me through.

"You're sure?" Cado's voice is deathly soft as I finally reach the front. He stands tall, spine straight but his face is leached of colour, mouth pressed in a firm line. Dervla stands to his left, shoulders hunched forward, hands clasping the leather gauntlets round her forearms. Neither react to my approach.

"Certain," the scout replies. "The rebels were expecting us and wanted us to know it. They used him as a signal."

My heart is in my throat. An icy trail of dread floods my body. I take my place at Dervla's side, eyes fixed on the familiar cloak. It lies on the mossy tree stump, covering something large.

Dervla's gaze is fixed ahead, staring over the heads of the sailors and out towards the tree-line. Under my breath, I ask what's happened. She shakes her head and I see tears well in the corners of her eyes. Her hand stifles what I think is a sob before she turns and pushes her way out of the crowd.

Cado sees her move and gestures to one of the sailors to follow. When he sees me at his side, his gaze changes, becoming hardened and unyielding.

I don't see the command for others to disperse but the sailors file away, leaving Cado and me alone, standing next to the covered stump.

"Did you betray us to the rebels?" Gone is his melodic, honeyed voice, it's replaced by a deeper, harsher tone.

"No, never. What's happened?"

"Do you know who did?" His unearthly, cold voice scratches like gravel down my spine.

"No. What's wrong?" I barely hear myself whisper, eyes still trapped on the tree stump.

He pauses at my response, anger dissolving. His face is stripped bare of the political blankness and has a look that approaches pity, as if he would like to unknow what has happened today.

"He's dead."

My lungs freeze in shock; my knees start to buckle. "Eskar?"

"Our scouts saw his body fixed to the watchtower walls this morning." He speaks gently, raising his deep green eyes to mine, the bruises underneath them wet.

"There wasn't a mark on him, not one that could have killed him anyway. I think he was suffocated. That is Kitto's trademark, after all." He walks forward and pulls back the cloak covering the tree stump.

No!

I scream, throat shattering. My knees hit the floor and fingernails dig into the dry earth. Eskar's body lies prone on the mossy tree stump, eyes closed, arm hanging limply by his side. He's gone, truly gone. His dark hair has fallen back from his forehead and tangles with the moss, the old tree stump recognising a companion in death. He ventured out alone and met his match. Kitto won again.

I make myself take in his body, his neck streaked with red grazes, from frantic hands likely trying to find air. The grazes are so similar to the ones he inflicted on himself when she tortured him, when I was forced to watch. But this time, I wasn't there to save him. Nobody welcomed him home to Chi An Mor and nobody fought for him when he died.

My legs refuse to move, even though staying here is the last thing I want. Outsmarted again and again. Each time, the price of losing is higher. We failed. I lost Eskar to my arrogance. It was our plan but my retribution.

I force myself to stand, to walk through the small encampment, feet leaden, body heavy, leaving Cado to keep vigil. The usual busyness of the morning returns as the sailors organise themselves, presumably to leave for Tanwen – to destroy the rebels. I can't bring myself to share in their anger, their desire for revenge yet. Without a particular route in mind, I walk wherever is most empty, stepping over discarded equipment and half dismantled tents. My cheeks are wet, my chest cracking in two.

I'm at the far edge of the camp, teetering between here and wandering into the forest and losing myself in the trees when I hear the first garbled shouts. Initially, I ignore them, my fingernails scratching deep into my arms as I try to hold myself together, sobs rising in my throat. The shouting changes to piercing shrieks cut off mid-scream and there's a clashing of metal. I turn. An animal instinct – existing through generations of evolution – calls me to the forest. To run. I'm not a predator here: I'm prey.

Chapter 65

I push my grief away as I watch thick, acrid smoke encircle the camp, causing confusion. The smoke's movements are unnatural. Then I realise, the rebels have us surrounded. My legs lock in panic. Zephyrs are controlling the billowing clouds of smoke, inciting chaos. The fires are small but multiply. As soon as some are put out, more are lit. The smoke provides cover and is disorienting the sailors. Shouts from Cado carry over the wind but his words are muffled and ineffective.

We're hopelessly outnumbered: the sailors in the camp are overrun with rebels. Where is Dervla? She has enough magic to defeat the intruders – to wash them all away. Our sailors are comfortable with water, they can navigate a manufactured flash flood and wait for it to recede. The rebels won't. I wait for her to act but the fires burn brighter and the panic from the sailors is thick in the air. Flecks of glowing ash rise up to the moody sky. The tall trees protecting the clearing are bone dry and I watch in horror as the brittle pine needles catch alight in the wind.

The flames in the trees spread, a fiery halo, damning

all of us. I need to get Dervla out of here before it's too late. Taking control of my body, I sprint for the centre of the burning camp, calling her name loudly.

Smoke burns my lungs with every inhalation, my eyes stream and I dodge figures appearing through the plumes. They're not Dervla and I don't pause to see if they are friend or foe.

An errant gust clears the air momentarily and I see the ring of fire working its way down tree trunks, sealing us in. I'm running out of time; if the fire reaches the floor and cannot be contained, we'll all die from the smoke or burns. The heat from the small fires becomes all-consuming and the flames are spreading fast. I double-back several times through the smoky haze to avoid being consumed by the crackling flames.

A piercing cackle rips through me. I've heard that maniacal laugh before. My body is thrown violently sideways and my vision goes dark.

Screams of pain rouse me. The smoke in front of me sways, then flickers dark again. I lift my head from the dirt and vomit, black streaks coating the ground. This sets off a coughing fit and, as I wipe my eyes, another explosion rocks me. The laughter pauses, then starts again, closer now.

I turn, catching a glimpse of Dervla through the parting smoke and scramble towards her. She staggers, blood leaking from a gash on her forehand, one hand stemming the flow as she struggles to stand. Before I can reach her, a wall of solid air slams into me and I'm frozen in place.

We're separated and I can't break through. I'm

pummelling my fists, when out of the mists walks Kitto, fresh-faced and full of maniacal glee, her band of rebels close behind. As she opens her mouth to speak, a mighty pine falls with a huge crash which shreds the air. It clears a path through the mist, blowing it apart, revealing Cado fighting hand to hand with a rebel.

He sees us frozen in place and dispatches his attacker whose body crumples on the spot.

Kitto's solid air stops him in his tracks and traps us in a swirling, misty cage, sweating as the flames tickle the sky around us.

Dervla's thin voice barely carries over the flames to Cado, "There's not much time. You need to stop the fires."

His face is grim and his head turns to survey the raging flames above and around us, then looks back at Dervla. She stumbles and hits the ground, her blood spattering in the mud.

Kitto's laughter fades and her focus is absolute, studying Dervla and Cado. It looks as if she's assessing them for any weakness.

While she's distracted, I reach into my magic, bringing it close to my fingertips. I don't have much to offer if it comes to a fight against Kitto; she's stronger than I ever realised. But, if I could get close enough, I could blind her. If she falters with these solid walls of air, we might have a chance. I need Cado to be ready to act, to give me a sign.

But his gaze is fixed on Dervla and the fires surrounding us.

"Cado!" I shout. "Kitto – we have to take her out." I

interrupt his indecision, desperate to stop her.

Dervla catches my eye; she looks like she did in the aqueduct when we arrived in Pentargon – completely broken. "The fires, our people. We need to save them," she counters weakly.

I open my mouth to respond but the familiar choking sensation, a weight of air crushing my windpipe makes my eyes bulge. A small smile plays across Kitto's lips.

I turn desperately to Cado, as his hands start to move. Static builds, making the magic in the air oppressively warm. I stand and wait for floods of water to pour from his hands or ribbons of steam to erupt, but nothing happens. Something feels wrong. The King's body is relaxed, eyes closed, hands drawing complex patterns. Dervla's eyes are locked on Kitto, she pulls herself upright. I hope she has something left to take Kitto out, or to hold her in place until Cado can deliver justice.

The smoke clears a little. I breathe more easily and the burning in my lungs dissipates. Around us, rebels clash with Cado's Navy, the metallic clang of swords battles with disorganised shouts of orders from both sides.

Cado's body shakes and the fires creeping down the pines around us recede. He's extinguishing them. They're being sucked into nothingness by the vacuum which has enveloped them.

I clear the ringing of war from my ears and turn to Cado. "You are not a Mordros," I accuse, venom leaking from my voice.

His shoulders sag. "No, I'm not."

The walls of air have disappeared. I stride towards

him, incensed. This man and his family are responsible for the repression of Aubades for years. He hides in his fancy palace, ruling Trevesiga from afar, perpetuating the oppression of people like me. If his secret were discovered, the Mordros would exile him too.

"I can explain." He catches my wrists, preventing me from raining ineffective blows on his chest. "But not now. You need to trust me." His face is strained, his body covered with a fine sheen of sweat and I realise he wasn't wielding, he was channelling. He sucked the fire into his body, turning its energy into a huge amount of magic and I think he's struggling to control it.

"You need to run." He pushes me away, and I turn back to Dervla, to ask for her help. If he combusts in the middle of the battlefield, everyone will be annihilated. She's standing with Kitto, looking mildly pleased and not at all exhausted.

Chapter 66

For the first time I notice Kitto's leather bracelets match the tassels on Dervla's hunting glove. As if on cue, Kaens calls and descends from the clearing sky. Kitto reaches out her arm, as does Dervla and the beautiful kestrel lands on Kitto's bare, outstretched forearm.

"She always did prefer you over me," Dervla's words confirm the worst. The scars littering Kitto's arm are from bird claws, where she's foregone wearing a protective gauntlet. One for every message exchanged between them.

My head flicks between Dervla and Kitto. The traitor and the rebel. They exchange a pointed glance before Dervla positions herself in front of Kitto.

"Sage, come here. We need to get you away before he combusts."

I don't move, "I need answers now."

"It's not a rebellion, it's a revolution." Cado's voice is strangled. Sweat pours down his face, his fists clench as he wrestles for control. "They mean to rule Trevesiga."

"It was necessary. Sheltered in your palace, you refused to be a proper leader. You allowed your paranoia of your magic being discovered to rule you," Dervla snaps coldly. "I achieved more as your Almanac than you ever have."

"Then why continue the rebellion, if being the Almanac got you the power you wanted?" I ask.

"I've lived a life pandering to weak men. It was always going to end sometime. Your research helped accelerate that," she retorts.

"You used me?" I hate the tremble that slips through my lips as my oldest friend shows her true colours.

"So did he." She points to Cado who quakes behind me. "His support of your research was for his own gain. He would be able to use serpentine to mimic Mordros power, to protect himself outside the palace's enchantments. To keep himself hidden. I supported you because I knew how important it was to Trevesiga, to Aubades."

"And to yourself," I snap.

She shrugs. "Yes, but that's good business. I would have supported you in anything. I just happened to have an angle of my own."

"An angle? One that ends with you ruling Trevesiga?"

"What's wrong with that? Your double standards with ambition are getting tiring. It's okay for you to crave power and freedom because you came from nothing, but, according to you, because I was born to privilege, I shouldn't ask for more."

"The Concord won't support you."

"The Concord will have to. I'll return with what's left of the rebels and tell them about the deadly secret Cado has been harbouring. That outside of the protection of

Chi an Mor, he turned in battle and wiped out his own forces. He can't keep control for much longer. Come away from him Sage before it's too late."

I unconsciously take a step towards her. "Cedar?"

"In Pentargon. Safe, I promise."

"The charged serpentine that Kitto sent?" A hint of reproach flickers across Dervla's face.

"We've discussed Kitto's methods; she regrets the turmoil she caused you." A smug smile crawls across Kitto's face; there's no regret.

"Turmoil? She nearly murdered us! And Eskar's death?" I challenge.

"I will live with that guilt for the rest of my life. He was my friend too." Dervla's eyes glitter and harden. "But, it was a deliberate choice. Him or the woman I love." Kitto looks smug, confident at Dervla's side.

"I regret causing you pain but, in the end, that too was an easy choice, one I would make again and again. There's no competition with Kitto." This might be the first honest thing she's ever said to me.

I turn to Cado. It might have been Dervla's decision that got Eskar killed but he used him as a weapon, going back on his promise to grant Eskar his freedom. Cado shoulders some of the blame. He reads my accusation and furrows his eyebrows unable even now to voice his apology. I take a few more deliberate steps from him.

"Sage, I won't hurt you. I promise. Don't choose her." His body shakes and the ground beneath me heats.

For the first time, Dervla looks uncertain.

"I can't lose you too, Sage. But it's your choice. It has

always been your choice." She reaches a hand towards me, waggling her fingers in a pleading motion to take it so we can leave together. I realise it's never been my choice, not when she's been the mastermind all along: setting us up like game pieces, changing the rules as it suits her. How can I win when someone is always looking at my cards? My brother, Haelyn, Eskar – her journey to Trevesiga's crown is littered with the bodies of the people I love.

I face Cado, meeting his emerald eyes. "I don't trust you."

My voice cracks on the second word; our gaze holds until I turn. I take Dervla's hand, she grabs Kitto's with her other and Kaens takes to the sky with a hollow, victory cry.

We run, not looking back at Cado or the battle around us. The ashy pines are within reach when I stumble. Kitto runs ahead, saving herself but Dervla stays, pulling me up from the floor. Then we hear it. A booming cacophony of fire explodes from the centre of the ruined war camp. Dervla throws a wall of water up in an attempt to protect us but it vaporises. The steam scalds my skin and the pain has me fighting for consciousness.

Dervla kneels beside me, her body curled around her hands. The wound on her head seeps blood again and the silence is deafening. The battle is over: Cado lost control. There's nothing standing in Dervla's way now.

Chapter 67

The cells are dark. Quiet, save for water dripping from the ceiling. I pull my Concord robe tightly around my shoulders, aware my footsteps echo too loudly. The sea frost from my journey back from the laboratory melts and runs down my face in tiny droplets.

Dervla's first autumn in power has been cruel so far. The harvest failed, people are starving and the Concord are squabbling. There's only one of her and too many fires to extinguish. Where she makes one decision, another three battles appear. Everything must be run past her. She may have repealed the Difan but the people of Trevesiga are bristling at the return of a dictatorship. The ramifications of imbuing serpentine with magic remain a secret.

Haelyn meets me at the darkest cell, face pale and taut, hair pulled back into a neat braid. On our return, she was released with a full pardon. But her time in the cells sapped her of her previous warmth. Now, she has no interest in light-hearted gossip, no interest in lending a helping hand to those in need and certainly no interest in being my friend.

She has just one focus. One driving need to compensate for the lonely days she spent terrified in the dark: she wants revenge. I'm well aware she views my participation as a partnership of convenience. If we're caught, it's every woman for herself.

The dripping stops. The walls are dry, my magic replenished. That precious little strand from Eskar is still buried deep inside me and writhes happily now it's fulfilled. Haelyn gives me a subtle nod and we start to channel. Her Zephyr magic and my combination of Aubade and Mordros together.

The crystals of serpentine we've hidden in the walls start to glow.

Acknowledgements

To Luke – you held me together through the broken nights and rollercoaster of our first baby and the first draft of this novel and I am forever grateful. You are my rock and your complete confidence in my abilities has never wavered, even when mine did. You and Miles are my everything.

Thank you to Aby, the first person to read this book end to end and my incredible cover designer. Your feedback and critique whilst we both multi-tasked juggling babies and toddlers is a testament to your determined friendship and your total enthusiasm for the side plots – some of the characters wouldn't have survived without you – no promises for book two though…

To the *Saucy book club* – thank you for the laughter, the hilarious notes and suggestions, the enthusiasm and the full-body warmth that comes with deep friendships with such an incredible group of women; I admire and love you all, I don't say it often enough!

To my local writer's circle, and Laura in particular,

who gave and continues to give invaluable feedback on my writing. Thank you for building my confidence and teaching me that there's nothing to fear from sharing your work, and so much to gain. I continue to be blown away by the creativity and talent in the group and am in awe of you all.

To Lesley Hart at Author's Pen – thank you for being my editor. You are the font of all knowledge when it comes to publishing. Every piece of feedback has been gratefully received and has made this book shine.

To thriller author Jessica Huntley – thank you for your endless patience in answering my self-publishing questions. Your guidance has made all the difference to me as a debut author and saved me several mishaps and I'm really grateful for all your wisdom.

To Helen Jones, thank you for your typesetting and proofreading; self-publishing is a daunting journey, made less so with a fantastic team by my side.

Finally, my parents and Luke's who support us in everything (shout-out to my father-in-law who proofread my drafts and no doubt despairs at my inability to understand the possessive apostrophe or where to put a comma). Thank you for being our biggest cheerleaders.

Dear reader,

One last thing before you go …

I hope you've enjoyed Aubade Rising. As a new author, reviews and visibility make a huge difference so if you have a chance, please consider sharing your thoughts online via Amazon, Goodreads or on social media

Thank you so much for reading book one in Sage's journey.

Best wishes,

HAYLEY PIERCE

For news about Hayley Pierce's next publications, including the sequel to Aubade Rising, please follow this QR code to her website:

https://hayleypierce.com/

Or:

HAYLEY PIERCE

Biographical notes

Currently based in Sussex, Hayley is a West Country girl at heart. She craves being by the ocean and when she's not parenting, writing, or working, she can be found rock-pooling, swimming and digging her toes into the rough red sand of South Devon.

Printed in Dunstable, United Kingdom

67158201R00211